The TRAGEDY OF US

R.G. ANGEL

The Tragedy of us

By R.G Angel

Cover: Red Leaf Book Design
Editing: Writing Evolution

Dedication:

To my Mom for always believing in me and pushing me to share my stories with the world.

To my Squad – You are amazing women!

And to all the geeky smartasses out there. You girls rock. Never let anyone tell you, you're not worth it.

Contents

CHAPTER 1 _____ 6

CHAPTER 2 _____ 17

CHAPTER 3 _____ 27

CHAPTER 4 _____ 42

CHAPTER 5 _____ 52

CHAPTER 6 _____ 60

CHAPTER 7 _____ 67

CHAPTER 8 _____ 77

CHAPTER 9 _____ 86

CHAPTER 10 _____ 99

CHAPTER 11 _____ 106

CHAPTER 12 _____ 115

CHAPTER 13 _____ 121

CHAPTER 14 _____ 127

CHAPTER 15 _____ 135

CHAPTER 16 _____ 146

CHAPTER 17 _____ 154

CHAPTER 18 _____ 163

CHAPTER 19 _____ 173

CHAPTER 20 _____ 182

CHAPTER 21 _____ 191

CHAPTER 22 _____ 196

CHAPTER 23 _____ 200

CHAPTER 24 _____ 214

CHAPTER 25 _____ 220

EPILOGUE – 1 year later_____ 227

ABOUT ME _____ 232

ALSO BY R.G. ANGEL _____ 233

CHAPTER 1

I looked at my phone and groaned. Today was the first day of junior year, a day just like all the other seven hundred and twenty odd days that high school typically lasted.

Up late, I jumped into a pair of faded blue jeans and grabbed one of my homemade "cause of the day" T-shirts. Glancing in the mirror, I shook my head. I didn't have the time to sort the bird's nest on my head. Throwing my hair up into a messy bun, I ran downstairs. I'd barely managed to put my flip-flops on when I heard rap music blaring outside, followed by a couple of quick horn blasts.

I grabbed my backpack and ran to the black Chevrolet parked in my driveway. Chago sat in the driver's seat, a grin on his face.

"Chula! Estas bien?"

I chuckled. "Si Guapo." I patted Chago's knee. "I still can't believe your brother gave you his car. And why on earth are you listening to this? You don't even like rap."

"I decided to give it a try." He twisted his mouth, pretending to listen intently. "No?"

I shook my head, trying my best not to laugh.

He shrugged dismissively, backing out of my driveway. "Okay, well, tomorrow we should try Celine Dion," he decided before looking at me with crossed eyes.

I couldn't contain my laughter anymore. Chago Valdez was my best friend, my brother in all aspects of my life other than blood. His name was Santiago, but nobody called him that unless they wanted to get beaten up. I did use the "Santiago" card when I was mad at him though.

Chago and I'd met right after I'd moved to Montgomery back in second grade. My mother had been a young lawyer then. After my father passed away, my mother had started working at the East Side Legal Aid and put me in Elementary school there. That was where I'd met Chago. He'd defended me after a girl had threatened to beat me up. The connection between us had been instantaneous, and we have been friends ever since.

My mother hadn't approved of the friendship. She had been a widow with a stubborn child and wanted me to stay out of the

Eastside. She'd thought Chago would be a bad influence given the color of his skin and his slight accent, but I had proven her wrong over the years. I was the one getting Chago in trouble, not the other way around.

My mom had soon started to work for a big corporate law firm. The more she'd worked, the more responsibilities she'd been given, and the less I saw her. Now it had reached the point I was not even sure we lived in the same house anymore.

Despite what she'd initially thought of Chago though, my mother had helped him join Montgomery High School to be with me. As he lived on the other side of the freeway, he'd been meant to go to Eastside Preparatory College - a bad school with one of the lowest success rates in California and deemed dangerous because of the high gang activity. Originally, she had been rather pleased we wouldn't be together in school anymore. It made her cringe whenever I used Spanish rather than English at home and in our many arguments. I'd even told her that Mama Valdez had been more of a mother to me than she had ever been. It had been pretty harsh, I knew that, but sometimes, I wasn't able to help myself.

When I was twelve, my mother had organized a work cocktail party and, as an act of rebellion, I'd invited Chago. My mother had been mortified, but unknowingly, I'd actually helped her. A potential big client, worth billions of dollars, was also from the Eastside. He'd thought that my mother, my obtuse mother, was a very open-minded woman to let her only daughter befriend a boy from the Eastside. He had been so impressed that he had signed with her, making my mom an associate of the firm.

Now Chago was studying with me at Montgomery High School, which counted only a meager number of students from the Eastside. These students were usually invited to join based on their unique talents or exceptional test results.

Despite the stereotypical view of the Eastside, not everybody was in a gang. Both Chago and his older brother Mateo were gang-free. Their father Paco had died protecting some gang boss. As a form of gratitude, Mateo and Chago were free to not join the gang, and they were smart enough to enjoy that freedom.

This may have been another reason why we were so close. We were part of a very exclusive club; we had learned only too early what it was like to grieve a parent.

However, Chago being from the Eastside had an undeniable advantage. My smart mouth got me into loads of trouble with the pretty and popular, and it was only the fear of facing Chago that made them keep their distance from me.

"Man, I just lost five bucks," he whined, detailing my clothes while we waited at the traffic light.

"Why?"

"Mateo and I bet on your shirt. He said you would wear something about animal protection and I thought it would be something related to the environment."

"Stop betting on me! It's degrading!" I exclaimed in mock hurt.

Chago winked. "So, Chula, do we need to go pick up Gaygan?"

"You know he wants to kick you when you call him that!"

"Nah, he doesn't. He loves it."

I chuckled. "Yes, he does."

Gaygan was the nickname Chago had given to Logan Brier, the only other student that Chago and I were fond of. He was a year older and the Chief Editor of the school paper. We'd met Logan in Junior High when a band of seniors had wanted to beat him up and Chago had defended him. That was a recurring theme with Chago; he was always there to defend the weak and defenseless. He never judged anyone. He had been judged way too many times himself to ever do the same to others.

We gave Logan a place in our usual duo at school because misfits were stronger together. None of us really fitted in with the rest, but we loved it that way. Most people couldn't wait to leave high school, and others, the popular ones, dreaded leaving it one day. Us? We just went along for the ride. We were El Bandito, the Anarchist and the Eccentric.

"He is probably already there. He is a senior now. He has to prepare the freshman-whatever-stuff."

"Very eloquent," he teased.

"I know, it's a gift," I sighed. "I hope we'll have more classes together. Last year was painful."

"I don't know, Charlie. I sure as hell didn't try to get into Advanced Literature."

"Well, except that," I admitted, adjusting my bag as he parked the car.

"Dork!"

"Baboso!" I stuck my tongue out.

"Very mature." He wrapped an arm around my neck after joining me on the pathway.

"You're the one talking." I nudged him with my hip as we walked through the school's main doors to check our schedules.

Everybody in school presumed that Chago and I were dating. We never cared enough to deny it. Truthfully, we could never date; we knew way too many embarrassing things about each other. We'd gone through the awkward phases of puberty together, confiding in one another since we didn't have anyone else. I could never see Chago as a potential boyfriend after that and I knew he felt the same.

"Charlotte Miller," I heard a commanding voice say as soon as we crossed the threshold to the main hall.

I did my best not to roll my eyes. "Principal Webber, I missed you this summer!" I exclaimed with an angelic smile.

"Of course, you did," he replied before locking eyes with Chago. "Mr. Valdez, why don't you go check your schedule?"

Chago nodded, understanding it was a dismissal and not a suggestion.

"I'll see you later, Guapo." I winked at him. "Worst case scenario, meet me for lunch at our usual table."

I knew the principal didn't like me much and it had all started when my mother had convinced the school board to let Chago join the school. He was living at the limit of the district, and she'd scared them with parity and other legal gibberish. To be fair, the principal had had no problem with Hispanics or even people from the Eastside, but he didn't like being overruled and he particularly despised the rules being bent.

To be fair, I'd also given him a lot of reasons to be exasperated over the past two years. I was an activist and regarded as a "troublemaker," which I thought was unfair. I was only speaking my mind loud and clear, trying to think outside the box they were forcing us into.

"You are a junior now. It's time to think about your future, college, and career." He walked beside me down the corridor toward the administrative office.

"I'm thinking, sir, thinking hard." In truth, whilst I wanted to be a journalist, I was still unsure about all the steps I would follow to get there.

"You finished last year with very good grades in almost every subject," he continued.

I nodded. I knew science was my weakness and I was dreading Physics class this year.

"You know, tutoring would look good on your college applications."

I looked up, my eyes slanted with incredulity. "Have you met me?"

He furrowed his eyebrows in a disapproving scowl.

"I'm not what you can call sociable. I'm not very patient and I don't like people that much. I would be the worst tutor Montgomery High has ever seen." I chuckled. "Hell! I think Mau Tse Tung would even be a better tutor in Human Rights than I would be."

The crease between his eyebrows deepened, showing that my attempt at a joke had fallen flat.

"Maybe it's time to change," he stressed, his tone reproachful.

Maybe it's time to butt out! I sighed, knowing that this discussion would only cause me an hour-long speech of painful boredom. "I'll consider it."

"Good, good." He smiled, pleased with himself. "Here's your schedule. You're lucky to have been accepted into the Advanced Literature class. The selection process was very competitive."

I bet! "Thank you," I replied with fake cheerfulness, then left before I said something I would regret. Payaso!

As soon as I exited the office, Logan dropped his group of freshmen and trotted toward me. It always amazed me to see that despite his gangly 6'4" frame, he could be as graceful as a ballerina.

"And here we have our little Miss NGO," he leered with his usual cheeky grin. "She is a member of PETA, Amnesty International, Red Cross, Greenpeace, and I don't know what else."

I turned around and looked into his eyes. His contacts were violet today to match his Converse shoes.

"I'm also a member of 'Leave me alone, or I'll kick your ass'," I added deadpanned, nudging him. "How are you doing, bud? Ready for the fresh blood?"

"Yes. I want to know if 'The Cure' has some new comics ready for the paper or even a small, acerbic chronicle."

I shrugged, looking down at my schedule, taking the direction of the lockers, knowing full well that Logan would follow me until I gave him an answer.

"I don't know, but I can ask him if you want," I replied playfully.

"You do that. Where to?" he asked, glancing at my schedule over my shoulders.

"Locker first, then Calculus."

The Cure was a sort of pirate writer for the paper. He also drew funny, engaged comics that were both loved and hated by the students. No matter how entertaining The Cure was, the students all feared being the target of his cold abrasiveness. Everybody thought it was a guy, probably a senior, as you had to be, and I quote, "gutsy" to write those things. The principal would have loved nothing more than to forbid his publications, but it was satirical, and he knew Logan was a fervent defender of the freedom of speech. The "pretty and popular" would have probably paid good money to find out The Cure's identity, but only two people in school knew the real identity of The Cure: Logan and Chago. I was him. Yes, Charlotte "Charlie" Miller was The Cure! The underground chief of an inexistent rebellion. I was saying "out loud" what everybody thought. I wondered how that would look on my college applications.

"Very well then." Logan rested his back on the locker beside mine, legs crossed at the ankles while scanning the corridor up and down. "Oh, by the way, we've got a new teacher in charge of the newspaper, thank God!" he exclaimed dramatically. "Old creepy Miss Jane is no more."

"Uh huh…" I replied absentmindedly, organizing my locker. I knew better than to listen to him when he was in "Gossip Queen" mode.

"Yeah, it's the new lit teacher, Mulligan. In his forties, but he's damn hot."

I looked at him with my best "dude-what-the-freak" face, making him chuckle.

"First of all, eww, and second, who don't you find hot?" I shook my head.

"I don't know," he said and shrugged. "Him." He pointed at a random guy in the corridor.

"You know what, let's stop the crazy talk. It's only day one, but who knows, I might get inspired by the end of the day," I trailed off.

He nodded. "Where is Chago? You guys are usually joined at the hip."

"Yes, we are, but Principal Webber wanted to have a talk with me."

Logan winced.

"It was speech number 2316, AKA the classic 'It's time to think about your future' talk." I shoved a book in my bag with a sigh of irritation.

"Also known as the 'it's time to fit the mold and stop questioning everything or you'll fail in life' speech," Logan jested, but I could hear the cold edge in his voice. He was the president of the teen LGBT association, and that was why he had a certain status and power within these walls. The principal couldn't be too hard on him without risking a discrimination accusation. But everybody wanted to make him change, and I knew it was taking a toll on him even if he was doing his best to hide it. It seemed that Chago and I were the only ones who accepted him without restriction.

I reached for his hand and squeezed it tight. "We're still on for tonight?"

"Tonight?" Logan cocked his head.

"Yes. Chago, you, and I. Pizza at my house? You know the first day back ritual I-" I stopped, staring at him. "You forgot?!"

Logan grimaced, his neck reddening with embarrassment. "Sorry, the new boss wants to see the whole team tonight and I still have to finish preparing the senior-freshman gathering. Do you mind if we do that tomorrow?"

I shook my head, starting to walk to my first class as I was now running late. "Tomorrow's fine; it's not like I have any obligations at home."

Logan grabbed my hand and pulled me into a hug before I could escape.

"Chula, Gaygan," Chago greeted, wrapping an arm around my neck as soon as Logan let me go. "'Sup, dude?"

"Busy, busy." Logan fist-bumped Chago. "I'll tell you at lunch. See you guys later."

Chago reached for my schedule. "Calculus too, chica? They really like to torture us as soon as we wake up."

We sat at the back, side by side. Chago gave me his own schedule. We had three classes together. First-period Calculus, third period PE, and fifth-period History.

"French?" I gasped. "That's hard shit, Chago."

"Yeah, well, I wanted Spanish, you know." He rolled his eyes. "An easy way out, but they outsmarted me. They gave me French, my second option. I never thought they would."

I smiled encouragingly, giving him my schedule. "Worst case scenario, I'll find you help. Logan aced it last year."

He pointed an accusing finger at my schedule. "How come you managed to get Spanish? You speak it almost as well as I do!"

"I know, but I'm a gringa." I rubbed my pale arm, a striking contrast to the warm bronze glow of his skin. "And my name is Miller. I'm a winner." I winked.

"Humph…" He pouted, looking forward as the teacher entered the classroom. "Now I'll finish thirty minutes after you three times a week."

I snorted. "I think I can survive thirty minutes without mi hombre," I whispered to him.

"If you keep your mouth shut, you might," he muttered, and I knew he was only half-joking.

The rest of the morning went fast and I knew I would be paired with Chago in PE. It was not a surprise because nobody else wanted to pair up with him. If only they could see past appearances and area codes, they would meet such an amazing guy.

By lunch, Logan had all the first-day gossip ready for us. Truth be told, neither of us cared, but he enjoyed it so much, so we played along.

"You really sound like Perez Hilton; do you know that?" I asked, biting into my cheese sandwich.

"Don't go around complimenting the guy," Chago said, elbowing me teasingly. "He might dye his hair pink."

Logan snorted. "And let go of my magnificent blond hair which took me months to achieve? I think not!"

I looked at Chago, and we shared a smile at Logan's outrage as we let him go on. Logan often listened to Chago talk about cars or sports, and he listened to me rant about political crises, human rights, or animal rights issues, so we did owe him this much.

13

We had our table just by the emergency exit. It was funny, but I couldn't remember sitting anywhere else. It was our table, a silent lease, as most of the tables were tacitly assigned. The center of the room, or rather the center of the high school world, was occupied by the jocks and cheerleaders. The further you were from this inner circle, the more of a social outcast you were. We were even beyond that invisible limit; the only difference was that, for us, it was a choice, not an obligation.

The afternoon classes went smoothly. My classmates and I had a mutual understanding to ignore each other. I did well until History class came around.

I sat in the back, resting my bag on the table beside mine, waiting for Chago to arrive.

"That's my seat." The high-pitched voice made me cringe.

I looked up to meet the brown eyes of Brittany, whatever her surname was, the co-captain of the cheerleading team.

"This is your seat?" I asked, touching the chair.

"Uhm, yeah." She played with a strand of her blond hair, chewing her gum loudly. I couldn't believe it; she was trying to kick me out of my seat and was giving me attitude about it.

"Oh, I'm so sorry, I didn't see your name on it." I half stood up and turned around. "Oh wait…no." I frowned. "No, your name is not on it." I let out an overplayed sigh as I sat back down. "Well, tough job, doll, you'll have to pick another seat."

"Douuuug, she doesn't want to move!" she whined, resting her hands on her hips.

The big guy sitting on the other side of me stood up, glaring down at me.

I returned his glare even though I had to crane my neck up to look at him. Maybe Chago was right. I wouldn't survive half an hour without him if I kept the attitude, but I just couldn't help it. I hated bullies.

"Maybe she didn't hear you clearly." He stood closer to me, all tall and menacing. "She told you it's her seat," he hissed, tightening his hands into fists.

I did my best to hide my smile. If he was trying to scare me, he was in for a treat. "And maybe you didn't hear me with your steroid damaged brain. I. AM. NOT. MOVING." I enunciated each word slowly.

He bared his teeth at me. "I'm warning you, you little—"

"Oye, Pendejo," Chago greeted coldly, entering the room and coming to stand behind me, his hands tightly anchored on my shoulders. "If you've got something to say to her, you say it to me. Entiendes?"

Doug's eyes widened slightly as he took a step back. Doug might have a few inches on Chago's 5'7" height, but Chago's taut frame, buzz haircut, dark eyes, and impressive tattoos were enough to make anyone with half a brain step back.

"So, what's the problem?" Chago insisted, tightening his hold on my shoulders almost painfully. He was clearly mad at me too.

"There is no problem," Doug conceded before taking his bag and moving row.

"That's what I thought," Chago confirmed, taking Doug's seat.

"You didn't need to defend me," I whispered, slightly angry after Doug and Brittany left. "I can fight my own battles."

"Come on! Have you looked at yourself lately? You're 5'2"! We need at least four of you to make one like him." He pursed his lips in disapproval.

"So?"

He grunted in frustration. "Yeah, well, we'll see what Mateo thinks of you provoking a football player."

"You wouldn't dare!" I hissed, narrowing my eyes.

"Try me," he challenged, returning my glare.

"Soplón!"

"I love you too, Chula," he chuckled as the teacher called the class to order.

The last period was actually enjoyable. The new literature teacher, who I now knew was called Adam Mulligan, was rather fun. The list of books for Advanced Lit were surprising, yet interesting choices.

"Some of the books you have to read are the same ones required by the seniors in normal Lit class, so don't go around showing off like you're smarter."

It wasn't stupid advice as some of the geeks here seemed to have a masochistic streak. I had to admit I also had this masochistic streak more often than not.

"In this class I want you to learn to think outside the box. Don't try to express the dictates of our society. When you write a paper on one of these books, I want your opinion, your real opinion, supported by your own logical argumentation." He sat on the edge of his desk, burying a hand in his pocket. It was what I called the "casual-cool," the friendly teacher style.

I rolled my eyes, but smiled. He seemed nice enough, and even if I wouldn't admit it, Logan had been right for once. He was attractive for an old man. Well, not "old." My mother would have kicked me hard if she had heard me refer to a person in his forties as old, but for me, it still seemed like an eternity away.

"I don't want to read a general opinion I could have gotten straight from Google. You will never get a bad grade for expressing and explaining an opinion, even if it's the opposite of what the majority think." He smiled. "Even if it's completely different from what I think." He stood up and walked up and down the aisles. "Think for yourself, that's all I'm asking for," he added, tapping my desk as he walked by.

I frowned, deciding to ignore the gesture. Usually, teachers didn't spend much extra time on me. I spoke my mind way too much, so they found me challenging at best. This teacher probably needed a week or two to figure that out. When the class was over, I found Chago leaning on the lockers across the hall, arms crossed on his chest, looking all dark and menacing.

I couldn't help but laugh. "You're not helping with the rumors, you know," I whispered, interlocking my arm with his.

"Nothing will, Chula, and you know that. They had me pegged as dangerous and psychotic the day I crossed the threshold. I'm just giving them what they expect to see."

"Not that you enjoy it or anything," I teased, throwing him a sideways glance.

"Not that I enjoy it or anything," he confirmed with a half-smile. "So where are we going?" he asked as we headed in the direction of his car. "Since our usual 'first-day' ritual has been pushed back."

I shrugged. "It's not like my mother will be home," I sneered, not able to conceal the bitterness in my voice. I knew she was working hard. I knew people were counting on her, but what about me? I was counting on her too! She had let me down too many times to count. I'd lost my father in a car accident years ago, and progressively I had lost my mother too.

Chago just looked at me for a couple of seconds before starting the car. He knew better than to try to make me feel better about that.

"Let's go home. I bet mama and Mateo are dying to know about our first day," he soothed, his face softening as it did only for me. "You're always making them laugh with the offensive version of you. I swear sometimes Che Guevara had nothing on you."

As we headed in the direction of the freeway, I realized that for the vast majority of students in school, it was crazy to go to the Eastside, and if you were white and rich or from the upper middle class, it was even worse. They usually did it out of stupidity, on a dare, or for the thrill of danger, but for me, it was my second home. There I was the "Gringa Valdez," a part of the vecindad. It was somewhere where people cared for me.

CHAPTER 2

On Sunday morning, I was surprised to find my mother in the kitchen. She had her iPhone in her hand and her laptop was on the kitchen counter, but she was dressed casually, which for her, meant no suit. I knew she wouldn't be home for long, but still, my mother home during the weekend? I needed to mark the date on my calendar.

"Hello, Charlotte, honey." She kissed my forehead between two sentences with her interlocutor.

"Hello mother," I mimicked her professional tone. I knew it hadn't been voluntary; it was just who she was. I think she'd forgotten how to be a mother when my father had died. The change had been progressive. I'd believed it was her way of dealing, but the more she'd become engrossed in her work, the more she'd forgotten her role in my life.

I couldn't help but miss the mother she had once been. I missed little things such as the sound of her laughter which had always filled the house and the clown shaped pancakes she'd made on Sunday mornings.

I looked at her as I put two frozen blueberry waffles in the toaster. We did look a lot alike. We were both short with the same brownish-red hair, even if hers was almost always tightened in a strict bun. However, where her eyes were blue, mine were an unusual, metallic grey, which I'd inherited from my father, and I could see nostalgia on her face sometimes when she looked into my eyes.

I poured myself a steamy cup of coffee and sat at the table with my waffles.

"So, what have you got planned for today?" she asked, finally off the phone, but keeping an eye on her computer screen.

I shrugged. "Chago's madre organized a—"

"Santiago's mother," she corrected. "It's mother, not madre." She hated it when I used Spanish in our conversations as if I didn't know how to speak properly. I spoke perfect English when I needed to.

"Fine!" I snapped. I couldn't believe she was trying to correct me when she hadn't been to one PTA meeting since grade school. "Santiago's *mother* is organizing a party for Angela's baby christening and she is also using the occasion to throw us -" I smiled - "and by us, I mean Santiago and myself, a 'back to school' party."

"Isn't that nice?" she commented, finally closing her laptop.

"Do you want to come?" I asked, already knowing her answer.

"I would love to, but I need -" she checked the clock on the kitchen wall - "to go in fifteen minutes. I know it's the weekend, but it's a very important merger I'm working on. A lot of money and jobs are involved, and our client has to fly to New York tomorrow."

I nodded. "It's okay." *Like it would have changed anything,* I added to myself. "Then later we're going to the movies with Logan. There is a retrospective on Hitchcock, and Logan is a massive fan," I added with a small smile, thinking about how much fun we had re-enacting the Psycho shower scene, except that I had been the killer and Logan had been Janet Leigh. He really did scream like a girl; it was impressive.

"So how's school?" she asked, putting her laptop in her bag, car keys already in hand.

I shrugged. "School's cool, nothing special."

My mom stopped moving around and looked at me, and I mean really looked at me. It was scary; it had been forever since I'd had her undivided attention.

"What?" I asked warily.

"Are you thinking about college?" she asked, playing with her keys, clearly uncomfortable. "It's closer than you think. Your acceptance curriculum is being shaped right now whether you like it or not."

My eyes widened as understanding filled me. "You talked with Principal Webber?!" The man was really an evil manipulator.

She nodded once. That was something good about my mom; she never tried to sugar-coat things. "He phoned my office."

And you found the time to take his call? I thought. It took all my willpower not to say that out loud.

"You wouldn't imagine my surprise when he told me you'd refused his very generous offer to make you a tutor." She sighed. "You don't know how good it would look on your college applications, Charlotte."

"I'm still weighing my options here," I replied evasively. I wanted to tell her I was studying guitar and that that was an activity, but it would only lead to an old argument - the "piano over guitar" war. She wanted me to study the piano; it was classier to her, but I wanted to study guitar. I pretended it was because it was cooler and that I wanted to study an instrument I could carry with me. But the truth was, I wanted to play guitar as my dad once had. I also suspected that was the main reason my mom refused to let me.

She put her bag back on the table and rested her hands on her hips; it meant big trouble ahead.

"Listen, you might not care about your future, but I do. I don't want to be a controlling mother, but- "

I couldn't help but snort, which earned me a bone-chilling glare.

"Sorry, continue," I apologized, my tone lacking any contrition.

"You need to find an extracurricular activity. I don't care what."

Yeah, that sounded more like her right now. I couldn't help but smile slightly, hiding it by biting on my waffle.

"What about the school paper? Your friend Logan is working for it, isn't he?"

"He is the editor-in-chief."

"So even better. I'm sure he can find you a little task, anything really."

I looked up, dying to tell her I was working for the paper already, that I was the mysterious and outspoken "The Cure," but it wouldn't serve my cause.

"I'm thinking about it. Either that or the auto body shop."

She stood straighter, her whole body a tale of how frustrating she found me. "Stop being so rebellious all the time! It's tiring, Charlotte. You are acting like a child."

"Why is speaking my mind and doing what I want so rebellious, mother? Please tell me in these rare five minutes you are keeping for me."

She sighed wearily. "You know what? I really don't have time to deal with your teenage drama, Charlotte. I have people counting on me right now and I'm already late." She pointed at the clock. "This discussion is going nowhere." She grabbed her bag and stormed toward the door, but as she reached it, she turned around swiftly, pointing her index finger at me. "I give you two weeks to find an extracurricular activity, young lady. Two weeks or I'll pick for you," she added, her face taut, her lips a thin white slit of barely contained anger.

After she left, I looked at the door, replaying what she'd just said. People counting on her? She didn't want to let them down? How many times had she let ME down?!

I shook my head and took a deep breath, willing the frustration away. Chago would come to pick me up soon and he really didn't need to worry about me. He worried way too much already. He was suffering from what I called "big brother syndrome," and I didn't help him with my big mouth and short temper.

I would figure something out before the end of the ultimatum. I always did.

After a quick shower, I changed into a green knee-length summer dress with matching flats. I almost never wore dresses. I didn't feel comfortable in them, but it was sort of customary for this kind of party in Hispanic families.

"Chula, you're all cute," Chago complimented as I sat beside him in the car.

"You too, Guapo. You look really nice." He was wearing a white dress shirt with a black tie and black dress pants. "I bet Eva will keep her eyes on you all afternoon." I wiggled my eyebrows suggestively.

"Callate!" he shouted in mock anger as he started the car.

I chuckled, patting his leg as we took the direction to the Eastside.

Eva was the girl Chago had had a crush on for as long as I could remember. Most of his relationships didn't last long because girls felt threatened by our friendship, which was completely stupid. If we had wanted to be together, we would have been. Girls ended up asking him to choose between them and me, and of course, he always chose me, as I would always choose him. Not that I had really had to choose since I'd never had a real boyfriend. It was true that, with such an overprotective best friend, it was hard to meet someone. Plus, most guys didn't like my smart mouth.

I was not completely innocent. I had been kissed before by Chago's older cousin, Diego. It had almost caused World War III between Chago, Mateo, and Diego. After that I'd sworn to myself to stay away from anyone related to the Valdez brothers.

When we parked in front of the house, we could hear the Mexican band getting ready to play.

"Mateo?" Chago's mother, Antonella, asked from the kitchen.

"No mamá, somos nosotros."

21

"Ah, m'hija!" She came into the living room, hugging me tightly. I did get a lot of motherly affection, even if it was not from my own mother.

"¿Cómo está hoy? ¿No demasiado cansada?" I asked, hugging her back. I knew she loved it when I spoke Spanish.

"I'm doing fine, no stress. Things are running smoothly. Thank you for asking." She glared at Chago.

"I was about to ask too!" he whined, offended.

"Of course, you were." Antonella gave me a playful smile. "I was just wondering where your brother was." She pursed her lips with disapproval. "Los invitados are already arriving."

"He is probably in the garage. I'll go look for him," Chago offered.

"No, stay here, help mama. I'll go. It's only down the street." I smiled.

"Gracias." Antonella sighed with relief before going back to the kitchen where I could hear multiple voices.

"Yeah, right, you go," Chago teased with a suggestive grin. "You are so selfless."

"Cállate idiota!" I turned around just fast enough for him not to see my creeping blush.

Chago was always picking on me because when I was ten and Mateo was fifteen, I'd had a major crush on him. But that was a lifetime ago, even if both brothers still liked to tease me about it. But really, nobody could blame me after seeing him. He was like Eduardo Verastegui's twin brother. The girls around here had even nicknamed him "El modelo caliente." My crush had died quickly though, especially after all the embarrassing puberty moments he'd witnessed. He was the one who'd had to go buy me tampons when I had my first period because I was at their house and Mama Antonella was at work.

Even though the crush had died years ago, the attraction was never fully gone. I was only human and Mateo was beautiful.

I knew Mateo was never late. If he was not there already, then there was a ninety-nine percent chance he'd forgotten. I stopped by his room and picked up a blue shirt and black dress pants before heading out.

I was at the garage five minutes later, knocking at the back door as loud as I could.

"Quién es?" I heard Mateo's deep voice.

"The most beautiful girl you've ever seen!" I called back.

He chuckled, opening the door.

I looked at him from head to toe. His long, curly hair fell to his shoulders. He was very tall at 6'2" and he had his mother's green eyes, which were even brighter with his jet-black hair and dark skin. He was wearing ripped jeans covered with car oil and an old tee shirt.

"Oh, mi reina, you look fantastic." He moved from the door, letting me in.

"Yeah, and you don't." I pointed at his outfit.

"Ouch, ego bruised." He brought his hand to his heart in mock hurt.

"You have no idea why I'm dressed like this, do you?" I asked, skepticism oozing from my tone.

"To seduce me? If that's the case, it's working," he teased with a wink.

"You've really forgotten?" He looked at me with wonder. "Let me give you a hint... Clara?"

"What, Clara? I—No!" His eyes widened. "The Christening?"

I nodded.

"It's next week!" He pointed at the calendar where "Clara Bautizo" had been pencilled in next week.

I shook my head. "Nope, it's today, and almost everybody is there."

He cursed under his breath. "I'm screwed! I didn't buy anything, and it's my cousin's baby! I—" He sat heavily on a chair. "You know how bad it will reflect on me?"

I smiled. "Don't worry about that now." I pointed to a door by the entrance. "Go shower, here are some clean clothes."

"But—"

"Go! I'm waiting!" I shoved him toward the shower room before hanging his clothes on the door.

As he showered, curiosity won, and I went to look at what was keeping him so occupied on a Sunday morning. What I saw took my breath away. Since meeting the Valdez brothers, I had become a car aficionado, and this was a blue 1968 Chevrolet Corvette Roadster. A pure beauty.

I let my fingers trail delicately over the body.

"Beautiful, right?" Mateo startled me.

"Magnificent," I breathed reverently. "I understand why you've forgotten everything else, and why you gave your car to Chago."

I turned to face him and was surprised again by how handsome he really was. "You scrub up well. Blue looks good on you."

He smoothed his shirt. "You picked well."

"I sure did."

"Now how long do I have to find her a gift?" he asked and I caught him looking around.

"What are you going to give her? A tire?"

"Uh…" He pretended to ponder the idea. "Por qué no."

I chuckled, slapping his arm playfully. "Don't be silly." I looked in my backpack. "Here." I handed him a little blue package with a silver bow.

"I—no, I can't take your present!" He shook his head vehemently. "I'll figure something out."

"It's not my present." I took out a pink box with a white bow. "I—" I started and sighed. "Chago is usually the one to forget these kinds of things, so I always get two gifts." I stuck my tongue out. "Today he bought something. Who would have thought it would be the big and responsible brother that would need a major ass saving?"

"I'll give you the money back," he affirmed, taking the box.

"I know you will. You need to change shoes as soon as you get home." I pointed at his trainers.

He nodded. "Thanks, mi reina." He hugged me, kissing my forehead. "You really saved my ass here."

"You're welcome. Don't you want to know what's in the box?"

He chuckled. "I trust your taste. I trust you with everything." He took my hand, pulling me to the exit. "Come on, let's go. And I meant it before, you look very pretty in this dress. Green really suits you."

"It usually suits redheads."

The christening party went well. Mateo's gift, a medallion of the "Virgen de Guadalupe" engraved with Clara's name and date of birth on a golden chain, especially touched Angela. She hugged him hard on the edge of tears.

I gave her a nice summer dress with the peace symbol on the front.

"I love it; it's totally you," she laughed.

"That's what I was looking for," I replied, kissing her cheek loudly.

Chago and I stayed for another hour with him whining about the gift I'd given Mateo and how he should have forgotten his present like he always did.

"Don't be a baby." I nudged him. "We need to get ready to meet Logan."

"Si." He nodded. "Let me change and I'll meet you by the door."

I'd just exited the garden when I felt an arm wrap around my waist.

"Abandoning me already?" he whispered in my ear.

"Mateo, come on, go have fun. There are plenty of girls waiting to dance with you." I jerked my head toward the garden.

"Lo se, pero a dónde te vas?"

"I've got a date with your brother tonight." Seeing his face made me burst into laughter. "And with Logan for the Hitchcock retrospective."

"Have fun. Keep those guys in check." He gave me a quick hug before going back to the party.

"Chula? Ready to go?" Chago was himself again, his faded blue jeans and white tank top showing off his tattoos.

I nodded. "Let's stop by my place first. I really need to change."

"Aww, why? You look like a muñeca." He grinned.

"Yeah, well… We'll see if I look like a doll when I kick your ass."

He raised his hands in surrender. "God forbids."

"I can hold my ground, you know," I added stubbornly with my head high.

"You sure can. I taught you everything you know." He laughed. "Okay, let's go, but you've got to be fast. Logan will be waiting for us in less than thirty minutes and you know how he gets when we're late."

I scrunched up my nose. "I know." The last time he'd made us pay for a week.

"I'll be quick." I rushed into the house, jumped into a pair of jeans, threw on a random shirt, grabbed the red folder hidden under my mattress, and headed out.

The folder contained two comics and a small article comparing school cliques to jungle animals. This was written with my trademark sarcasm and wit, of course.

We made it to the movie with minutes to spare, having run like there was no tomorrow, hand in hand, laughing like silly kids. It felt so good to be carefree. I missed being a child sometimes.

"We're here," Chago gasped breathlessly as I tried to catch my breath, hands on my knees.

Logan checked his watch. "Two minutes early." He grinned. "See, my constant drama queen act actually works."

It *worked,* I thought.

"Here." He handed us two passes.

"This is for you." I gave him the folder.

He nodded, knowing what it was. "Let me put it in the car." He jerked his head toward the blue-green Dodge parked down the street.

"But the movie?" Chago asked, waving his ticket.

"I didn't trust you guys to be on time, so I lied. We still have fifteen minutes."

"Did he just outsmart us?" I asked Chago with disbelief.

"Chula, I think we created a monster," he agreed with such a dramatic tone that we both burst into laughter.

Somebody snorted behind us and I felt Chago tense.

"Chago…" I warned him as we turned around.

Unmistakably, there was a group of jocks and cheerleaders from school.

"Told you they accepted anyone in that cinema!" Doug sneered. He surely felt a lot braver with his buddies around. The problem was that I knew Chago was reckless enough to challenge them, and I knew I was stupid enough to fight alongside him.

They were standing in line for the new action movie. At least we wouldn't be in the same room.

I could see Chago's hands tighten into fists.

I grabbed his bicep. "Please, Guapo, let's go." I rested my other hand on his chest. "You know they are only looking for it. They are not worth it."

"Pero se burlan de nosotros!" he growled, glaring at them. Chago reverted almost exclusively to Spanish when he was furious.

"So what? Let them mock us. It's not like they are important," I replied as calmly as I could.

"Hey, Jeff, is that gonorrhea of yours healed by now?" Logan asked, coming up beside us. "You can't ignore those kinds of things for too long. Ask Mary." He pointed to the overly made-up blond with bright red lipstick. "She regretted it."

Chago and I chuckled. Logan could humiliate people with a few words; it was a gift.

"Come on, guys, Janet Leigh is waiting for us," he added, nudging us.

Chago nodded sharply. "You're lucky I love you, Chula," he grumbled, grabbing my hand again. His tight hold was the only true tell of the extent of his anger.

"Love you too, hot Latino bad boy," Logan teased, trying to ease the mood.

"Not even in your dreams," replied Chago, following him into the theater. When his muscles finally relaxed, I sighed with relief.

"Oh that, my friend…you can't stop," Logan wiggled his eyebrows suggestively.

"I—" Chago started.

"Stop it, you two!" I kissed Chago's cheek. "Let's enjoy Janet's screams even if she has nothing on you!" I added for Logan's benefit.

"I know, right?!" He sighed dramatically. "And when you think Hollywood will never know about my talent."

"It proves there is a God out there," Chago teased right back.

I chuckled, resting my head on my best friend's shoulder. I was just so lucky to have them in my life.

<u>CHAPTER 3</u>

"So, did your mother move on already?" Chago asked on our way to school.

I grimaced. "Not really, no." I showed him the red Post-it.

"The red one?" He whistled. "That's bad."

I nodded silently, looking at the little piece of paper that said, *Three more days and I'll pick for you. Love, your mother.*

My mom was not present in my day-to-day life, but the Post-it color code was something she loved to use in our "control center" which, at home, was on our fridge. She didn't leave notes often, but depending on the color of the paper, I knew the degree of importance or urgency of the message. It could be green, yellow, orange, or red. I'd only received three red notes in my life, and they'd never been pleasant.

I sighed. "Of all the things she's forgotten in my life, she didn't forget this one!"

Chago chuckled, but didn't comment. He knew better by now.

"She managed to forget my birthdays, Christmas, your Holy Communion, my spelling bee challenges…" I trailed off.

Chago gave me a chastising side look. "We both know she never 'forgot' those things, Chula. No matter what you say, we both know she loves you…probably the only way she knows how."

"Humph." I pouted, crossing my arms on my chest. It was true she never forgot. I always had expensive presents on the day, but all I had ever wanted was for her to be there.

Chago frowned. "Come to think of it, you never joined the spelling bees," he retorted, parking the car close to the school entrance.

"I know, but I'm sure she would have forgotten if I did," I replied, sticking my tongue out.

Chago burst into laughter, getting the attention of a popular group. I threw them a cautious glance, hoping they wouldn't look for trouble today. I really needed to be on my best behavior if I wanted to gain one or two more weeks of freedom.

"Only you can say something like that, you know that right?" he asked, wrapping his arm around my neck.

"That's why you love me." I grinned.

"One of the many reasons, yes," he confirmed. "Seriously, what are you going to do?"

I shrugged. "Have a word with Logan. He knows all about the school extracurricular activities. I need one of the least crowded and least constraining activities possible. I will also try to pacify the situation a bit."

"How do you intend to do that?" he asked with curiosity.

"Tonight, she is having a sort of party with her biggest clients and she wants me to go. You know -" I smiled bitterly - "to show she is not only the perfect lawyer, but also the perfect mother."

"Want me to come?"

I shook my head. "Nah, I'll go by myself for once, be everything she expects me to be in public, and maybe I will negotiate another week of reflection. I mean, she is a lawyer, after all; negotiation is in her blood."

"I hope it works, Chula." He nudged me gently before we settled into calculus.

"Yeah, me too." Worst case scenario, I could always try to join the Debate Team, but I'd had fights with most of them, and they literally hated me so much that I knew they wouldn't take me in. The Model United Nations was another interesting choice, but since I'd called the teacher in charge a 'Nazi in sheep's clothing,' my chances of getting in were low.

"What are you thinking about so hard?" Chago whispered, bringing me back to reality and to the teacher completely engrossed in her lecture.

"That if I am forced to join the philatelist group, I'll run away and join a group of guerrilleros in Colombia," I replied deadpanned.

Chago chuckled as quietly as possible, but still received a glare from a math geek. Did that guy have a death wish or something? I glared back to make him turn his head before Chago noticed him.

"You know what, Chula? I actually can picture you as a guerrillera. You'll take control of the group in less than a month!"

"You don't have much confidence in me, Guapo. I'd give myself a week."

We both chuckled, pleased that the teacher was so lost in her lecture she didn't notice our lack of attention.

During lunch, Logan promised to have a look at the activities available and the teachers in charge of them. We needed to find one led by someone I hadn't smart-mouthed yet, which wouldn't be an easy task.

"We'll figure something out, Charlie honey. Trust the "Logan." You know there is no problem to which I can't find a solution."

Chago snorted. "You can still walk with those ankles, Chico?"

"Of course! Unless you are ready to carry me everywhere, in which case, I'll say no."

I slapped Logan's arm. Today his eyes were a pale blue to match his shirt. I didn't even know how many pairs of contact lenses he had.

"If you want, you can come after class to the journal. I only have one class this afternoon."

"Yeah, I appreciate it." I looked at Chago. "Since you're finishing half an hour after me."

"Don't forget your mother," Chago offered.

"I'm not expected there before six; plenty of time." I waved my hand dismissively.

"I'll see you later, after Advanced Lit."

"Yeah, I—"

"Logan? Do you have a minute? I have a slight problem with my article," a sophomore boy called.

Logan looked down at his barely eaten food and grabbed his apple.

"Yes, let's go to the newsroom; it will be easier to work there." He stood up and sighed dramatically. "Sorry guys, but the work of a celebrity never stops."

"Whatever helps you sleep at night," Chago mocked.

"See you later, Lonnie."

"Can I ask you something?" The amusement shining in Chago's eyes made me wary.

"You can try."

"You are going to dress for the 'job' tonight, right?"

"I guess…" I trailed off suspiciously.

"Wearing what? One of those outfits your mother has been trying to force on you for the past few years?"

I grimaced, thinking of the lacy, girly, preppy dresses that my mom, well her assistant, kept buying for me.

"Can I come over just to take a picture? I would love to see you wearing one of those dresses," he teased with a wide, mischievous grin.

I shook my head vigorously. "¡Sobre mi cadaver Santiago!" I growled, knowing it annoyed him when I used his full name. "Some things are better left unseen."

He laughed. "I'll see you in one of those eventually."

"Scary shit."

"Probably," he agreed, still laughing.

The rest of the afternoon passed in a blur, I was much too busy thinking about how to approach the negotiations with my mother. What could I offer in exchange for her giving me more time? It was more a question of what freedom or principle I was ready to give up to keep my freedom of choice.

"Today I'm going to give you back your essays on 'The Picture of Dorian Gray'." Mr. Mulligan stood by his desk with a pile of papers in his hands. "I know it's probably far earlier than most of you would have expected or hoped, but they were just too interesting to read. Some of you have very unique views on the book; it helped me figure you out a bit more."

That wasn't something I'd expected. We'd turned them in on Monday, and he was already done correcting them? That was impressive.

"Some of you are still very close-minded and getting too much inspiration from other opinions," he added, going through the aisles, giving back the papers. "But it's all right. We're here to work on that."

"Brilliant," he whispered as he settled my paper in front of me. An A and it took all of my willpower not to gloat out loud.

'Please see me after class' was penciled just below the grade. I looked up at him and frowned when I met his eyes. I didn't like it when the teachers called me after class. Usually, it was to complain about my attitude and ask me to tone it down, but I thought that was what he was looking for - free spirits. The small smile he gave me startled me; I didn't know what to think anymore.

"Miss Miller." He leaned back in his chair, crossing his arms on his chest when I joined him after the bell had rung.

"You wanted to see me?" I asked wearily, playing with the keychain on my backpack strap.

"Yes, your work was fantastic quality." He seemed genuine. "The way you described and compared it to modern society with Lord Henry Wotton being today's magazines and TV commercials influencing the minds of the naïve teenagers like Dorian Gray today." He chuckled lightly. "That was pretty original."

"And sadly, so true," I confirmed, still not seeing his reason for asking me to stay after class. "You wouldn't even imagine the number of students in this school ready to sell their 'pseudo-soul' for new boobs or some muscles. Dorian's naivety is transposed today by people's vanity."

"Why are you saying, 'Pseudo-soul'?" he asked curiously. "You don't believe we have a soul?"

"Let's keep theology for another essay, sir." I tried to sound as if I was joking, but I always hated when people were trying to figure me out. "All I'm saying is that even if they have one, and believe strongly in it, they wouldn't mind selling it for physical beauty. The whole debate between Heaven and Hell is irrelevant. We create our own heaven; we create others' own hell."

"So young and already so cynical." He shook his head.

"That's all you wanted?" I asked, trying not to sound too rude; it was good to have a teacher who didn't see me as a smart mouth just yet.

He cleared his throat. "Your essay's perfect, that's true. You think outside the box. You've got one hell of an opinion, but it's not all black and white in life, you know." He detailed me. "It would be too easy. Sometimes you have to choose the lesser of two evils even if it's evil. The line is blurry, in shades of grey."

"What if I don't want to be like that?" I challenged him.

A smile tugged at his lips. "Yeah, we'll see. No, actually, I wanted to ask you a favor."

"A favor?"

He nodded. "I have a student, a senior who has a small problem with his literature essays. He can't get into them, and it feels like he cannot express his own opinion."

"Maybe he doesn't have a mind of his own, like 95% of the students here," I let out snidely. "He can go to the tutoring center, plenty of help there," I added dismissively.

"He doesn't want to. He wants to get into an ivy league University, and he thinks tutoring may affect his chances."

I shook my head. "I'm not a people person. I don't know why people keep thinking that, but I would be a terrible tutor."

He cocked his head. "I could make it worthwhile."

I narrowed my eyes suspiciously.

"I've heard you were having trouble concerning your extracurricular activities for College applications and—"

"Was it in the newspaper or something?" I snapped, throwing my hands up in annoyance. "And why does everyone keep pushing me toward tutoring?"

"It's only one student for a limited period of time and it won't be listed as tutoring on your curriculum."

"Keep talking," I replied, intrigued.

"I might be able to say that you were an active member of 'Spread Literacy,' which is the charity I am taking care of. An excellent extracurricular activity if you want my opinion."

I narrowed my eyes. "Why would you do that?"

He shrugged. "Why wouldn't I?"

"Let me get back to you on that tomorrow, okay?"

"Why wait?" he asked, reaching for the papers on his desk and putting them in his bag.

Because I want to talk to Logan first. Because I hate favors. Because I want to see if I can manage a delay from my mother tonight. "Because I hate making rushed decisions and right now I have Logan waiting for me," I said, looking at my watch; I only had fifteen minutes to see Logan before Chago was done. "I like to make decisions after thinking for a little while." I took a step back and gave him a small smile. "Plus, I always thought that, if something looks too good to be true, it probably is."

Mr. Mulligan laughed, his eyes shining with genuine mirth as if he didn't expect any less from me.

"I'll see you tomorrow and…thanks."

"You are just as smart as Kate and as opinionated as David, an explosive combination," he commented just as I reached the door.

Of all the things he could have said, he'd said one of the only things that could stop me right in my tracks; he'd mentioned my father.

I turned around slowly and met his expectant eyes; nobody, except for Chago and Logan, knew my father's name. I never talked about him and my mother sure as hell didn't either. She didn't even speak to me about him.

"You know my parents?" I gasped.

"We were together in school. We were friends, your father and I." He took a deep breath.

"What happened?" I asked eagerly. I didn't know much about my parents' teenage years. I didn't even know my grandparents on my mother's side, and I'd only known my grandmother on my father's side while we lived in Montana.

"Life happened," he replied wistfully.

"But—"

"I'm not going anywhere, Charlotte," he assured with a kind smile. "We'll have time to talk. I understood you were expected somewhere, no?"

I nodded. "See you tomorrow," I repeated before rushing out, still under the shock of his revelation.

As expected, Logan didn't have much news for me.

"Well, I did find something…" He trailed off and I knew only too well where he was going with that.

"Please, if you're about to say the philatelist club, just shut up right now or I'll have to beat you dead with Chago's crowbar, and we both know you don't want that to happen."

Logan nodded. "Please, not the crowbar." He gave me a lopsided grin. "But I'm not going down without a fight. I still have tomorrow, don't I?"

"Yeah, you do, Lonnie, even if I know it's tough."

"I can try, but not tonight. I still have all that to organize." He gestured toward a huge whiteboard full of pictures, notes, and articles.

"It's alright. I need to get ready for my mother's 'one ticket to hell' evening. You know how much I hate cocktail parties."

"At least as ardently as I love them."

"Why are we even friends?" I asked with a heavy sigh.

"Because I'm awesome?" he offered.

"Yeah, that's probably it," I replied with a wink.

"Ready to go, Chula? Logan needs to work," Chago called, leaning against the door frame. "Don't give him an excuse to do nada! His middle name being 'slacker' and all."

"Chago, Chago, Chago…" Logan rested his hand on his chest in mock hurt. "You are breaking my heart." He shook his head. "Especially coming from the guy who tried to get into Spanish class." He grinned. "But it's true though. I really need to get some work done."

I hugged Logan quickly before following Chago to the car. Chago was silent the whole drive back, but I didn't miss the twitch of his jaw muscles, the tell that he was deep in very unpleasant thoughts.

"What are you thinking about?" I finally asked as we parked in front of my house.

"I want to ask you something, Chula." He looked so serious that I knew it was not a trick to see me in my dumb dress.

I sighed. I didn't like when he looked serious. It made him say very wise things I usually didn't want to hear.

"Okay, come in. Can we discuss while I get ready?"

He nodded and got out of the car, playing with his car keys.

Oh, it was big, I thought, feeling the weight of anxiety settling in my chest.

He followed me into my room and sat on my bed, his back to me while I picked up the least girly cocktail dress my mother had bought me. It was a satin black single-strap dress, stopping about two inches above the knees. The only frivolity was the black satin rose on the strap.

"I was thinking," he cleared his throat. "Is it true that this tutoring thing is so great for your college applications?"

I shrugged before realizing he couldn't see me. "I don't know, Chago."

"Because I can't help wondering why you are refusing so vehemently?" he questioned and sighed, shaking his head.

I stripped off my clothes. "I'll get in the shower, but I'm going to leave the door open. Come stand by it, so I'll hear you."

"So, as I said," he tried louder. "You keep saying you would be a terrible tutor, but I saw you helping the kids at home. You're patient, funny, nice. I-I don't see what's wrong with your tutoring methods."

"I don't know. It's maybe *them* I don't want to help? You know there is a difference between helping the kids back in the vecindad and helping the spoiled, ungrateful brats from our school."

"I just hope you're not trying to mess up your chances to explore your full potential." The worry in his voice tightened my chest. "If it's how you feel, I'll say go for it, but if it's to mark your difference, or rebel or anything like that, it's not worth it."

I closed my eyes, turning off the water. "I'm getting out," I replied, hoping I would not have to answer his question.

"You're exceptional, Chula, bright, unique. You need to leave your mark on this world," he insisted with conviction. "You can be anything, a lawyer, a writer, an architect, a doctor. Well, maybe not a doctor. You really suck in chemistry and physics, but you get my point."

"Where are you going with this, Guapo?" I asked as I tightened my wet hair into a tight bun. My hair needed to be wet if I wanted to do anything with it.

"I can't expect much from my future. I'll go to community college at best. I'll become lower middle class hoping that my kids will be able to do better and that's fine by me, I swear. It's much better than what I could have expected at first." I could hear the earnest truth in his voice.

I scowled at his words. "That's not true. You deserve to be so much more."

"Of course it is." He was lying on my bed, looking at the ceiling. "But I want you to be that...whatever you want to be and marry that great doctor or whatever. I know that fulfilling your potential doesn't mean you'll forget me or mama or Mateo. I know you, Chula; I trust our friendship more than that." He had a smile in his voice. "I give you more credit than that."

I smiled as I tried to find a pair of shoes that could both go with this dress and weren't a death trap. "I could never let go of you, my Chago, whatever I become, wherever I go," I confirmed affectionately, but my smile transformed into a wince as I looked at a pair of black stilettos I found in the back of my wardrobe. My mom had acted all offended when she'd seen my face as she'd given them to me for my sixteenth birthday.

"They're Christian Louboutin!" She had exclaimed like it meant everything.

"Of course, they are," I replied, disappointed as all I'd wanted was a Taylor Baritone 8-String acoustic guitar.

I finally managed to find a pair of plain black shoes with a very thin green line around the toe. They had squared large heels of about two inches. At least I would be steadier in those.

I applied blush on my cheeks and pink gloss to my lips before putting on the baroque style Taxco Sterling silver Malachite necklace Chago had given me last Christmas. It was a way of bringing that part of my life with me.

"Look at me, Guapo," I asked, swirling around.

"You're very pretty." He sized me up before pointing at my outfit. "You deserve all this."

I laughed and sat beside him. "I swear the reasons why I refused have nothing to do with you or any desire to sabotage myself. It's mainly because I can't stand 95% of the students at our school. And I know it's not my career or my future life that could separate us. You're a part of me like I'm a part of you, and you know what Santiago Valdez?" I winked, patting his knee. "Mark my words; you'll do extraordinary things one day."

He nodded. "Anything is possible," he agreed, but I could see he was only humoring me.

"And please God take back the 'I deserve all this'" I groaned, pointing at my outfit. "I've never felt more uncomfortable in my whole life."

"Including when you fell in caca de caballo last year and ended up losing the pants, wearing only Mateo's dress shirt as a summer dress, in front of all those horny young Mexican guys at the cowboys training day?"

I thought for a while. That had been pretty embarrassing, but I knew that, with Chago and Mateo by my side, none of the guys present would have had a chance to even lay a finger on me.

I nodded. "Even then, hermano."

"You'll survive tonight. You're a tough cookie. I mean, you deal with my idiot brother daily."

"I sure do. But those people," I faked a shiver. "Son malvados, compadre!"

"No, they're not evil, just...assy." He pointed at my cell. "You've got my number on speed dial. If it gets too much, I'm just a call away." He checked his watch and stood up. "Your car will be here any minute." He hugged me, holding me tightly against him. "Sabes que te quiero mucho, ¿no?

"I love you too." I kissed his cheek.

We heard a horn and sighed simultaneously.

"I'll call you when I get back." I tried to sound far cheerier than I felt. "Do you want to stay here and watch movies?" I asked, knowing how much he loved the flat screen TV and home theater system. I'd left him alone at my home more than once; it was not like my mother was here enough to care.

He shook his head. "No. I'll try to get some hours at the garage. Mateo could use the help anyways. Business is pretty good these days."

I nodded. "I'll speak to you later."

The car took me to the hotel where the party was taking place. I was planning on finding my mother discreetly to show her the effort I'd made, then staying in a dark corner for a couple of hours before sneaking back home.

"Aww, Charlotte sweetheart," my mother squealed as soon as I walked into the room, attracting the attention of the people around her.

I forced a smile, walking toward her. The discreet entrance I'd dreamed of making went straight out the window.

She opened her arms to hug me. Okay, it was the "loving-caring mother" act tonight.

"I'm glad you made it!" She rubbed my back. "How was school?"

"Fantastic, as usual." I smiled brightly to the people she was talking to. I started to feel sorry for the actors who had to do that all day long. Their cheeks had to be so painful by the end of it.

I introduced myself politely before excusing myself to get a drink, in other words, it meant getting away from my mother and her associates who were checking me out from head to toe. At least I could see the genuine appreciation in my mother's eyes. Would she be grateful enough to drop the extracurricular issue once and for all? Unlikely, but one could dream.

After collecting my juice, I took two quick steps back from the bar without looking and collided with someone.

"I'm so sorry," I apologized automatically.

"That's alright," crooned a deep and slightly accented voice.

I turned around to see a tall Hispanic man with graying hair. He was still very fit for someone who was probably in his early fifties.

"Charlotte Miller." He extended his hand to shake mine.

My face brightened with recognition of Andres Cardenas Ruiz, my mother's biggest client and the man who, involuntarily, had played a part in my mother easing up on my friendship with Chago. I genuinely liked the man because of that, even if he didn't have any knowledge of his help.

"Mr. Ruiz, it's a real pleasure to see you." I smiled brightly, shaking his hand energetically.

"It seems to be," he jested. "Your smile switched from generic to genuine in a second."

I cocked my head to the side. "Very observant." I was impressed. I'd only met the man a handful of times before.

"In business, you have to be," he confirmed. "People are most revealing in their posture."

"I wouldn't know," I admitted, even if I could tell at school just by the way some people walked in the corridors, how important they thought they were.

His smile widened, making his eyes crinkle. "I like your honesty, Charlotte. Would you have a few minutes for me? I wanted to talk to you."

"Of course." I followed him to a remote table.

"I don't know if your mother mentioned it, but I'm going to recruit an intern for the summer." He looked around the room as if he was always trying to be conscious of his surroundings. "It might not interest you to apply, but it comes with a full scholarship to the University of your choice and an employment contract upon graduation."

When I heard the words 'full scholarship', I could only think of Chago. It could be his way out! He was the one interested in business. He was gifted and he had a lot of instinct.

It was his shot, and he more than deserved it. I quickly glanced at my mother who was eyeing us discreetly. She wanted me to accept the offer, and she was going to be super pissed about what I was about to do. I would be kissing the extension of my parole goodbye because of this and would have to accept the offer made by Mr. Mulligan, but Chago was worth it.

"I'd never thought an internship offer could have such an effect. Did you just freeze on me?" he asked, and I could see he was trying hard to ease the atmosphere.

"I—" I shook my head. "No, I was just thinking, and you are asking the wrong person."

"Is that so?" he asked curiously.

I nodded. "I'm not good in business. It's not even a field I'm interested in, but Chago — Santiago would be an asset to you."

"Why is that?" he asked, and I could see I was doing Chago's preliminary interview right here and now.

I couldn't stop thinking about what an opportunity it could be for him. Chago who had to work part-time and thought he couldn't do better than community college. This could change everything for him. This had to change everything, and it was my shot to help him.

"Most of the people who've made it in the business world don't even have highly rated MBAs or other credentials. If I'm not mistaken you only went to community college, am I right?"

He nodded with a small smile as if he knew where I was going with this.

"See? I mean people who've really succeeded have this little something, that touch we call 'business sense' and he definitely has it." I smiled, remembering how passionate he had been when he'd taken the business class last year. He'd played it cool in front of the others like it was not a big deal, but he'd get so excited whenever he'd explain things to me or try to figure out some business plans for Mateo's garage. "I know you won't take my word for it because, let's face it, people don't get as far as you are now by trusting other people; it would be a mistake."

"Very true," he confirmed.

"Maybe…I don't know," I shrugged. "Ask the Business Studies teacher to give you the virtual business plans the class made last year. Chago didn't get the best grade, but his plan was probably the only one viable in real life. It was based on facts, not only on theories and assumptions."

"How would you know the others were not as good?" It was a legit question. He didn't know Chago. He didn't know the other students as well as I did.

I laughed. "Because I know the other students and because I know him. Plus," I blushed as I was about to admit to this stranger, my mother's biggest client, my criminal tendencies.

"Plus?" he encouraged with a mischievous light in his eyes.

"Plus, I was so offended he didn't get the best grade, I broke into the teachers' office to read the copy of the paper that had beaten him," I admitted. "And there was nothing proactive in it. Only basic meaningless theories," I added, my nostrils flaring with anger.

He settled more comfortably on his chair. "So, what do you want from me?" he asked with amusement. My pleading was entertaining him.

"I'm not telling you to give him the internship. You know better than I do. I'm just asking you to give him a chance, the opportunity to prove he would be the best for you because I know he will be. I wouldn't push you to test him if it was just a hunch. I know. You will be one of the few who will test him fairly, give him a real chance without looking at where he comes from or what he might look like."

"Would you bet on him being perfect for that job?"

I nodded.

"What would you bet?" he asked curiously.

I twisted my lips, thinking. "I might be biased here since Chago is probably one of the most important people in my life, but I'd bet everything I have." Even if I don't have much, I added to myself.

"Santiago Valdez is a lucky young man to have someone trusting him so fully, without restriction. I wish I'd had a person like you in my life during my youth," he admitted, and I could hear a faint trace of longing in his voice.

"You didn't turn out that bad," I retorted in a weird attempt to cheer him up. I couldn't believe I was sitting with a powerful, rich man I barely knew and was trying to cheer him up.

"But maybe there are some mistakes I could have avoided," he confessed, idly tracing the faint scar on the side of his neck.

I shook my head. "Chago is fantastic, with or without me. He would have managed just as well."

"Never underestimate your impact on his life. Having someone who trusts you, who forces you to try to become the person you ought to be... That pushes you to become the best possible version of yourself." He smiled. "Believe me; I'm old enough to know."

I smiled silently, not really knowing what to add.

"Well." He stood up. "I'll check out what you told me and I'll arrange for him to come for an interview."

"Don't tell him about my involvement please," I pleaded fervently, reaching up to seize his arm.

He smiled. "Ah, yes, that famous Latino pride we are all born with."

"It's both a blessing and a curse," I confirmed. I knew Chago. If he ever thought this was an act of charity or a favor, he would tell Andres to shove his internship where the sun never shines.

He patted my shoulder. "Don't worry. he won't know. Enjoy the rest of your evening."

"Sure!" I exclaimed as cheerily as I could.

He joined my mother's group. After a while, she threw me a discreet dark glance, and I knew he had told her I'd declined his offer.

I sighed, heading for the exit as subtly as I could. There was no point in me staying any longer—the damage was done.

As soon as I exited the room, I decided to call Chago. I wanted to spend a few hours with him; it would make me feel better. It always did.

"I can't believe you refused the offer!" my mother hissed from behind me.

I turned slowly, phone in hand.

"What do you want to do with your future?" She took another step toward me.

"I don't know yet, but give me some time to figure it out. All I know is that it's not business," I replied as calmly as I could. She was angry enough without me fueling the fire. "I'm just not attracted to business. I'm sorry."

"Well, you still have to pick an activity, young lady. Don't think-_"

"But I already did, Mother!" I sneered smugly. Calling me 'young lady' was the best way to send me into "sassy mode."

Her eyes widened slightly with surprise.

"I'll be part of 'Spread Literacy,' which is run by my literature teacher. See, I did listen." Sort of.

She sighed wearily. "One day, you will realize I'm not your enemy and that I'm just trying to help you make the right choices."

"And maybe one day you might realize that I'm not defying you just because I'm saying 'no.' I'm just making the decisions I truly believe are right for me." I shook my head. "Please, Mother, don't you realize that I've got to live my life the way I feel is right for me? You might think it's all wrong for you, but it can be right for me. At least try giving me the benefit of the doubt. You're a lawyer, right?"

My mother opened her mouth to reply when one of her associates appeared.

"Kate? We're waiting for you."

"She was just telling me goodbye, Mr. Goodman." I apologized with my best angelic smile. If only I were being filmed right now, I would totally run for the best actress' Oscar. "I'll see you later, Mom," I added, concentrating on her.

"See you later," she answered, apparently grateful. Maybe she wouldn't be too mad about me refusing the internship offer.

I rolled my eyes as I got into the taxi. I would be tutoring after all, but I was not so reluctant now, knowing it might help Chago get everything he deserved.

CHAPTER 4

"Okay, I'll do it. I'm accepting the offer," I told Mr. Mulligan Friday after class.

He nodded "I'm glad you decided to do it. You are really making the right choice."

It was my only decent choice. "So how do we do this?" I asked, leaning back on the table across his desk.

"He should be here any minute. He had practice today."

I couldn't help but snort. "It's a Viking. I should have known." The Vikings were the players of our various varsity teams.

"Don't be so quick to judge him. He is on the honor roll in every other subject," Mr. Mulligan chastised me.

I looked away, pursing my lips with disapproval. "Yes, well, if the shoe fits."

"I think you're really perfect for the job." He scratched his stubbly jaw as if he was having some internal discussion.

"What about my parents? I—"

"Mr. Mulligan, I'm here." A deep voice interrupted me. I turned around with a glare, but the Viking I faced was not one I'd expected.

"Mr. Johnson, I'm glad you could make it." Mulligan stood up, gesturing him in.

Gabriel Johnson was "Mr. All-American-Hero." He was captain of the soccer team and was dating Darlene Freemont, the perfect co-captain of the cheerleaders' team. He was bright and sort of good looking. About 6'1 with thick dark brown hair, tanned skin, emerald eyes, a flawless face, strong jawline, and straight nose. Okay, he was totally hot - if you were into the almost perfect, Greek god type. But for me, he was actually too perfect. I felt pride in thinking, it was their flaws that made a person beautiful.

At least this Viking was not the worst of the lot though. I'd never seen him pick on the weak in the school's corridors, but of course, I'd never seen him jump to protect them either. So, while he was still in the Douchebag category, he didn't make the top of the list. Just thinking about that made me mad and it was not the best plan, I was supposed to help him, not curse him.

When I was done with my internal condemning, I realized that Gabriel was eyeing me curiously, an eyebrow arched in wonder.

Did I just zone out? I thought, not able to stop the slight blush creeping onto my cheeks.

"Charlotte Miller." I extended my hand to shake his, acting as if nothing had happened. "But you can call me Charlie," I added, not even knowing why.

"I know who you are," he replied, shaking my hand. His hand felt huge around mine, and it was so soft compared to Chago's and Mateo's scarred and calloused hands. You could see the difference in their lives right there, with a single handshake.

"Oh, angels of Heaven, sing for us! This Viking knows my name! How did I get so lucky?" I marveled sarcastically.

Gabriel's jaw clenched, but he didn't comment. He was smart enough to know it wouldn't be a great idea.

Mr. Mulligan cleared his throat loudly to get our attention.

"Not that this exchange is not fascinating to watch, but I need to get to the Editorial office." He grabbed his bag. "I'll let you discuss the details." He took a couple of steps toward the door before turning toward us again. "And of course, I intend to get feedback for our agreements to stand…from both of you." He smiled. "I'm your teacher, after all."

"Of course," I replied as Gabriel just nodded.

When Mulligan exited the room, I quickly glanced at my watch. I still had fifteen minutes before meeting Chago.

"Are you expected somewhere?" he asked curiously, sitting casually on a desk.

None of your business! I too, a poor mortal, have a life… kind of.

"Anyways." I ignored his question. "Mulligan gave me the list of books you have to study this year. I will help you for the first two." I looked at the titles, almost wincing. The first one was "Romeo and Juliet" and boy did I *hate* that book. "How do you want to meet? I guess school is not an option since you want to keep it as quiet as possible." I was rather happy to keep this tutoring agreement a secret because I couldn't help but feel slightly ashamed at helping a Viking. Those people already had everything.

"The library?" I tried. "It's not like we'd risk seeing your friends there. I bet they don't know where it is and books—" I pretended to think. "Isn't that like Kryptonite for your kind?" I couldn't help but snigger at my own joke.

"You are a hoot, aren't you? No. As shocking as it might be, some of us go there. And I don't think it's the best place to discuss books because that's what we would do most, right? Talk?" He gave me a superior smile, leaning back on the desk. "I might not be as bright as you are, but I've heard the library is supposed to be a quiet environment."

One for the Viking! I was somehow impressed by how quick on the draw he was.

His smile widened. He knew he had won this round and I didn't like the idea of being bested.

"This leaves your place or mine, but since all your friends live in the same haughty neighborhood as you, it leaves mine," I added, biting my bottom lip. I was not comfortable with someone new invading my environment, even for a limited period of time. *He doesn't care, Charlie; you're not even a blip on his radar.*

He straightened on the desk, giving me a roguish smile. "There are simpler ways to get me into your house." He completed his comment with a wink.

"Get over yourself!" I snapped. "If you don't want to take this seriously, better drop it now. I've got other things to do!" *Not really.*

He threw his hands up in surrender. "Geez Louise! I was just trying to make a joke here," he sighed, standing up. "What did he promise you to agree to this? Because you don't seem to be such a people person and you're clearly not my biggest fan."

"It doesn't really matter what I gain out of it, does it? As long as it's good for you." I looked at my watch again. Five more minutes. "Listen, here is my phone number and address." I scribbled on a piece of paper out of my notebook. "I think we should give you a week to read the book. Is that okay?"

He nodded.

"Do you have some time next weekend?"

"I have a game Friday night. What about Saturday afternoon? At two?"

"That's fine. Give me a call if there is something you don't understand in Shakespeare's unique writing. And don't worry; we're not the same. I would never mock someone who's trying to learn something."

I stood even straighter, muscles so tight it hurt my neck. I expected him to take the bait. I shamelessly realized I really wanted this fight.

"I—" he started, but apparently decided otherwise. "You better go. Your boyfriend will be waiting. See you next week."

I nodded, not even bothering to set him straight. Who cared anyway?

I rushed and arrived just as Chago exited the room.

"Hey, Chula! Where were you?" he asked as we walked to his locker.

"You know. My English project," I pressed on the word project.

"What is that exactly?" he asked curiously as he threw books into his backpack.

"I'm tutoring a student with what I can say are 'special needs'."

He eyed me, eyebrows furrowed with wonder. "I thought you didn't want to tutor anyone."

I shrugged. "It's only one person for a limited period of time and it won't be 'tutoring' on my resume, which won't give colleges a wrong idea about who I am."

"And who is this student?"

"I plead the fifth," I chuckled, sitting down in the car.

"Damn! I knew that one was going to come back and bite me in the ass!"

When Chago and I 'pleaded the fifth,' it had nothing to do with the Constitution and the protection against self-incrimination. When we were about thirteen or fourteen, we'd gotten extremely bored one day during the summer holidays, so we'd invented our own friendship Constitution. Our Fifth Amendment was the right to keep a secret from each other if the desire to keep the secret had been invoked by the third party involved and if this secret wouldn't have a real impact on our lives. Gabriel had expressed his wish to keep the tutoring a secret. It was not my place to talk about it as his name wouldn't change anything. And truth be told, I didn't think Chago would be pleased I was helping a Viking. He wouldn't say anything, of course. He was way too supportive for that, but he didn't like them or trust them, and I knew he would be even more protective of me if he knew.

"You use it a lot yourself," I reminded him, thinking of all the bad things that had to be going on where he lived, but which he kept from me. I knew it was to protect me and stop me from worrying too much, but...

"What are we doing tonight?" he asked before starting the car.

"It's Friday night and we're careless teenagers with minimum parental supervision on my part."

"I see…" He wiggled his eyebrows suggestively.

"You know what it means, right?" I asked with a cheeky grin.

"It means watching movies and eating junk until we crash?"

"Yahtzee!"

He laughed, shaking his head. "Your bed or mine?"

"Well, you know I love your place, but Saturday mornings?" I winced. "If your little cousin wakes me up at 8:00 am again, there will be a murder in the Valdez house."

"Good point." He nodded. "Your bed then."

At first, my mother had thrown a fit when she'd come home late at night to find Chago asleep in my room. I'd told her that if we'd wanted to do something "reprehensible," we wouldn't have done it in the open. She'd still grounded me for two weeks and had been suspicious of us for a long time, but a year or so ago, she'd finally realized that Chago and I didn't see each other that way. The fact that I kept pushing him into dates with girls was probably a part of it. And the fact that I'd taken him to buy my first bra instead of her because she'd been too busy that week.

Now Chago was sleeping at my house at least two or three times a month. He even had half a drawer there.

"But let's not forget about Eva's party," I reminded him, quickly glancing his way.

He sighed. "Chula…" he started with exasperation.

"What? Are we going back at pretending you don't like her?"

He continued to drive silently, but the whitening of his knuckles as he grabbed the steering wheel tighter was a sign of his growing irritation.

"You know she won't stay single forever, right?" I shook my head. "She is a great girl and I'm pretty sure she likes you too."

"It never ends well," he let out somberly, parking in front of my house. "I don't want to fight…not with her."

I looked at him silently for a minute. I could see his point. Every girlfriend he'd ever had had started okay, but after a while, they tried to break us up, and Chago hated that. It was all or nothing; I was part of him like he was part of me. I knew he liked Eva a lot more than he'd liked any of the other girls before. I could see the longing in his eyes. He didn't want things to end bitterly with her. For once, he truly cared.

"She is different…" I said, hurting for him. "Eva, she is not like the others. She knows us well. She won't feel threatened."

"Yeah…" He trailed off. "Anyways, is Gaygan coming to watch movies with us tonight?"

I rolled my eyes at his not-so-subtle way of changing the subject. "No. Tonight he has his meeting with the LGBT club and I think he might have a new boyfriend."

"Really? As long as he is better than the last one." He grimaced, falling heavily onto the sofa.

I faked a shudder. "Yeah, that one was pretty messed up." I recalled the half-goth, half-alien college freshman he'd dated for a couple of months before the summer.

"What did he want to be called again?" Chago asked with a smirk, arranging the cushions around himself as a comfortable nest.

"Natas? Yes! That's it!" I burst into laughter. "He explained it was Satan in reverse."

Chago laughed too. "You honestly have to give Logan some credit; he really has a gift for finding the crazy ones."

I swatted his legs, so I could sit down. "What do you want to watch?" I asked, scanning Netflix.

Chago rested his legs on my lap. "Whatever you like. I'm so dead, I think I'll be out in five." And true to his words, he was snoring lightly less than ten minutes into the show.

****

The weekend was uneventful except for Sunday when my mother was home. It seemed that what I'd told her on Thursday night had touched her a lot more than I'd expected. She asked me if we could talk as soon as I woke up, and there was no iPhone or Laptop or any other electronic device in her surroundings. I couldn't remember the last time she was not connected.

"I thought about what you told me," she said, setting a plate of frozen waffles and a cup of coffee in front of me, which was the best breakfast she'd made in years. "I know you might think I'm trying to destroy your life, but I'm not. I never wanted to hurt you."

I looked at her silently. I'd never seen her so raw, so "real," so…human. At least not since my father died. Before that, it'd been different. She'd been happy, and maybe a part of me longed for the mother she had been back then.

"I know that's not what you are looking for, Mom. I never thought that was what you wanted to do." I reassured her, and it was true. She had many flaws, but I knew she wouldn't purposely do something that would damage me.

"Oh." She rubbed her neck. "I thought teenagers always thought parents were trying to destroy their lives."

I wanted to tell her that she, unfortunately, didn't know me enough to try to analyze me or pretend to know the way I was thinking. The more I became autonomous, the further down I went on her list of priorities. She was not a bad mother. She was just— What was she? A careerist? She dealt with her grief the only way she knew how.

"It's just that I'm scared to see you make mistakes I could prevent. I was in your shoes not so long ago, baby. I was sixteen too, and I know how full of certitude we can be then. We think we know it all, but truth be told, we don't." She gave me a wistful smile. "I was once young enough to think I knew it all, but it goes so much faster than you think."

"You're trying to shield me from mistakes I've never heard of. You -" I shook my head. "You never talk about the past, Mom. What is it you did that was such a mistake? You are a lawyer. You are healthy. You were a decent mom. What did you do that was so wrong?"

She looked at me silently for a second, pain etched in her face. "I just don't want you to mess up your life and suffer, that's all," she said, ignoring my questions.

"Are you regretting choosing dad? Having me?"

She recoiled at my words and I didn't think I could have hurt her more if I had slapped her. "How could you say something like that?" Her voice broke and the desperation in her eyes made me regret opening my mouth.

At that moment her phone started to ring, but she ignored it. This was even bigger than I' thought.

"I'm sorry. I shouldn't have—" I looked down at my plate as shame overwhelmed me.

"No, you shouldn't have, but I wonder what made you say that." Her voice carried the pain I had seen on her face.

"I know you love your job but--" I looked up and saw that the pain was now mixed with obvious weariness. I took a deep breath, deciding it was better to change the subject; there was no point in hurting her. It was too late to change anything anyway. "I'm smart, Mom, and if I make mistakes, well, so be it." I cocked my head to the side with a small sad smile. "It's better for me to make mistakes than resent you for forcing me into choices I might end up regretting. Don't you think?"

She pinched her bottom lip between her thumb and forefinger, lost in thought. "I guess so, but it wouldn't hurt you to listen occasionally, would it? Because sometimes you don't get a second chance, no matter how much you want it."

"I think it's never too late for second chances. I think only death can stop you. I-" I was interrupted by the phone again. "Maybe you should get that." I pointed to her laptop bag.

She grimaced. "We have new juniors and-"

I raised my hand to stop her. "It's cool mom. I may be sixteen, but I do understand." I shrugged. "I will spend the afternoon at Chago's anyways. Mateo is still working on that beautiful car and--"

"You like cars?" she asked, surprised as if I'd told her I'd wanted to quit school and join the circus.

I nodded. "I love them! I didn't join the auto shop last year to annoy you, you know."

She nodded slightly before cocking her head to the side as if she was talking to herself. "I'll try to be more present; I guess I don't know you as well as I should."

I wanted to deny it, make her feel better, but I refused to lie. "Probably not, " I admitted.

"I'll try harder, spend more time with you." She stood beside me, resting a tentative hand on my shoulder.

"You don't have to. I just wanted to know about you, your life, why you keep burying yourself in your work." I raised my head to lock eyes with hers. "Loving your job is one thing, but the amount of time you spend working? It's more like running from something. I might be sixteen, but I know that much."

"When you get older, you'll understand," she replied as the phone resumed its annoying tone.

I looked at her retreating form as she took the phone and walked briskly into her office. I hated the whole 'When you get older, you'll understand'. What did that even mean? I'd understand better if she tried to explain. I was not six anymore, but maybe explaining things would be harder on her than on me, like putting salt on an open wound.

I sighed, concentrating on my now cold waffles, maybe things would be different from now on. She seemed to want to try harder. I just had to help her.

As I walked back to my room, I stopped down the hall and looked at the small picture in the ugly frame I'd made in preschool. It was the only picture of us as a family that was out to the public eye. The only picture with my dad. I closed my eyes for a second, reliving that day at the park. It had been two months before his death. It had also been the last bright smile I'd ever seen on my mother's face. When my father had died, the happy, carefree part of her had died with him.

My heart sped up as I remembered the last time I'd seen my father. Every time I relived that moment, it took my breath away as if I was being punched in the stomach. It never got any better. Every time I thought about it, it hurt just the same.

I had started first grade four months earlier and we were all excited as my mom, freshly graduated from law school, had just gotten her first job at a law firm downtown. I'd kept hearing Dad tease her about him being married to a sexy lawyer even if, at the time, that hadn't meant much to me. I'd lost him when the two of us were in the car, driving back to Dallas from a water park. We'd been playing the color game. I'd loved that game when I was a little girl. The goal was to quickly match the color of a passing car with something of the same color: red/strawberry, yellow/sun, blue/Smurf etc.…

My father had always made me laugh by making mistakes. I knew he'd loved to humor me. He'd used to say that hearing me laugh was like hearing the angels sing.

"Green like a leaf!" I'd shouted, laughing from the back seat.

"Orange as the sea!" my dad had quickly answered, looking at me in the rear-view mirror.

"Nah!! The sea is blue, not orange! Silly."

"Are you sure?"

"Yes, I'm sure! You lost again."

"It's because you are very good, baby."

I nodded, looking out the window.

"Blue like… Like your shirt."

My dad had gasped, bringing one of his hands to his chest. At the time I didn't know what was happening. It hadn't alarmed me.

"Your turn daddy," I'd tried when he hadn't said anything. The car had decelerated. "Daddy?" I'd tried again, but his face had fallen on the steering wheel. "Daddy!!" I'd screamed as the car had left the road, but at a speed slow enough not to cause much damage when it had connected with the tree. I was young, but I'd known something was wrong, terribly wrong… I had felt it in my flesh and bones.

I'd struggled to unlock the safety belt and had awkwardly gotten in the front seat.

I'd shaken my father. "Daddy, please wake up, open your eyes." I'd sobbed. "Daddy, please."

I'd buried my face in his neck and cried for at least twenty minutes before someone came to help us.

I heard words like 'coronary emboli' and 'heart failure,' but all I'd known at the time was that my dad was gone and that I would never see him again.

I opened my eyes and realized I had been crying as the picture was blurry in my shaking hand.

"He was only twenty-seven. How fair was that?" I whispered, putting the picture back on the mantle. *Life is not fair, Charlie. It never was and never will be.*

I remembered everything as if it had happened yesterday. It was also one of the reasons why I had never tried to get my driver's license. Chago and Mateo had tried to teach me a couple of times, but I had panic attacks every time I sat behind the wheel. I was grateful they never insisted. They kept saying I'd be ready when I was ready.

We all had our dark secrets, memories weighing us down, but dealing with them? That was another story.

I was a pretty good preacher on how to let go of things weighing us down; I was just not that hot on the practicing part.

<u>CHAPTER 5</u>

I was barely through the school doors on Tuesday morning when my phone beeped in my pocket, announcing a text. I frowned, the only people who usually texted me were Chago and Logan. I was beside one and facing the other.

I looked at the number I didn't know. "Uh, " I let out absentmindedly before opening the text.

I'm done with the book. I've Qs, meet 2day?

I stupidly looked up, finding Gabriel at the end of the corridor with Doug, the moronic football jock I'd almost fought with on the first day. *So much for not being a douche,* I thought.

I hit the reply button before saving his number.

Nope, I have plans tonight. Even us dorks have lives. Sry.

I glanced in his direction and I didn't miss the smile creeping on his lips as he looked down at his phone. I sighed.

2moro? I sent, remembering that Chago would be working with Mateo then.

Soccer practice. Thursday?

I let out a growl of exasperation. He needed me more than I needed him. He could try harder.

"Estas bien Chula?" Chago asked, eyeing my phone curiously.

"Yeah, it's nothing. Just stupid spam texts." I quickly glanced at Gabriel and met his amused eyes.

"So anyway, when are you planning to work on your French?"

"I don't know," Chago rolled his eyes. "What do you think?"

"Thursday? Seems perfect because you are not working, and we have plans Friday." I shrugged. "Your call."

"I have plans for Friday too!" Logan blurted, radiating with excitation. "I've met a guy online and we have a date on Friday. Yes, he is a bit different, but…" Chago and I looked at Logan warily. Usually, the 'normal' guys he found were halfway to Crazy Town. If he was saying this guy was 'different', it was a scary thought.

"What?!" Logan asked, looking at us. "It's not like you didn't know I was dating."

"No, it's just --" I started.

"Nada." Chago nudged me slightly. He knew how sensitive Logan could be and expressing my doubts would have hurt him. "Are you available Thursday?"

Logan grinned.

"Stop the perv jokes hombre." Chago glowered. "Yes or no?"

"Yes, Thursday is fine for me. I have the editorial meeting, so what about seven at the library?"

"Thank you."

"Anything for my buds" he replied with a very dorky 'peace out' sign, which made both Chago and I laugh.

"See you at lunch," I called, as I pulled Chago toward our calculus class.

Thurs, 6.30, my place. I texted Gabriel.

"Thanks for stopping me from saying something stupid to Lonnie," I whispered as the teacher started to set her material down.

"No problem, I really want to meet that one and if you had said anything, Logan would have refused."

I threw him a fake death glare. "That's mean."

"Like you don't want to meet him yourself," he teased.

I pretended to look angelic. "No…Of course not!"

"Pendejada." Chago chuckled, throwing me a pencil.

I caught the pencil before it hit me. "I will keep this, thanks; and yes, you're right. I want to meet this guy. Should we play Nancy Drew on Friday night? I bet the dude is a vampire wannabe or something."

"Miss Miller, Mr. Valdez, I would love to teach you some calculus, so if you don't mind finishing your mind-blowing discussion after class, it would be highly appreciated."

I looked up dumbfounded. I hadn't expected to be caught.

"Of course, Signora, please go on." Chago leaned back on his seat smugly.

I grinned, looking down at my book.

Mrs. Walters sighed heavily, but concentrated on her blackboard again.

Five minutes later, I received a little ball of paper. When I opened it, I had to do my best not to laugh loudly.

Deal. You can be Nancy. I'll be Sherlock. Vampires are too common. Gaygan wouldn't think it's weird. I'll go with a time-traveler, space alien or

Jesus' resurrected soul. Imagine the title, 'The Time Traveler's Gay Boyfriend'. We've got a box-office champion right there.

I shook my head and winked at him. Nobody could make me laugh the way he did.

****

I was watching TV when a quick knock at the door startled me. I looked at the time on the screen. Six thirty-two.

"Uh, at least he is on time," I muttered, turning off the TV and walking lazily to the door.

I couldn't help the sardonic smile forming on my face when I opened the door. He was standing there in his vintage green polo, beige khaki shorts, and black leather flip-flops. Yes, he was the poster child for the new "Abercrombie & Fitch" collection.

"What is making you smile?" he asked, crossing his arms on his chest.

I shook my head. "Not much." I moved out of the way. "Please come in."

He looked around the hall. "Are you going to give me a tour of your home?"

Was he joking? I looked at him through narrow eyes. Apparently not. I snorted. "Right, since we're friends and all…." I trailed off. "This is the living room." I pointed to the left. "this is the corridor." I pointed ahead. "these are stairs going to the first floor, which is filled with goblins, fairies, and unicorns," I added sarcastically. "Here is the kitchen where we'll work." I pointed to the right. "This way, please."

He nodded with a small smile. He seemed to be enjoying my smart mouth. Well, he sure hadn't heard the end of it.

"Want something to drink before we start?" I asked politely. I couldn't just drink something in front of him.

"Sure, thanks." He seemed surprised by the offer. I couldn't blame him. I hadn't been particularly forthcoming.

"Coke?" I tried.

"Yep, thanks." He set a notebook on the table before sitting heavily.

I gave him the can of Coke before sitting on one of the kitchen stools, putting as much distance between us as I could.

"So, you wanted to discuss the book. What's on your mind?"

"Tell me why you smiled that way when you opened the door," he said, playing with his pen, completely ignoring my question.

"I--What?" I jerked back with surprise. I hated being taken by surprise.

"When you opened the door, you looked at me and smiled. But it was not the 'I'm pleased to see you' kind of smile, it was." He shrugged slightly. "I don't know. It was a sarcastic smile, a kind of 'I knew it!' smile and I just wondered why."

I looked at him silently for a couple of seconds. "You don't even know me and you pretend to be able to decipher my smiles? Really?" I arched an eyebrow in mock wonder. "I'm impressed."

"I'm trying to get to know you since we're teaming up for a while," he replied before taking a sip of Coke.

"There is no need, really, but what made me smile is the way you're dressed."

"That bad?" he asked, not letting go of my eyes. Someone who really cared would have given himself a quick look over, but he didn't. He was confident in his looks.

"No, there is nothing wrong with your clothing. On the contrary. It's like you've just been vomited from the new summer catalog of Abercrombie and Fitch."

"Is there something wrong with Abercrombie and Fitch? Are they using some sweatshop in China's back alleys or killing dolphins or even polluting the lakes or anything else you're defending this week?" he asked sarcastically.

I glared, pursing my lips. I knew the reputation I had in school - a trouble maker, defending causes just to piss off the students.

I shook my head and raised my hands in surrender. I didn't want to have this discussion, not with him. It was not worth it. I didn't need him to understand me.

"You know, you're playing the Almighty right now, but I'm pretty sure your clothes don't cost a fiver either," he insisted, detailing me from head to toe.

I looked down to my faded blue jeans and yellow tee-shirt promoting the Paris Agreement. I couldn't help but smile. The jeans had come from a shop in the Eastside and the shirt had been custom made at the tee shirt shop where Chago's aunt was a supervisor. So, actually, I wasn't wearing more than fifteen dollars' worth of clothes, but that was not the point either.

"It's just so generic, I bet all your friends are wearing more or less the same thing right now and-" I frowned. The look on his face told me he'd just baited me and I'd been too quick to bite. "Whatever, you're right, I'm sorry. I'm probably just jealous of your fashion style."

He opened his mouth to say something, but dropped it. Smart boy. I was a step away from showing him the door.

"Let's go back to the book. You seemed pretty eager to work on that," I continued, toying with the rim of the can. "What can I do for you?"

"Okay. I've read it and yes, I understood everything even with my little brain. "

I gestured for him to continue.

"I just wanted to talk about how to start this whole creative writing bull."

I nodded. "Okay, well first you have to write a little synopsis of the book. You know, just the basics to show you've read it. Plus, it will help you keep the main points in mind."

"Then?" he asked, opening his notebook.

"Then you ask yourself questions."

"Questions?" he asked, confused.

"Yes. You see, to express a unique or at least *your* own opinion, you have to ask yourself questions. As an example: when I read Dorian Gray, I asked myself, what are Dorian's main flaws? His ingenuity, his beauty, and then his vanity. Can I transpose that to the modern world? How?"

He nodded, apparently genuinely interested and it felt nice to be listened to, especially by one of them.

"So for Romeo and Juliet, you can... I don't know. Why not approach the notion of cliques? Is it still like that? Can we mix?" I knew the answer was 'hell no!' but I kept it shut. My opinion was not needed. "What if Romeo decided it was too high of a price to pay to be with her? On what is this love really based? Is it really love or merely passion? What would have happened if Rosalind had given in?" I finally stopped, blushing slightly, realizing I'd gotten carried away. It happened often when I talked about literature.

Gabriel was looking at me with something I couldn't really decipher. He seemed amused, yet impressed too. It was odd.

"You're passionate, aren't you? All flushed and all." He grinned. "It's cute."

"Rah! Shut your cake hole!" I snapped with embarrassment, jumping from the stool. I pretended to put some order to the kitchen to give myself something to do. "So you get it?"

"Yes, I think I have it. I can work on that for Saturday. It's still good, right?"

I nodded. I knew Chago would be working Saturday like every other weekend. "Since we're good, I think it's time for you to-" I was interrupted by the phone. I quickly looked and it said 'Office'. It was my mother. I really had to get that. "One second," I said quickly before answering.

"Take your time." I heard him reply as he leaned back on the chair.

"Yeah?"

"That's no way to answer the phone," my mother complained, her voice cold and professional, suggesting she was not alone. She was always taking that weird tone when she was with her colleagues. I was not even sure she was conscious of it.

"Hello Mother, what can I do for you?"

She sighed heavily. Apparently, she could pick up my attitude even through the phone. "We're expecting paperwork for a merger we intend to do in Japan, but it seems they've sent it to our home. How they got our address is a mystery, but I need you to check if it's there before I phone them up and throw a tantrum."

"We know how much you love your tantrums, Mother," I replied.

"Uh huh. Do that now please." I was sure she wasn't really listening anymore. She was probably working on some documents or talking to her colleagues.

"Yes, I'll do that," I continued. "I'll be right back." I mouthed to Gabriel before going to my mother's office. "Then I'll go back to make out with all the strangers I brought home from the club where I work as an exotic dancer, okay?" I told her, looking through the pile of mail the cleaner had left on her desk.

"Sure, it seems fun," she replied absentmindedly.

Yes, she was clearly not with me anymore.

I looked up from her desk to see Gabriel leaning against the door frame, the prick had followed me.

"Do you mind?!" I asked coldly. "Where are your manners?!" I added, shooing him with a gesture of my hand.

"What?" my mother asked, annoyed.

"Nothing."

"I don't have the time to joke around, Charlotte. Do you have it?" she muttered, clearly frustrated.

"Is it Kiogy Synergy?"

She sighed with relief. "It's okay. She has it," she reassured someone on her end. "Scan it now please. I'll see you later. Thanks," she added quickly before hanging up.

I sent the papers to her office and walked back to the kitchen, already preparing what I would tell Mr. Johnson about his behavior. This was my home, my space. He couldn't act like he owned the place! This was not a social call and I was not one of his groupies.

I found the kitchen empty. I thought he might have left, ego bruised, but I noticed his car keys and notebook on the table.

I frowned. "Gabriel?" I called going to the living room. "Gabriel?" I called louder, walking through the corridor. It was getting creepy. I had seen way too many horror movies in my life, and I couldn't stop some scenes of *Scream* from popping into my mind.

I saw lights on the first floor and felt the flush of anger creep up my cheeks.

"Johnson! If you don't answer right this second-" I stomped up the stairs.

"You'll do what?" I heard his voice coming from my bedroom.

I walked in on him going through my vinyl records.

"How dare you? I--" I was just too mad to even talk, I lost my wit and that was a first.

"Good one." He turned around holding my copy of 'Charlotte Sometimes' by the Cure.

I brusquely snatched it out of his hands and put it back in place, my hands shaking with anger.

"How dare you go into my bedroom without me!" I snapped, trying to fight the urge to slap him.

"You know us jocks are not that smart. We take things pretty literally and don't understand sarcasm. I was just looking for a fairy to take home to my troll."

"Who do you think you are? I mean, really? This is *my* house, This Is *my* space. I-" I shook my head. "Get out...*now!*" I ordered, pointing at the door.

"I was just trying to get to know who you are." He gestured at my walls covered with photos I'd taken and drawings I'd made. This was my private life. It was like he was reading my diary.

"I don't want you to know me!" I barked, quivering with anger. "We're not friends and we never will be!!"

"But-"

"I said get out!" I pointed my index finger to the door once more.

He buried his hands in his pockets. "Out of your bedroom or out of your house?"

"Both I--Just get out." I added, tightening my hands into such tight fists, I was sure my palms would bleed.

"Are you really that mad?" he asked, eyeing my fisted hands.

I looked up at him incredulously. Did everybody let him do whatever he wanted just because he was him? Gabriel Johnson? Probably.

"Of course, I'm mad! You not understanding shows how superior you think you are, Mister Soccer Star!!" My breathing was shallow with anger, my heart hammering against my ribcage.

"I'm not like that. It's..."

"I said get out" I repeated, pointing to the door again. I might have been a dwarf compared to him, but I could hold my ground and fight dirty. There were some things in my room, I didn't want him to see. It was the raw me - my art, my music, my pictures...*my life.*

He nodded silently, walking out of my room. I followed close behind him until he got his notebook from the kitchen and walked out.

I was about to close the door when he turned around. "We're still on for Saturday, right?" he asked like nothing happened, like I hadn't shouted at him, like he hadn't just invaded my privacy.

I let out a weird grunting sound. "Yes, 2:00 pm. Don't be late." I closed the door, not waiting for an answer.

I went up to my mother's room and discreetly watched him through her window. He walked lazily, one hand in his pocket, totally casual. I frowned. Where was his car?

He turned left down the next street. Two minutes later, his black Mercedes drove past. It seemed he didn't want to be seen here either.

I let out a heavy sigh, leaning my forehead against the cool glass of the window. Man, it wouldn't hurt for that guy to learn a bit of humility. He needed to see that he was not omniscient, that not everybody would crawl on their knees for him.

CHAPTER 6

"He will spot us straight away!" I laughed as we took our seats in the fifties retro café close to our Ivy League university. "There is no one here," I added, scanning the unusually empty coffee shop.

"How could he even do that with our super spy disguises? I mean, look at you!" He grinned. "How could he ever think that the girl wearing black sunglasses at night with a UNESCO cap is you, uh?" he asked sarcastically.

"Ahaha, very funny," I muttered, sticking my tongue out. "And what about you, Chago Valdez?"

"What about me?" He looked down at his clothes. "This is Mateo's senior year Halloween costume; he won a prize with this."

"You look like a douchebag." I sized him up, not able to stop myself from rolling my eyes. He was wearing a grey shirt, black cargo shorts, and flip-flops. He was a mix of Abercrombie & Fitch, Aeropostale, and American Eagle. So different from the tank top, greasy, old jeans, and black boots I was used to and loved.

"Exactly! Who would think I would be such a douche?"

"And what was this costume called again?" I asked, quickly browsing the menu.

"It was the 'stupid & rich gringo' look," he joked. "You like it?"

I shook my head, trying not to laugh. "Yes, you totally nailed it." We couldn't see any of his tattoos except the tribal one on his right calf.

I remembered how my mother had freaked out when Chago had come to my house after he'd gotten his first tattoo at the ripe age of fifteen. She had waited for him to leave before making me strip down to check if I had any tattoos. It had been hard for her to believe I didn't get one as well. "Not even a little 'save the whales' slogan or the WWF panda trademark?" she had asked before biting her lip, cursing herself for giving me ideas. I'd told her that if I wanted a tattoo, I would wait to be legal but, truth be told, I didn't like the idea of a needle poking into my skin repeatedly, injecting ink which would stay forever. It just gave me the creeps, but it didn't stop me from admiring Chago and Mateo's tattoos.

"Anyway, I- oh! Wait, he is here?" I whispered, lifting the menu to just under my eyes.

"Go on Nancy Drew, tell me what you see," Chago said playfully.

"Clearly a date. He is wearing the baby blue shirt with matching contact lenses and converse."

"The shirt he says makes him look like a model?"

"Yep, the one and only."

"Oooohhhh, it's getting interesting." Chago rested his chin in his palm, looking at me with a playful grin.

"He is sitting in the corner booth. Apparently, the guy is not here yet," I continued, feeling like an awesome ninja. I couldn't really take that much credit; this retro cafe was where Logan had all his first dates.

Chago chuckled. "I can't believe we're doing this."

"Just shut up. It was your idea," I hissed, still keeping my eyes on the door. "Plus we have no life... Did you have anything better to do on this charming Friday night?"

"Something better than playing 'iSpy'? I think not!" he exclaimed with fake offense.

"I thought so." I put the menu back on the table.

"Are you ready to order?" the waiter asked, looking at me strangely.

"It's okay, Nancy. You can take the sunglasses off."

I took my sunglasses off before concentrating on the waiter, showing him I was not embarrassed. "A spy job is never over, my friend," I added, deadpan.

"Are you ready to order?" he repeated, ignoring my joke.

I sighed. "A strawberry milkshake please and some apple pie."

The waiter turned to Chago.

"I'll take the man's version of her order. Chocolate milkshake and Brownie. Brown, the color of men!"

"Uh huh, is that all?"

Chago threw me a look. "Yes, thanks."

"That guy was so fun!" I snorted after the waiter left.

"You have to give him some credit, Chula. The guy probably deals with haughty, self-proclaimed geniuses from the university every single day. It wouldn't make you a hoot either."

"Nah, it would make me unemployed," I admitted, knowing I would probably punch the first or second disrespectful asshat I encountered. Self-control had never been a quality of mine and one of my biggest pet peeves was disrespectful people.

"That's what I thought," Chago confirmed, shaking his head.

"But you wouldn't want me any other way." I winked.

"No, I wouldn't."

The waiter came with our order as a tall reddish haired cute guy walked in.

"Oh, this one is cute, but he looks way too normal to be him." I watched him cross the room to the booth where Logan was sitting. "Oh my! It's him" I almost shouted, slamming my hand on the table.

Chago steadied our glasses before turning around as discreetly as possible, but the guy was already seated. "What do you mean by 'he looks too normal'?"

"No Goth clothes, no fangs, no weird hair color, no fake claws." I looked at Chago with big puppy eyes. "Do you think he might be...oh my God, I can't say it," I shuddered for dramatic effect. "Normal?" I scrunched up my nose as if that word was disgusting.

Chago rested his hand on his chest in mock horror. "Please don't say stuff like that, Chula. It could be dangerous." He took a long sip of his milkshake. "No, that guy has to be even weirder than the others. Logan usually loves rubbing his dating life in our faces. Always saying he has more fun than both of us combined."

"Not a hard thing to do," I conceded begrudgingly. My dating life was limited to two or three kisses, and Chago, well... His longest relationship had lasted about three weeks.

"Maybe," he conceded, dismissing my comment with a gesture of the hand. "But that's not the point. He did hide this date from us which means he has to be a total crazy ass."

I nodded. "Okay then, you know what's left to do guapo?" I wiggled my eyebrows.

"Should I be afraid to ask?"

"We need to approach the subject!" I exclaimed like it was evident.

"What's our cover?" He rested his elbow on the table, playing along.

"Young love, meeting one of their dearest friends unexpectedly."

"Young love?"

"Yes, so the guy won't think you are just a jealous suitor wanting a piece of that fine man Logan."

Chago crossed his eyes, lolling his tongue to the side.

"You stay here for a moment and wait for me to call you." I took the last bite of my apple pie before putting ten dollars on the table. "Can I have your car keys?" I extended my hand.

He looked at me with one eyebrow raised. He knew I was terrified of the idea of driving. I didn't even have my driving license.

"It's part of the plan," I insisted.

He sighed, dropping the keys in my hand. "I swear, Chula. One day, you'll be the death of me."

"That's the plan, boy." I stood up and walked in a straight line beside the booths. When I reached the corner booth occupied by Logan and his date, I dropped the car keys. "Damn!" I reached down, looking idly at their booth. "Logan? Hey, how are you, buddy?! It's such a surprise to see you here!" I exclaimed as genuinely as I could, putting the keys in my jeans pocket.

His eyes widened with surprise, his smile slowly vanishing when he realized I was the one standing in front of their booth. "Yes…a real shocker," he replied as calmly as he could, but the 'I'm going to get you' look he threw me was clear enough.

"Santiago, honey, come see who's here." I beamed at Chago.

Chago walked toward me, pursing his lips, trying hard not to laugh.

"What is it, angel?" He wrapped his arms around me from behind, resting his chin on my shoulder.

"Look who is here? Our dear friend Logan!" I kept my bright smile on.

"What a coincidence!" Chago played along, keeping himself positioned behind me. "How are you doing on this beautiful night?"

"I'm doing peachy!" Logan replied, throwing us a dark look we knew only too well. He was going to make us pay for a long time. I could already start to hear the week-long drama queen speeches.

I turned my head toward Logan's date. Even from this close he looked perfectly normal.

"And you are?" I tried as invitingly as I could.

"On this planet, I am known as David, " he replied neutrally.

"I see…" I trailed off.

"Okay, I'll bite," Chago whispered in my ear, tightening his hold around my waist. "Well, our names are Charlotte and Santiago, but what is your real name?" he asked, and I was really impressed with how he managed to keep his composure.

David smiled, oblivious to our teasing. "Well, my real name cannot be pronounced in any human language. Only people from my home world can."

"Of course," Chago replied and I didn't need to see him to know he had his 'omg-one-ticket-for-the-Looney-bin' face on. "I have to give it to you, hombre. Whenever I think you've managed to reach the top...you still surprise me, and that's a real challenge. Where do you find them? That's the question."

I elbowed him gently. "Well, we better go now, but it was nice to meet you, David. I hope you like life on this planet. I know we ruined it, but you know -" I grinned. "It's home."

"It's fine, Charlotte. I find your motherland welcoming enough. Thanks for the concern. My home is pretty hostile. It has been for centuries since the Spatial Quest started."

Oh, it's getting good!! I marveled. He was totally cuckoo for cocoa puffs!! "I-" I started, but was stopped by Logan's loud throat clearing.

"Aren't you expected somewhere?" he asked through clenched teeth.

"Yes, yes we are," I confirmed, as Chago let go of his hold around my waist.

"But don't worry. I'll call you later." I could hear the underlying threat in Logan's voice. He was going to bitch for hours about how childish and rude we had been.

When I turned around, I met Gabriel's amused eyes. He was sitting at a table with three other jocks, including Doug, my number one fan. Why did he look so amused? I hated being the source of his amusement without knowing why.

"Right?" Chago asked as we walked to the exit.

"What? I didn't catch that," I apologized, concentrating on him again.

"I said we're going to pay for a while, but it was worth it, don't you think?"

I nodded. "Yes, but you are not the one who is going to face his wrath tonight." I was not bothered. Logan would argue and argue and argue. It was not different from his usual self anyways.

"It's just because he knows I'm working in the morning, but don't worry, he'll bitch at me soon enough."

"True. But a space alien? Really?" I asked as we drove back to my house.

"I'm starting to think he is going on a website called 'freaky dates' or something like that." He shook his head. "I really don't see any other way."

"I think it runs deeper than that. It's like -" I took a deep breath - "like he is choosing the most messed up guys, knowing it could never lead to something serious... I think he is just terrified of growing attached."

"Like the fear of intimacy, right?"

"Have you been watching daytime TV guapo? I told you not to. It messes you up."

He grimaced, but didn't comment. "Still on for tomorrow night? Eva's party?"

"Duh! Like I would miss that." I really liked Eva. Even if we didn't go to school together, it was nice to talk to a girl sometimes. I also really wanted to work on Chago and her getting together because I knew that, if they did, they would be in it for the long run.

"What are you going to do tomorrow?" he asked me.

I shrugged. "Nothing much. Working on my lit." That technically wasn't a lie.

"Pick you up at six?"

I nodded before kissing his cheek loudly. "Have a good night, guapo, and say hola to Mateo and Mama for me, okay?"

"Si Chula, have a good night. I'll call you before bed."

"I wouldn't expect any less from you."

I waited for Chago to leave before entering my cold and empty house.

I sighed. "I'm home!" I called for the benefit of the furniture. I shook my head and walked heavily into my room. Picking up my guitar, I played for a while.

I had taken classes for four years. The teacher had said I was a natural and that he had taught me everything he had to teach. Now I just played for myself or Chago from time to time. It always helped me feel better. Every time I played, it felt like I was reviving a part of my father that existed inside me.

I looked at his photo on my dresser. I knew so little about him that even the most trivial things meant the world to me. I knew his favorite color was green and that he loved to joke around. I also remembered that he used to play guitar for me almost every night.

I closed my eyes, playing a Cure song as I imagined my father sitting beside me on the bed. I never felt as close to him as when I was playing guitar.

"I love you, dad," I whispered. I could almost hear him reply, *'I love you too, Lottie, my sweet angel. Heaven must have loved me more than I thought to have given me its most beautiful and precious angel'*. I replayed his words in my head repeatedly. They were perfectly engraved in my mind, except that now the voice in my head was not my fathers' anymore, but mine…only mine.

CHAPTER 7

I was not surprised to find the kitchen empty when I came down for breakfast on Saturday morning. My mother had been home for two Saturday mornings in a row already, making that almost a miracle. Three would have been a sign of an imminent apocalypse.

"Morning, " I mumbled to myself as I poured a cup of coffee.

I was halfway through my first cup when I noticed a green Post-it on our 'Control Center' board. Green meant good news. Well, good news as far as my mother was concerned, which didn't always mean it was good news for me, but it was all relative.

I took the time to finish my coffee. Green was not an emergency.

I don't have to work tomorrow. How about lunch and shopping? Love, Mom. Even her notes had this professional vibe.

I sighed and wrote 'yes sure, why not' on the note before pouring myself a second cup of coffee. I had never been the biggest fan of shopping with my mother. The last time we'd done it was two years ago for some Christmas shopping and we'd ended up fighting in the middle of the mall. It didn't matter what we wanted. We were just too different, but I did want to try again. Our moments together were so rare and life was so short.

Feeling finally alive after my second cup of coffee, I decided to give Chago a quick call. I knew him well enough. It would be very socially awkward if he went to Eva's birthday party without a present.

"Valdez mechanic," announced a deep, accented voice I recognized at once. It was Diego, Chago's older cousin, but for me, he would always be my first kiss.

"Diego, it's me. Can I have a word with Chago please?"

"Hey, gringa Valdez!!" he shouted cheerfully. "Chago, Chago, siempre Chago." He sighed. "Me destroza el Corazon."

"Right, of course I'm breaking your heart. Find some chica to heal it."

He chuckled. "Un minuto."

"Chula, what's up? Is everything alright?" Chago asked, worry laced in his voice. It was true that I never bothered him at work.

"Estas bien, sorry to bother you, but you know the party tonight is for Eva's birthday, right? Did you buy anything?"

"Yes, actually I did." He cleared his throat. "I have what I need."

I nodded idiotically. "And what are you going to wear?"

"Clothes?" he teased.

I sighed. I might not be the most fashionable person on the planet, but I wanted Chago to look nice tonight. "I'll figure something."

"Chula--"

"I'll figure something, Santiago!" I snapped with as much authority as I could.

"Do I even have my say in this?"

"Nope," I said, popping the 'p'. "You don't. Wear a decent pair of jeans, no oil stains or rips, or so help me God…"

He sighed heavily. "Si, six?"

"Come at 6:30. It's better."

"Did Gaygan call you last night? Was it bad?"

"Not so bad really. Not as bad as I expected." I grinned. "It was merely a four on his bitch-fits' scale."

Chago chuckled as I heard Mateo shout in a rude way for Chago to move it and come back to work.

"Talk to you later. Love you and say hi to Mateo," I said.

"Will do. Love you too."

I decided to go to the mall near my house because whilst Chago might have bought a present for Eva, I hadn't. I looked at the clock. It was only 10:30. I still had plenty of time to take a quick shower, find a present, and grab a bite to eat before the visit of Gabriel 'The Great'.

I browsed the shops, not really knowing what I was looking for. I liked Eva. I'd known her for years, but I couldn't say I really knew her, and that was a real dilemma. I knew her enough that a generic present would hurt her feelings, but not enough to buy her a present that would be truly personal.

I tried to think of what I knew about her and remembered that she collected perfume bottles. That was a good present. There was a beauty shop by the main entrance, and I was pretty sure I had seen a collection of small bottles. It was two presents in one.

When I turned around, I froze, looking at the window of Hugo Boss and for once, it had nothing to do with the giant poster of the hot, dark haired model. There was a beautiful dressing shirt on a mannequin. It was a light brown, a sort of mix between amber and golden brown - the exact color of Chago's eyes! I knew he would complain, telling me he had enough clothes at my house without me having to go buy some more, but I had to. I'd never seen a shirt matching him so perfectly before. This was made for him. He had to wear it tonight. As I purchased the shirt, I looked at my watch. Perfect, it was barely one, which left me with plenty of time to grab some lunch to go before heading home. I stopped by the sandwich store to get a tuna sandwich with lots of red onions. This was one of the perks of being currently single; I didn't have to be careful with my breath.

When I got home with what I thought was plenty of time, I found Gabriel sitting on my front steps.

"What are you doing here?" I asked as I got out of the car, bags in hand. "I thought we said two?"

"Sorry. I'm set on central time," he teased with a half-smile.

"Then you're late," I replied, pushing past him to open the door.

He stood up and followed me without being invited. "Well, maybe I've been here for an hour. Who knows."

I sighed, setting my two shopping bags down on the console in the lobby before turning to face him. He looked totally at ease, leaning against the wall, peering into my shopping bags like he belonged here, like he owned the place. Damn this guy really had the talent to get under my skin.

"Yes, I'm sure you are just so eager to spend time with me that-" I shook my head dismissively. "Nevermind. You have to give me time to eat."

"You went clothes shopping? Did you find yourself something cute?" he asked, pointing at the Hugo Boss bag.

I glared, but didn't take the bait. "Come, please." I gestured toward the kitchen. I was aware that my tone was anything but inviting, but he didn't seem to mind.

He chuckled as I sat down at the table with the sandwich, a bottle of water and a can of Coke.

"What are you laughing at?" I asked as he sat across from me, setting his book and notepad down on the table.

"Nothing. It's just-- You gave me a hard time on Thursday about my - How did you put it? 'Fashion sense'?" he said using air quotes. "But I can't help noticing you've bought something from Hugo Boss, Miss Non-Fashionista."

A slight blush of anger crept onto my cheeks. I raised my forefinger. "First, it's none of your business." I raised my middle finger. "Second, don't try to explain what I do; third, don't give me your opinion on what I do or don't do because truth be told, I don't give a rat's ass. And *finally*, it's a present, so just shut it!"

"The final point, the 'shut it'? Very eloquent, bravo!" He smirked, clapping slowly, apparently pleased to have gotten under my skin.

"Eloquent? Nice! Is that your word of the month?" I asked sarcastically.

He beamed. "Yes, yes, it is. Do you like it?"

I snorted, looking down at my sandwich, only too aware that I was about to eat in front of someone without offering them something to eat too. As much as I wanted to annoy Gabriel, I'd never been able to eat when someone was staring at me.

"Do you want some?"

"Will you have enough?"

I sighed. "I have plenty, but don't answer a question with another question. It's annoying. Here, plenty." I jumped from my chair. Taking a big bag of chips from one of the cupboards, I laid it on the table. I'd almost thrown it. This guy was really gifted in being able to bring out the worst part of me. I was never this rude. Mama Valdez would have chewed me out if she'd seen me act the way I had.

"So, do you want some?" I asked, sitting down again.

"What is it?"

"Tuna, lots of red onions, cucumbers, and mayo."

"Mayo?" he asked, an eyebrow raised.

"What? Are you lactose intolerant? Or don't you get how a girl can have mayo? It's full fat too! Not all of us have the goal to be a size zero, you know."

"No, it's—Yes, I would love some, thanks."

I nodded, cutting the sandwich in half. "Careful, it's nasty for the breath."

He chuckled." It's okay. I'll go home and brush my teeth. What does your boyfriend think of your taste for breath destroying food?"

I simply shrugged, not wanting to lie. "I like what I like. I don't care if it's not good for my breath or that it won't turn me into a fen-phen addict."

He smiled brightly, the kind of smile that showed all his perfect teeth. "That's refreshing. I like that."

"I live to please you," I replied dryly.

"Good to know." He winked.

I grunted with exasperation, finishing my half of the sandwich in silence.

"Okay," I started as soon as I'd swallowed the last bite. "You done with the questioning? Why don't you tell me what you have?"

He finished his sandwich slowly, probably doing it to annoy me, but I did my best to hide how easily it was working.

"Well," he started after a while, wiping his mouth. "Romeo is the hot shot in town. He has all the girls at his feet. I mean, he is a Montague for God's sake!! He is like royalty, so …why on earth did he settle for a chick when he was sixteen? He should have played the field, get as much action as he could, you know?"

My face probably showed my disbelief. I would have imagined something that stupid coming from Doug 'the beef-head', but not from him! Gabriel was on the honor roll! I knew it would have been far too presumptuous to say I knew the guy, but I never would have put him in the 'chauvinist pig' category.

"What?" He leaned back in his chair, crossing his arms on his chest, apparently pleased with himself.

"Are-Are you serious?" I hated showing him that he'd thrown me off.

"Of course! Did you expect anything else?"

I shook my head dismissively. It was crazy, but I couldn't help but feel disappointed in him.

"No. No, I guess I didn't. Let's work on writing this essay with your…opinion of it." I didn't even try to conceal the disappointment in my voice. He'd given me what all the jocks before him had served repeatedly. But this jock had a brain! I knew that, but if he wanted to play it this way there was not much I could do. "Okay, open your notebook and start writing down the questions you asked yourself after reading the book," I explained, not able to stop myself from grimacing. He was bound to get an F, this way, but to be fair, I only had to help him think outside of the box. I was not obliged to get him As'.

He picked up the pen in his hand, ready to write, but then he put it down again. "Tell me your opinion on it," he said, propping his chin in his hand. He looked straight into my eyes as if he was trying to figure something out.

I shook my head. "We're not here to express what I think. Believe me, I'm doing that enough. We're here for you."

He nodded. "Tell me what you really think, and I promise to tell you what I really think too."

"Why? The magnificent moronic macho-man argument you just served me was not *really* yours?" I raised an eyebrow in mock wonder.

He crossed his arms on his chest, leaning back in his chair. "Who knows..." I swear he was crossing his arms just to flex his admittedly impressive muscles.

I pondered it. I was sure there was more to him than met the eye. I might have been wrong. I was probably wrong, but I needed to know. That was the damn journalist gene I had... Damn it! I sighed. "You win."

He shot me a wide grin. "I'm listening."

"Romeo was in love with Rosalind for months. Like head over heels in love with her, and then he sees Juliet and everything flips?" I rolled my eyes. "And what about her? She sees him and goes crazy too? They don't even know each other. It's a 'love' -" I used air quotes - "based on appearances and appearances only I mean." I snorted. "Can you be shallower than that?"

Gabriel looked at me in silence. It felt like he was seeing me for the first time and I was not comfortable with him trying to figure me out. But now that he'd gotten me started, I had to finish my argumentation.

"Nothing is more ephemeral than physical appearance, you know. There could be an accident, late acne, a disease, or... I don't know." I shrugged. "This love is nothing more than hormones and external beauty. It's nothing else! It's not deep. I mean, for all we know they could end up married and Juliet gets fat after having a baby, and he turns out to be an idiot and then what, huh?"

"I don't know."

His reply surprised me. I hadn't expected him to answer my rhetorical question, but it felt good to be supported.

"Exactly! You don't know. Nobody does, and yet they are using this relationship as the best, most romantic love story of all time?

I'm sorry, but that's bull. This was not a love story; it was a tragedy." I took a deep breath. "Anyway, that's what I really think."

Gabriel nodded silently.

"What about you? You promised."

He stared into my eyes silently for a couple of seconds. I knew perfectly how I looked now - pupils dilated, cheeks flushed. It was always the same whenever I got into a heated argumentation. It was an incomparable rush of energy.

He shrugged. "Real or not, deep or shallow, I just hope that one day I will love someone as much as he loved her and that she will love me back just as strongly."

I looked at him, mouth agape. I probably looked like a fly trap right now, but out of everything I could have possibly imagined him to say, that was, by far, the last one...Was he a romantic? No, impossible!

"I'm not self-sufficient or cocky enough to want her to sacrifice everything to be with me. I just want to know we love each other enough that nothing else matters if we're not together," he added, looking down at the pen he was twirling between his fingers. "That's what I really think, but that's not what I want to say," he added quietly.

I couldn't stop looking at him. Was he really longing for love? I thought he was in this perfect relationship with that cheerleader.

"What about your girlfriend?" I couldn't help but ask. This guy was a mystery and I didn't like mysteries. I had to understand things around me. I hated being confused and he was messing up my preconceptions.

"Darlene? What about her?" He asked, looking up again.

"Don't you love her? I mean…I don't know."

"She is the co-captain of the cheerleaders' team, I'm the soccer superstar." He didn't manage to conceal the underlying frustration in his tone. "We're supposed to date, it's how it is supposed to be."

"Right," I snorted. "I almost forgot who I was talking to. My apologies." Could he be shallower? Sometimes I forgot that even smart people could be shallow.

He flushed with anger, his emerald eyes turning dark. "You don't know anything! You're judging, but you don't know shit. You don't know me! You have no idea what my life is really like! You're caught up on appearances just like us jocks. Stop being so condescending!"

"Tell me then!" I barked back. "I'm here listening. Tell me what it's like," I challenged, leaning closer.

He seemed to ponder it for a minute before shaking his head. "Let's get back to work, I can't stay much longer. I have a date tonight," he added, having retreated back into his shell.

"Yeah, maybe you're right. God forbid I get a glimpse of the real you," I stated, somehow hurt. Well, it was not like I cared anyway, right?

He mumbled something under his breath I didn't get. It sounded a lot like 'not much to see' but I couldn't be sure.

"I just don't understand why you want to pretend to be someone you are not," I couldn't help but add.

"Oh, yes. Since when are we friends? You don't know anything. You clearly don't know me. You are so judgmental and yet you don't like being categorized." He snorted with an eye-roll. "This is so ironic! I figured out what you are now," He slammed his pen on the table. "A hypocrite nothing more! I'm pretty sure you are pretending as much as anyone else - if not more!" he sneered, his jaw locked.

Fury blurred my vision. I had let so many things slide with him: his rudeness, his social inadequacy, his 'all-star' behavior, but I wouldn't let anyone judge me and insult me in my own home.

I jumped out of my chair and pointed in the general direction of the front door. "Get out!" I commanded coldly, trying to keep my voice leveled. I didn't want him to see how easily he could get under my skin.

His eyes widened with surprise. "Are you serious?"

"Umm, let me think…" I tapped my forefinger on my chin, pretending to think. "Yes, yes, I'm sure."

"That's twice now!" he hissed with anger, standing up stiffly and grabbing his things. "It's becoming a habit."

"Well, it will be this way as long as you keep being an ass!" I pointed at the door again. "Out!"

He walked to the door, then decided otherwise and came back to stand in front of me. "What didn't you like, Little Miss Perfect? Having your flaws pointed out?" He leaned down, towering over me, but I refused to step back or let go of his eyes. I needed to show him I was neither impressed nor scared. "Yes, it's easy to judge everybody, but it's not fun when it's the other way around, is it?" A mirthless laugh escaped him. "And remember, only truth hurts!" he added before stomping out, slamming the door as loudly as he could.

"Douchebag!" I muttered through gritted teeth. I hated to admit that he hadn't hit too far from home.

It took me a long time to calm down. I'd tried to draw a Cure comic strip to help. Usually, drawing was a good way to channel any overwhelming emotions, but what I'd drawn today annoyed me.

I incorporated The Cure, well myself, into most of my comics. I'd drawn a little androgynous character with a Zorro mask. I usually represented the jocks as wearing Viking helmets - not so original, but effective - and depending on what sport I was targeting that day, the ball on the character's shirt was different. As for the cheerleaders, it was all in the hair.

In today's drawing, I'd decided to bash the captain of the soccer team - no surprise there - and his super preppy girlfriend, Darlene. I'd drawn Gabriel standing in front of a mirror. He was taking his face off as a mask and once it was off, you could read 'fraud' on top of his head. It was the same for Darlene, except that on top of her head, it said, 'cheater.' And then I'd drawn The Cure. I'd almost drawn my own face under the mask, but I hadn't. I'd simply written the word 'coward' instead.

"Damn it!" I punched the desk angrily, and I was still mumbling when Chago arrived at six thirty.

"Chill out, Chula. What's wrong with you today? I can feel your anger."

I sighed. "Nothing." I pointed to the Hugo Boss bag. "Wear that tonight."

"Chula, I-"

"Wear that tonight, Chago," I insisted, cutting him off. I didn't have any patience left, Gabriel had used up every ounce of it.

"Ch--"

I picked up the bag and threw it at him. "Wear the damn shirt, Chago!" I shouted with exasperation.

He looked at me dumbfounded. It was true that I almost never shouted at him. "Fine, if it is that important." He took his white tee-shirt off before sliding into the shirt. "What's up with you, anyway?"

"PMS?" I tried sheepishly.

"Yes, right… Okay, I'll buy it this time. Come on, let's go."

The birthday party was a lovely garden party full of fairy lights. A delicious buffet of South American food was set up on the side. There was some of Eva's Eastside extended family and only a few of our own high school classmates, so Chago didn't have to pretend to be all badass and I didn't have to let my big mouth lead me into trouble.

Once I filled myself with some carb goodness, I noticed Eva looking discreetly toward Chago as he was talking with one of Eva's cousins.

Eva was a very pretty, 5'1" girl with a soft, round face, big expressive hazel eyes, and long, mahogany brown hair stopping just below her shoulder blades. She was perfect for my best friend because she was pretty both inside and out.

"You know," I started as I stood beside her. "I've seen a movie once about a guy who liked a girl so much that he stayed away because he was terrified to mess everything up."

Eva nodded, throwing me a grateful glance. "Yes, but if I remember correctly, in that movie the girl liked the boy too. Only she didn't want to wait forever. Life was too short."

"I know." I bit my bottom lip, not sure if I should reveal the cause of it all. I shook my head. She had the right to know. "But you see, this boy has a best friend he loves very much, she is essential to his life and he is scared that the girl he likes will eventually feel threatened and ask him to choose." I looked at Chago, my heart tightening with all the love I felt for him. "It happened often, and every time, it was an easy choice for him to make. But this time, he knows that if he ever had to choose, it would break his heart."

"But that would be stupid. The girl knows everything about him. She knows that trying to separate him from his best friend would change him to the core. He wouldn't be the same guy and -" she grinned - "he is pretty awesome."

"I can only agree with that! But don't worry, the best friend has more than one trick in her bag. It's not over."

"I'm just done waiting. What will happen, will happen," she murmured, looking toward a guy I had seen at school before. "It might just be too late." She turned and connected her hazel gaze with mine. "I like talking to you, Charlie. You're fun."

"It's never too late, you know. It might be harder, but it's never too late."

Eva shrugged, helping herself to a glass of punch. "Only time will tell."

CHAPTER 8

On Wednesday, I decided to go see Mr. Mulligan to tell him I couldn't work with Gabriel anymore. I had waited for him to apologize or to do something to show he genuinely wanted to try. But since I hadn't heard from him since Saturday, I thought it best to tell Mulligan before he got the chance to grade Gabriel's terrible paper.

"Miss Miller, what can I do for you?" he asked with a kind smile, seemingly happy to see me. His reaction to my visit was a pleasant change. Most of my teachers were wary as soon as I approached their desk. They'd all expected me to ask them to promote or raise awareness on a cause close to their field.

"I don't think the assignment you gave me is going to work," I admitted, trying to sound sorrier than I felt.

"Oh really? Why is that?" he asked, sitting back in his chair.

"Gabriel--" *is just a chauvinist pig.* I took a deep breath. "Gabriel and I, we are just too different. I'm not the right person to guide him and I'm sorry about that." *No, not really.* "But if you want, I don't mind joining the *Spread Literacy* association you are taking care of." Not that I really had the choice now as I'd told my mother I was doing it.

Mr. Mulligan smiled. "Really? Gabriel handed me his paper this morning and I have to say, I didn't really expect that."

I snorted. "I bet you didn't. It's-"

"Brilliant." He'd cut me off, probably to stop me from saying something stupid.

"Br-brilliant?" I gasped.

"Absolutely! I wanted to have a word with you about that, compliment you."

"I-- Don't understand." I sat on a desk facing him. Not many things threw me off, but this had thrown me big time.

"Do you have five minutes?" he asked, standing up.

I looked at the clock. Chago would still be in French for a little while. "Yes, absolutely."

"Good, come with me please." He turned, leading the way to the teachers' lounge. "I have an editorial meeting in a couple of minutes, but I think you need to read something," he continued, browsing a pile of paper before photocopying one for me. He winked. "I never gave that to you, okay?"

"Of course." I glanced at the front page. It was Gabriel's 'Romeo & Juliet' paper and Mulligan had given him an A. "Good grade," I remarked, folding it in two before putting it in my backpack.

"Good paper," he confirmed as we walked out of his office. "I will let you read it and think about your 'assignment'. If by Monday, you still want to change, we can do that."

"Why are you doing this?" I blurted out without thinking.

"Do what?" he asked, but his body language told me he knew what I was talking about.

"Help him and me…forcing us together."

He shrugged dismissively. "I just thought you two could shake things up and after reading that paper -" he pointed at my bag - "I realized I was right. See you tomorrow, Miss Miller," he added before hurrying toward the editorial room.

I sighed, looking around. The corridors were empty. Chago wouldn't be out for another fifteen minutes. I decided to wait by the car and read the paper Gabriel wrote. I was dying to read it, not knowing what to expect from him anymore.

Mulligan was right. The paper Gabriel had written was brilliant. It was full of smart wits and insightful comments. Reading his conclusion almost made me reconsider my views on the book.

'Some may claim that the love described in 'Romeo and Juliet' is shallow. With it based only on physical appearances, making it out to be an epic reference is an insult to love.

However, it is not the circumstances they meet in nor why they'd loved each other that makes their tale epic. It is the power of that love. Before falling for Juliet, Romeo valued his name, his connections, and his rank more than anything else. Once he had Juliet though, nothing else mattered. It had all become trivial in the face of their love. He would rather die than face this earth without her. This all-in romance is what makes them epic. Who wouldn't want to be someone's everything?

"Damn, that boy is smart!" I muttered, stuffing the paper in my bag as Chago made his way toward me.

"Got a B+!" He beamed, kissing my cheek soundly.

"Nice!! You need to thank Lonnie for that."

"I know. I might even introduce him to a guy who is not a freak," he agreed as we drove away.

"Uh huh," I grimaced, making him laugh.

"So…what are you going to give me as a 'well done' gift?" he teased.

"I can make you a sandwich."

"Si, I'm hungry. Gracias, Chula."

As soon as we walked into the house, Chago threw himself onto the sofa while I went into the kitchen to prepare us two sandwiches. But no matter what I did, I couldn't let go of Gabriel's paper. If I didn't know who'd written it, I would have wanted to meet the person. For me he would've been like the perfect match…the perfect friend.

I sighed, getting my phone out. *Be more mature than he is. Do the right thing,* I chastised myself.

Sorry about Saturday. I probably overreacted. Beep me when u r ready to work on the next book. I'll try not to kick u out. C

"Chula?" Chago called from the living room.

"Give me a minute, hombre! What do you want to drink? Coke?"

"Si, Coke esta bien."

I made two cheese and ham sandwiches before joining him. Seeing him sprawled on the sofa, I chuckled.

"All good?" I asked, nudging him to sit up. I turned toward the TV. "Oh no! I don't think so!" He'd put the monster trucks show on.

"But-"

"But nothing, guapo. Today there is the Tran-Siberian documentary on the Discovery Channel. You know I want to see that." I grabbed the remote and changed the channel. "And don't make your sad, puppy face. It doesn't work on me anymore."

"I don't see your fascination with Russia."

"And I don't see your fascination for monster trucks." I stuck my tongue out.

Chago stayed with me for about half an hour before giving up. "Sorry, Chula, but as much as I love you, this is boring me. I would rather be doing homework right now… See how desperate I'm getting?"

I chuckled, patting his knee. "It's okay, hermano. I'll see you tomorrow."

"Yep, bright and early." He kissed my forehead. "Have fun watching your show."

"Uh huh… And have fun doing homework."

"Have fun doing homework," he replied, mimicking me.

"Come on, you make me sound floozy!"

"So, I got you alright." He winked. "I'll give you a call later."

I nodded, concentrating on the TV again.

Barely a minute after he'd left, I heard him knock on the door. I rolled my eyes. He could be such a pain sometimes, especially when he was bored.

"Damn, Guapo, you're a pain!" I shouted from the sofa. "Come in and shut it! It will be over in less than thirty minutes."

"I promise I'll keep it shut." The deep voice startled me.

I jumped from my seat to face Gabriel. He was standing under the living room's threshold, his hands buried in his jean's pockets.

"Please watch your documentary. We'll talk later," he offered and for once he didn't have his cocky grin.

I nodded, sitting back down. I was thankful he'd given me some time to think. I was not the brightest when taken by surprise.

He sat down on the loveseat by the sofa and watched the TV along with me. I glanced his way from time to time, but he never had the bored look Chago usually had, he seemed to be truly interested.

"That's Saint Basil's Cathedral," he commented, pointing at the TV. "Don't you find its construction just breathtaking? It was such an innovation for the middle of the 16th century. Ivan IV of Russia ordered it and the legend says he blinded the architect to make sure he would never repeat such a masterpiece. He was quite a visionary."

I looked at him speechlessly. His eyes were lit, his cheeks slightly flushed. I didn't need to know him to see his passion.

"It has no comparison to any other Russian building. Do you see the uniqueness of the design? It's like a flame of a bonfire rising into the sky. Beautiful."

"It is beautiful," I confirmed, not able to stop myself from staring at him.

"What?" he asked, suddenly self-conscious.

"What do you want to do after high school?" I asked, turning fully toward him.

"Finance," he replied and the light in his eyes faded.

"Really? Why?" I'd expected something more creative like architecture based on his reaction to the documentary.

"I…That is a weird question!" he admitted with a low chuckle.

I shrugged. "Not so weird." I started to wonder if anyone really cared about what he wanted. "So, why finance?"

"It's a very interesting, always evolving field."

Could he have given a more generic answer?

"I mean my father did that, my grandfather too… It's a family tradition."

Yeah, that was more like it. "I guess so." I shrugged. "It's not really my thing."

"What's your thing?"

"Why did you come, by the way?" I asked, ignoring the question. "Didn't you have soccer practice or something?"

He looked hurt by my question and I felt bad. "When I finished practice, I saw your text, so I decided to come over for--" He rubbed his neck, looking embarrassed. "But your boyfriend was still here, so I decided to wait a while."

It would have been so easy to say, *'Chago is not my boyfriend',* but I stupidly wanted him to think that someone could love me. It seemed so grotesque that I was ashamed of myself. Since when did I care what people thought of me? I looked at him curiously. "Have you already started the book?"

"No, I- I know we're not friends, but-" He looked so uncomfortable, I cut in before I'd realized I'd spoken.

"Maybe we can try?" Damn, what was wrong with me? Since when did I want to befriend a Viking?

He relaxed immediately. "I would really like that." He smiled and it was a smile I'd never seen on his face before. I could almost see his soul through that smile.

"If we really want to be friends, maybe we should try being ourselves? No pretending. No saying we love finance when we clearly don't."

"How would you know?" he asked, but there was no anger in his voice, only wonder. "We can't say we've known each other for long."

"True, but I'm observant." I detailed him and didn't miss the weariness in his eyes. "You are not as good at hiding yourself as you think."

"I wouldn't say I've been trying"

"Then maybe people just don't care. This version of you is just so convenient, they don't want to look further," I proposed, but regretted it as soon as I saw a deeper hurt flash through his eyes. "Well, who am I to say that anyways? It's not like I know your friends. Forget what I said. I have a big mouth!"

"Wow, trying to spare my feelings? That is so not Charlotte Miller approved behavior."

I snickered. "Don't get used to it."

"Promise I won't." He concentrated on the TV again.

It felt weird watching TV with him. It was true that the number of men in my inner circle was very limited - one gay and two 'brothers'. I was very aware of Gabriel's presence. I couldn't fully relax no matter how much I wanted to.

Stop it, idiot. He is not your type… Of course, since hot like hell is not your type. "Yes, I'm screwed," I groaned loudly.

"Sorry?" he asked, confused. He seemed to have been just as lost in his thoughts as I'd been. "Why are you screwed?"

"I--" *Think, girl, think!* "Chemistry!" I shouted with a victorious tone. "It's confusing. I don't deal with it very well."

"Chemistry?" he asked as if he'd been expecting something totally different.

"Yes." I shook my head, internally congratulating myself for that save. "It's Chinese to me."

"I can help if you want. I mean -" he shrugged "you are helping me with my literature."

"Yes, but it's my job." I cursed myself. "I mean, you don't have to do that," I added, backpedaling.

"Yes, but we want to be friends, right? And that's what friends do - help each other," he explained with a big smile.

I smiled back. "That-- That would be very nice of you."

He thought for a moment. "What about we work on your chemistry on Thursdays and my literature issues on Saturdays?"

Chago was booked on Thursdays with his French tutoring and on Saturdays at Mateo's garage as business was doing really well.

"Or maybe you are just super busy…" he offered with an edge in his voice.

"No, it's cool, but what about you, Soccer Superstar?"

He chuckled. "I can manage." He winked, making my heart flutter. I didn't like that unfamiliar feeling. I didn't need to have felt it before to know it was a source of trouble. My stomach growled loudly, and I couldn't help but blush. This self-awareness was also annoyingly new. I was always myself. I had been embarrassed so many times in front of Chago, Logan, and Mateo that I didn't even notice such things anymore.

"Hungry?" he tried.

"Stating the obvious?" I replied, quick on the draw. I just couldn't help it as far as it concerned him or the other jocks.

He shrugged, turning his attention to the TV, making me feel guilty for my unwarranted 'knee-jerk' reaction. He wanted to be friends and I was pushing him back into his shell. Maybe something good could come out of this friendship if I'd just let it..

I looked at the clock. I knew my mother wouldn't be back for at least a couple of hours. She was teaching a college seminar on law once a week for the next month.

"Want to grab dinner with me?"

He turned to me briskly, clearly surprised by my offer. I couldn't blame him after I'd snapped a sarcastic comment at him.

He scratched at his cheek. "I…don't know," he admitted, looking at me with his eyebrows furrowed.

"Don't worry. I was thinking about ordering a pizza, nothing public. Nobody will see you with me. Secret friends, right?" I kept my face blank. Nobody had been ashamed of me before. It was both strange and hurtful.

"No, it's not that. I…" He growled, running his hands over his face. "Yes, I would love to stay. I just need to make a phone call."

I nodded. "Pepperoni, extra cheese good for you?" I stood up. "You can make your phone call from here. I'll be in the kitchen. Join me when you're done," I added, walking away without a look back.

I ordered the pizza. By the time he joined me, I was setting the table. He took a seat on one of the bar stools.

I wanted to ask him what had made him hesitate. Who did he need to call? But I knew it was out of line. We could try to be friends, but we would never be 'real' friends. Not like I was with Chago or even Logan, and not like he was friends with Doug, the moronic quarterback, or the other school jocks.

"Why do you want us to be friends?" I asked after I'd paid for the pizza and laid it on the table.

"Why wouldn't I?" he replied.

I hated his ability to answer questions with another question. "I dunno." I bit a big chunk out of my pizza slice, making him laugh. I'd done that to give myself time to think while I chewed. "It's just that, I'm not a geek or a nerd, so it won't help your jock karma to befriend me."

"Jock karma?" he asked, a ghost of a smile playing on his lips, his eyes full of amusement. I had never seen him so carefree before. It made his green eyes even greener.

"Exactly! I'm not popular or drop dead gorgeous." I was just stating a fact. It didn't bother me. It never had. "You are a good student and the only subject you're weak at, I have to help you with whether I like it or not. So I don't see what you have to gain, that's all."

"Maybe I'm not looking to gain anything." He put his pizza back on his plate and wiped his hands on a paper towel. "Maybe I would like to enjoy a friend who is so different from my usual friends."

I knew his comment was not supposed to be mean, but it still hurt me. I felt like an experiment, a try…a freaking guinea pig. "That's nice," I sneered, not able to conceal the frosty edge in my voice.

He cocked his head to the side, eyebrows furrowed, evidently thrown back by my reaction. "Well, I'm sorry, but I have to go." He stood up briskly. I realized he knew I was close to throwing him out again. I didn't know how he managed to always pull out the worst part of me.

I nodded, following him to the door.

He put his hand on the handle, but didn't turn it. His shoulders sagged as he sighed heavily with what seemed to be both annoyance and weariness.

"You know, I didn't mean it in a bad way," he confessed before turning around to look at me. "You are different - in a good way, a very good way." He kept his eyes locked with mine in a clear attempt to show he meant it.

I forced a smile, not really knowing what to do with that. I had years of experience with my poker face, but this guy, who I've known for barely two weeks, could already see through my pretenses. I didn't like that.

He opened the door slightly, still looking at me. "I know we'll need time to be good friends, but when we will be, I'll ask you why you think I'm a fraud and why you see yourself as a coward. Goodnight, Charlotte," he added with a small bow, leaving me frozen on the threshold.

He knew it was me! He knew I was The Cure. I could feel cold sweat running down my neck.

I closed the door, resting my forehead against it. I was certainly not ashamed of what I was saying through my comic strips, but I could only say those things because I had the cover of anonymity. If my identity was revealed, I knew the Principal would pressure me to shut it. I hated to know that someone I didn't trust yet knew something that big about me.

How had he even figured it out? I thought, pissed at myself. *Have I been reckless?*

The only thing I could now do was wait and hope he wouldn't rat me out.

CHAPTER 9

The next two weeks were quite uneventful, except for the fact that I started longing for those Thursdays and Saturdays to come. I hated longing for them so much, the way my heart fluttered when I woke up in the morning, knowing it was a tutoring day.

I couldn't say we were doing something wrong. We mostly talked, grazing the surface of who we really were. It seemed like both of us had problems showing the real us, but still, it was better than nothing, and I was sure that the little he shared with me was much more than what he was sharing with others.

I was rather grateful he hadn't mentioned *The Cure* again. Was he waiting for me to talk about it? If that was the case, he was going to have to wait a long time.

Today was Thursday, which meant I would be spending three hours with Gabriel tonight. He would probably end up eating dinner with me as he had been doing for the past two weeks. I had to admit that I really enjoyed his companionship.

As soon as I climbed into Chago's car for school, he threw an envelope onto my lap.

"I received a letter yesterday!" he exclaimed, excitement radiating from him as he backed out of my driveway.

"Yay!! How excited you must be! Your first letter!" I grinned. "Is it Hogwarts?"

"Ah ah divertido!" He shook his head. "Look where it came from." The header of the letter said 'Cardenas Corp.'

It was a letter from Cardenas Ruiz himself, inviting Chago to take tests for the internship he was offering. He'd specified that he'd looked through the business cases written by various high schoolers and found Chago's papers to be very promising.

I thanked the man for leaving me out of it. "That's awesome, guapo." I gave him a side hug as he was driving. "Told you, the best was yet to come."

"No te entusiasmes demasiado. It's just an invitation to take tests. It means nothing."

"Why shouldn't I get excited? I have every reason to. The tests are just a formality. You are awesome! I know that much."

He smiled, but shook his head. "You are just like mama. Do you know that? She is all excited about it. I think everybody in Mexico has heard about it by now."

"She is proud of you! Can you blame her? I bet Mateo is so proud too!"

"Well, you'll tell me tonight," he said, parking in front of the school.

"Tonight? Why tonight? I ha-- Don't you have a tutoring session?"

"I had one, but mama wants to have a family dinner to celebrate and there is no family dinner without gringa Valdez." He winked. "Don't worry about it. Gaygan will understand."

"I- Yes of course!" I hated the disappointment I felt at the idea of not seeing Gabriel tonight. I was deliriously happy for Chago, of course, and that was what always prevailed, but still, I hated to cancel my lesson with Gabriel. I wanted to spend more time with him even if I was not ready to admit it.

We found Logan in the editorial room. As expected, he was ecstatic for Chago.

"Damn. Now you won't only have a hot body and a face to make angels weep, you'll be a businessman too?" Logan wiggled his eyebrows suggestively." We should totally get together one day."

"Si, gringo loco, like it's ever going to happen," he mocked, punching Logan's arm. "I was thinking we could celebrate, the three of us, Saturday night with bowling or something."

"Saturday night?" I repeated. There was no way I could miss two tutoring sessions in a row. I was sure Gabriel wouldn't mind, but I would miss him. I liked the real him...at least the parts he showed me.

"Yes, why?" Chago asked curiously. "Well after work, of course. I can't let Mateo down."

Chago didn't finish work before five so it wouldn't be before six, long after Gabriel's departure. "That's fine," I agreed, bumping my hip with his.

"That's a deal. It seems like forever since we've spent an evening, just the three of us," Logan remarked.

"Well, who's to blame? You're always so busy," I teased.

"What do you want? I'm a senior and I'm popular..." He took a haughty posture. "You people cannot understand."

Chago and I snorted at the same time, but we couldn't add anything as the first bell rang.

"See you at lunch, amigo." Chago waved at Logan before taking my hand and pulling me down the corridor to our calculus class.

I met Gabriel's green eyes as Chago pulled me along. He was talking with Doug by our classroom door, apparently in no rush to get to class. We shared a discreet smile before Chago tucked at my arm, making us break eye contact.

I was sullen all morning. I knew it wouldn't be a big deal for Gabriel. He would probably be happy not having to deal with me and my stupid impairment in understanding science, but I still waited until lunch to text him.

Sry I have to cancel tonight. C u Sat.

I hadn't expected to get an answer, so I almost jumped out of my skin when my phone vibrated in the rear pocket of my jeans.

y? he wrote.

Plans with Chago. I can't cancel.

I waited for a reply, but nothing came, which put me in an even sourer mood. I spent most of the afternoon cursing myself for somehow liking to spend time with someone I surely shouldn't.

"Are you sure you are okay, Chula?" Chago asked as we drove back to his house.

"What? Yes! Of course, yes! My best friend is about to become this Mr. Hotshot finance king." I grinned. "How could I feel better?"

"No sé. It's just-- You seemed out of it today. Is your tutoring going okay? You would tell me if something was wrong, right?"

"Of course I would tell you! No, tutoring is going well." *Too well, that's the problem.* "I'm just tired, I guess." I sighed. "I didn't sleep well."

Chago reached over and kissed my forehead as we stopped at the traffic light. "Maybe you should call your mother to tell her you will be home later. She might worry if she gets home early."

I snorted. "Are we talking about the same mother? The woman is never home before nine? True story, she even sleeps at work sometimes when she wants to call Europe."

Chago didn't say anything, but he threw me a look full of reproach. The '*she-might-not-be-perfect-but-she-is-your-mother-and-she-loves-you*' look.

"Fine! Do you want me to invite her over?" I added sarcastically.

"Seguro! Why not?" he challenged with a mocking smile.

My mother didn't have a problem with Chago's mother, actually. I was pretty sure she was fond of the woman, but they were so different it was funny. My mom had once come with me to their house two Christmases in a row. She had been so caught up with work that she hadn't planned anything for us. Seeing the women side by side had been comical. They would have gone viral on YouTube if I'd managed to capture them on video.I called my mother to tell her where I was going, but I didn't tell her why. She might have realized I had been the one pushing Cárdenas Ruiz to consider Chago, and if that came out, I was pretty much screwed. She told me to be home by nine, which was quite funny. I'd bet she wouldn't be home by then, but I agreed anyway.

As soon as we made it to Chago's, I could hear a commotion coming from the kitchen. I looked at the table set for seven.

"Mama, it's us!" Chago shouted, throwing his book bag on the floor.

"Jesus, dude! Put the bag out of the way."

"You know what? It's times like these that I'm actually happy I don't have a sister."

"Why? Wouldn't you love having me around twenty-four seven?" I asked in mock hurt before taking my shoes off and putting my bag and phone on the sofa.

"We are almost together twenty-four seven anyway - well, a bit less these days because of work and stuff, but still."

I winked at him. "Let me go help mama."

As I reached the kitchen, I started to drool as the full aroma of spices filled my nose.

"Yum. You made Pozole?" I asked before kissing her cheek. "It's my favorite."

"I know it is, m'hija. That's why I made it," she replied, stirring the food.

"It's Chago's big day and you are making my favorite? He will be jealous, you know." I teased before washing my hands, getting ready to help.

"No, he won't. He loves it too. Plus, you are not coming around as often as you used to."

I knew she didn't say it to make me feel guilty. She was just stating a fact, but I couldn't help the rush of guilt.

"Sorry, but you know with Chago working and me tutoring, it's getting-"

"Don't apologize, please. I know that once the holidays start, you'll be around more often. No te preocupa. Here, taste this." She handed me a spoon full of Pozole. "Te gustas?"

"It's fantastic. It always is. Who else is coming for dinner?"

"Miguel y familia."

Miguel was Chago's uncle and Diego's father. "Cool. Want me to help with the salads?"

"Si, gracias." She patted my cheek gently. "I like having you here," she added fondly before checking the Flan Mexicano in the oven.

Chago came into the kitchen. "Ah, since you're both busy, I'll go watch TV." He chuckled, leaving the room before we could ask him to do anything.

"Don't worry. As soon as Miguel is here, he'll have to entertain them. He is the main attraction today."

I chuckled. "That's a good thing."

I was cutting the cucumbers into squares when I felt strong hands rest on my hips. I grinned, the faint car oil scent letting me know who it was.

"It's nice to see you in the kitchen. It suits you… Very sexy," Mateo whispered in my ear before kissing the top of my head.

I knew he was teasing, but he was still a macho guy. As much as I loved him though, sometimes it got on my nerves.

"Cabron!" I replied, bumping him with my butt.

"Carlota!" Antonella gasped, turning around to reprimand me, but it was a nice chastising.

"Sorry."

"Si, you hurt my feelings," Mateo whined in mock hurt, resting his hand over his heart.

"And you stop messing with her." Antonella pointed her wooden spoon at him. "Next time I will let her beat you."

"Well, I'll go watch TV with my brother. At least he shows me consideration."

"In your dreams he does," I mumbled, concentrating on the salad again.

Mateo smacked my butt before rushing out of the room.

I shook my head, but couldn't help but smile. I'd missed these little banters more than I'd realized.

I sat between Chago and Mateo at the table. I didn't think they were over the whole 'Diego and I' kissing thing… It had *only* been two years, after all.

Miguel was so proud of Chago. He asked him if he had any ideas to help his own dry cleaner/alteration business.

I could see the light in Chago's eyes becoming instantaneously brighter as he started to talk about refinancing. It was the look that Gabriel should have had when he talked about finance, but it was never there.

I helped Antonella clear the table and wash the dishes. When I went back to the living room, Chago was in deep conversation with Miguel about the best way to invest. Mateo was sitting on the sofa, watching TV with Diego. Antonella started talking about cooking with Diego's mother.

I sat on the sofa beside Mateo, hoping that Chago wouldn't take too long. I looked at the clock. It was already eight and I still had homework to do.

"You need to go home?" Mateo whispered in my ear.

"Yeah, but Chago is talking and--"

"So, what? Is Chago the only Valdez who can drive you home?" he asked, turning on the sofa to lock eyes with mine.

"No, of course not! Come on, Mat. You know me better than that."

"Si, I do. I also know you are a sucker for a guilt trip," he declared with a goofy grin.

I glared, but said nothing.

He kissed my forehead before reaching for the car keys on the table.

"Don't forget your stuff." He pointed at my bag and cell that was now on the armchair. "Oye, Hermano, I'm going to drive Charlie home, estas bien?"

Chago looked up as if he had forgotten we were even here. "I-- I can do it."

"No, it's okay guapo. Continue to do what you were doing. I'll see you in the morning." I hugged Antonella, kissed Chago's cheek soundly, and waved at Miguel. I was about to wave at Diego when he pulled me into a hug.

"Waving is so impersonal," he whispered in my ear. "And we have been close, no? Very close."

"Si." I hugged him back awkwardly.

"Okaaay, that's enough." Mateo broke the hug, throwing a quick glare at Diego who raised his hands in surrender.

"Let's go now." Mateo reached for my hand and didn't let go until we were in Chago's car.

"Your car is not done yet? I would love to get a ride in it," I admitted, remembering the 1968 Chevrolet Corvette Roadster.

"I'm almost done, but the business has been so good these days, I've barely had time to work on it. Not that I'm complaining or anything."

We remained silent for a while, but I could see Mateo wanted to say something.

"What is it Mat?" I finally asked as it was getting ridiculous. It shouldn't have been hard to talk to me, damn it! I'd known the boy my whole life. "Is it because of Diego? He was joking, you know. I certainly wouldn't go there again I-"

"No, it's not Diego," he replied, shaking his head. "It's-- Are you doing anything stupid?"

"What? Something stupid? You have to be a bit more specific now because I'm doing stupid all the time." I was trying to ease the mood, but it didn't seem to be working.

"I'm talking about a 'Diego' kind of stupid," he added, quickly glancing at me before concentrating on the road again.

"I really don't understand," I admitted.

"You know I don't like snooping around, but-"

"Right!" I snorted, rolling my eyes. Mateo was very protective of Chago and I. He was *always* snooping around to make sure we didn't get into trouble.

"Anyways, I was watching TV when your phone vibrated against my arm. I looked down and it was a text message from 'G'." He took a deep breath. "I know for a fact that when someone uses cryptic initials instead of names, it's usually a number they shouldn't have in their phone."

"I see…" I trailed off, keeping my eyes on the road. I didn't want him to see he was spot on.

"I know I shouldn't have done that. I truly do, but I opened the text and it said… I'm quoting. 'I missed you tonight, more than I thought I would'."

I couldn't help but smile. I was furious at Mateo, but Gabriel missed me and most of all, he'd admitted it! I was not the only loser missing someone.

"You are smiling? Dios mio, she is smiling! Why are you smiling?"

"You shouldn't have snooped in my stuff."

"And you shouldn't see guys you have to hide! He is probably a wacko if you do that. Does Chago know?"

"No! I mean there is nothing to say. I swear to God, Mateo, I'm not seeing anyone."

Mateo parked the car in front of my house. I was not even surprised that my mother's car was not there yet. He turned in his seat to face me. "Would you tell me if you were seeing anyone?"

"I don't know... Probably not since it ended so well last time." I couldn't help but wince, remembering the huge fight that had broken out when he'd found me kissing Diego.

"That's not the same, Querida, and you know it. He is a gang sympathizer and he knew you were off limits." He sighed. "You know I want to keep you safe. You and him was a *very* bad idea."

"Okay, I give you that one," I conceded. "But I promise I'm not seeing anyone. The kiss you interrupted with Diego was the last kiss I've had. I swear."

"Not that I mind you dating, but..." He ran his hand through his long, dark hair. "It's just - If you feel like you ought to hide it from us...it's maybe not a good thing. Also, if I know you well enough to figure you're hiding something... It won't take Chago long to figure it out too."

"I know," I admitted. I knew getting closer to Gabriel was stupid. He'd been dating Darlene since forever and even if she was cheating on him, it was not my place to interfere. We were also so different. I knew that if I ever were to fall in love with him, it would be unrequited and heartbreaking, something I was not eager to ever experience.

"-even heard a single word of what I just said?" I heard Mateo ask with clear annoyance.

Did I just zone out again? Damn it!! "Sorry," I mumbled sheepishly.

He sighed, shaking his head wearily. "I said it will all stay between us if you promise you'll come to me if things turn to mierda, si? I won't tell a soul, juro."

I looked at him. Seeing all the love and care in his eyes made me emotional. I reached across the seat and hugged him tightly. I buried my face in his neck, smelling the faint odor of cars with the fresh scent of soap that always made me feel better, safer. "I promise if things get out of hand, I'll tell you."

"Humph." He hugged me back. "Just don't do anything too stupid, bueno?"

"Si, but don't worry, I'll be fine."

He scratched his cheek. "Famous last words…" he mumbled before leaning down to kiss my forehead. "See you soon and don't worry. I'll take you for a ride as soon as the car is finished."

"I can't wait."

I got out of the car and waited for Mateo to leave before going inside.

I had barely put the key in the lock when I heard a 'Hey' that made me jump.

I swirled around. "Are you trying to give me a heart attack?" I asked Gabriel breathlessly.

"Sorry, I--" He buried his hands deep in his jeans' pocket, moving from one foot to the other, visibly uncomfortable.

"Have you been here long?" I asked when my heart calmed down. "You know, if I didn't know better, I would be totally creeped out. This looks really stalker-ish."

It was pretty dark outside, but I could have sworn he blushed lightly. "No, I came about twenty minutes ago. It's just that I sent you a text and-" He looked away, rubbing his neck. "You didn't reply. I thought you were mad about something, so I came around."

I shook my head. "No, I'm sorry. I didn't know about the text. It was deleted by mistake."

"Oh…right." He cleared his throat. "I better go now then. Since you are not mad or anything."

"D-Do you want to come in?" I asked, opening the door and gesturing him inside.

He smiled brightly. "I would love to, thanks."

"Just so you know, I won't be fun to be around. I have a bit of homework to do," I warned as he followed me into the kitchen. I sat at the table. "If you want something to drink just help yourself," I added before opening my calculus book.

He peeked at my book. "Need some help?" he asked, sitting right beside me. He was really getting at ease like he had been coming here forever. He was almost acting like Chago did.

I shook my head. "No, it's fine. I can handle calculus pretty well. So, how is the reading going?"

"I'm almost done with the book. I'm sure I will be all ready to discuss it next week."

"Why not Saturday?"

"I have a game Saturday afternoon. You forgot?"

"I - Yes, it must have slipped my mind," I said. That was better than admitting that sometimes when we were chatting, I got lost in his big green eyes and zoned out.

"That's why I was disappointed you canceled on us today."

I squealed internally. He would have missed me!! "Yes, sorry, but Chago had good news and his mom organized a family dinner."

His smile wavered. "You are family? Isn't that nice?" I didn't miss the cold edge to his voice. Was he jealous? It would have been the perfect moment to tell him that Chago was like a brother to me, and yet I remained silent. "What's the good news?" he asked, running his forefinger around the rim of his can of Coke.

"Oh, he has been invited to take some tests for an internship," I replied dismissively.

"Cardenas Corp?"

I looked at him silently, not confirming or infirming anything.

"You did it! You convinced the man to check Chago's paper. Nice!" He nodded approvingly with a wide smile.

"I—" I slammed my book shut. "Who are you? Some kind of spy with the goal to ruin my life?" I asked, not able to contain my aggressiveness. This guy knew enough things about me to make my life a living hell.

He recoiled with surprise, probably taken aback by the coldness of my tone. "I-" "How do you know that?" I continued coldly.

"I was at the party organized by your mother's law firm last month."

"Really? I didn't see you there." I couldn't believe I hadn't noticed someone as good looking as him.

"You didn't see me, but I saw you," he admitted with a small smile. "My father forced me to go because he'd wanted me to convince Cardenas Ruiz to give me the internship. So when he saw you talking to him, he went ballistic and forced me to spy on your conversation."

I opened my mouth, then closed it again. What could I say?

"Don't worry. I didn't tell him anything, but I did hear you trying to convince Ruiz to give Chago a chance." He shook his head. "To be honest, I was relieved and jealous at the same time."

"Jealous? Why?"

"Jealous to see you fight for your man that much and…" He rubbed his neck again, and I started to understand that was something he did when he was self-conscious. "Nobody has ever fought for me the way you are fighting for him."

"Maybe if you showed people who you really are, they would fight for you."

He shrugged, taking a sip of his Coke.

"But you know our friendship is far from being fair." I stood up, pretending to put some order to the kitchen to hide my nervousness.

"What do you mean?" he asked, and I could hear the confusion in his voice.

"You know my two biggest secrets. Two things that if you reveal, estoy arruinado," I admitted, turning around to look at him.

"What? Arruinado?"

"I'm screwed," I translated, leaning against the kitchen island.

"I won't say anything. Your secrets are safe with me. You can trust me," he added, turning in his chair, so he could have a good look at me.

It was not like I had a choice anyway. He knew everything and I didn't have any leverage on him. "Tell me something too," I said gently. "Something about you, anything that is not generic."

He nodded, licking his bottom lip. I could see he was thinking, deciding on the spot if he would let me in or not. He took a shaky breath. "You were right. I don't like business. I love architecture. My crazy dream is to study architecture at Columbia. I even have a notebook with some designs I've made."

Oh, that was a big one! I thought, pleased that he trusted me. "Will you show it to me?"

"Eventually."

"Tell me a secret," I blurted out.

"A secret?" he asked, coming to stand in front of me.

"Yes, you know, since you know two of my secrets. Tell me one of yours."

"A secret? Anything?" He took a step forward, standing even closer, so close that, when I looked up, I could see threads of gold in his emerald eyes.

"*Anything,*" I let out in a breath. This guy had some crazy effect on me.

He hesitantly brought his hand up. As he did, my breath caught in my throat.

He cupped my cheek in his hand. Very gently, he brushed my cheekbone with his thumb. His touch contained so much tenderness, it took all I had not to close my eyes and lean into his comforting touch.

He leaned down, towering over me. "Okay, here it goes." He took a deep, shaky breath, apparently as affected by the closeness as I was. "Since the first time I saw you in Mulligan's class, I've wanted to kiss you," he whispered, inches from my lips.

"Really?" I whispered back, letting my eyes trail down to his lips. His bottom lip was slightly plumper, giving his mouth a small perpetual pout.

"Oh yes, really. What about you? Tell me a secret." He was so close I could feel his hot breath on my lips.

"I might let you kiss me." I didn't get to add anything else as his lips brushed mine. It felt like a jolt of electricity running from the crown of my head to the bottom of my spine.

"Your lips are very soft," he breathed, keeping his lips on mine. "I wonder what they taste like."

"Why don't you find out?" I replied, keeping my eyes closed. He brought his other hand up, securing my face between his hands before pressing me against the island. I could feel its bite in my back, but it didn't matter. All that mattered now were his lips moving in sync with mine. He very gently ran the tip of his tongue across my bottom lip in an invitation to deepen our kiss. I cracked my lips open. As soon as his tongue met mine, it was like it was meant to be. I never wanted this kiss to end.

I wrapped my arms around his waist, holding him against me. My body felt like Jell-O, so it was good that I was trapped between Gabriel's body and the kitchen counter or I would have melted into a puddle on the floor.

I couldn't help the little moan from escaping my mouth when he started to lightly suck on my bottom lip. Gabriel took it as an encouragement. He deepened our kiss with a new-found ardor, making my toes curl. It was exactly how I imagined the epic kisses in the old movies felt like, but I'd never thought I would experience one.

When we finally broke apart, completely breathless, he rested his forehead against mine, keeping his eyes closed.

"That was---" he started after a while, still a little breathless.

"*Wow,*" I finished, finally opening my eyes.

He opened his eyes too, but kept his position. I could feel his furious heartbeat under my palm. It rested on his chest. I could smell his tanned skin. It was a strange, intoxicating mix of musky aftershave, sun, and sea.

We stayed in this embrace, staring into each other's eyes for a little while. I couldn't say if it was a minute or an hour. All I was aware of was the nice, tingling sensation of my swollen lips, his warm body against mine, and the almost eerie synchronization of our heartbeats.

"I better go," he whispered, bringing me back down to this sulky reality.

I nodded. "Yes, I think it's for the best." I reluctantly let go of my hold on him.

He let go of my face and took a step back. He looked at me with a scrutinizing gaze as if he was seeing me for the first time.

He brought his hand back to my face and brushed his fingertips from my temple to my chin.

"I'll see you soon, Lottie." He turned around briskly and rushed out, leaving me both numb and speechless.

"Lottie?" I asked long after he was gone. Only my father had called me that; it felt so weird to hear that nickname again. I'd never allowed anyone to call me Lottie after my father had died, but I knew I wouldn't object if he continued.

I sighed, sitting on a kitchen stool and resting my forehead against the cold marble. It was official. I made the mistake I'd sworn I wouldn't make. I was falling for that Viking. I was falling hard and I knew there was only one way for this to end - with my broken heart.

CHAPTER 10

When I woke up the next morning, I brought my hand to my lips, still hardly believing what had happened the night before. Gabriel Johnson had kissed me. *Me*, Charlotte Miller, and even more surprising, I had kissed him back, wanting more.

I couldn't help but smile, replaying the scene in my head. I knew it was stupid, wrong, and probably - no, not probably, *definitely* - a mistake, but I couldn't stop my heart from jumping every time I thought of his lips on mine. I really hoped this feeling would linger because I didn't expect to repeat that experience anytime soon.

I looked at the alarm clock and jumped out of bed. Chago was going to be here in less than fifteen minutes. I slid into the first pair of pants I found, threw on the first tee shirt in my wardrobe, tightened my hair into a ponytail, and I was ready to go.

I was just finishing my orange juice when I heard Chago's car in the driveway.

I grabbed my book bag and ran out to meet him.

"Wow, Chula." He chuckled as I sat heavily in the car. "If I didn't know any better, I'd thought your ass was on fire."

I glared at him. "I didn't sleep well and missed the alarm this morning… Sue me."

Chago made a cat noise. "I know how, ummmm, *'sensitive'* you get when you don't get sleep. I will keep it down today." He winked.

I couldn't contain my smile any longer. "Come on, guapo. Let's go get some education."

As soon as we crossed the hall threshold, I couldn't help but look around for Gabriel. I cursed myself for doing that. I had not expected the little pinch of disappointment when I couldn't find him in the crowd.

"Chula?"

"Uh?" I concentrated on Chago's questioning eyes. "Sorry, I guess I'm not totally awake yet. What did you say?"

"I was saying that I have to see the Principal about the day I have my tests for the internship. Meet you in calculus?"

I nodded and tried my best to concentrate on anything but Gabriel as I walked to my locker. What did I expect to happen?

What did I even want to happen? Did yesterday mean anything or was it a slip-up?

As I put my books in my locker, I heard Doug's laugh. My head turned toward it as if it was a magnet. I knew that usually where Gabriel was, Doug was there too, but this time the massive redhead wasn't with Gabriel. I couldn't help the little sigh of disappointment that escaped my lips.

"Who are we looking for?" Logan asked from behind me.

I turned around, startled. "I…You. I was looking for you."

"Sure, you were," he replied, looking behind me curiously. "So where is the conjoined twin?"

I laughed. Logan was not the first person to say Chago and I were joined at the hip. "He is with the Principal."

"Trouble?" Logan asked, frowning.

"I'm the trouble maker, remember?" I grinned. "I would be in there way before him."

"True… So, we're still up for Saturday, right?"

I nodded as the first bell rang. "Course! I'll see you at lunch," I called, rushing to calculus.

I didn't get to see Gabriel that day, not even during lunch at the central table where he always sat.

I was angry at myself for letting the situation affect me. It was making me different. I didn't want to become one of those silly girls who crushed on a guy that couldn't care less.

"What's wrong with you today, Chula?" Chago asked, wrapping a protective arm around my shoulders. "You didn't ask me what the Principal told me about the tests. You didn't mock Doug's stupid comment in Calculus *and* you didn't comment on that idiotic cheerleader's obvious collagen treatment," he added, pointing to a dark-haired girl who was bending over the central table.

Logan tsked, shaking his head. "Gemma…Gemma…Gemma. She really looks like a fish now."

"Did you get a new red Post-it?"

I shook my head, biting into my sandwich. "No, it's just… I'm out of it today. Maybe I'm getting a cold or something? But enough about me." I forced a smile. "What did the Devil tell you?"

"Principal Webber?"

"Who else, guapo?"

"Apparently, he is happy for me." He shrugged, finishing his can of pop. "He even wished me luck."

"That is…interesting," Logan commented, rubbing his chin. "Maybe the body snatchers got to him."

I pretended to ponder that. "Your theory is as good as mine."

"What was yours?" Logan asked curiously.

"Voodoo priests."

Logan grinned, nodding in approval. "You went exotic… Nice."

Chago shook his head. "Oye, you two are locos."

"Takes one to know one," Logan chimed, glancing at the clock above the door. "Well, my dear friends, I'm sorry to ditch you, knowing you will both miss me so dearly, but some of us have obligations from which we cannot derogate and--"

"Like being a pompous ass?" I asked, cutting him off.

He bowed. "Like that indeed."

Chago snorted. "At least he is not lying to himself."

Logan batted his eyelids. "See you later, hot stuff."

We looked at Logan's retreating back.

Once he exited the cafeteria, Chago reached for my hand. "Come on, Chula. Now tell me what's wrong?"

I looked at him silently for a few seconds. "Nothing's wrong"

He sighed and shook his head. "I know you. Don't lie to me. It's insulting."

"It's just a whole. I didn't sleep well and there is the chemistry exam that's bothering me." I shrugged. It was not really a lie. It was only the partial truth. I had my own definition of lies, which changed to fit the moment.

Chago looked thoughtful for a minute, but finally let go and concentrated on his plate again.

I looked away as a feeling of guilt submerged me. Lying to Chago was horrible. I'd never felt as guilty as I did now. But Mateo was right. If Chago knew who I was tutoring, it wouldn't take him a day to figure out my illicit feelings for Gabriel. The very 'not-single' Gabriel. Chago wouldn't support my choice, not that I could blame him. This was one of the first times I hadn't told Chago the whole truth and it felt wrong. *I'll tell him. I will tell him once I have everything figured out.*

I also couldn't help the rush of guilt every time I glimpsed Darlene in the corridors. I willed myself to forget, but how could I? It had been one kiss, just a kiss, and yet it was a kiss too many in our current situation.

The rest of the day was uneventful, but I had never been more aware of somebody's absence before today. Gabriel Johnson shone by his absence.

On Saturday morning, a knock on the door made my heart flutter. Even if I knew Gabriel had a game later today, I couldn't help but hope it was him.

However, who I found in front of my door was almost as surprising as Gabriel.

"Logan?" I asked with incredulity. It was not the fact that Logan Brier was in front of my door that was shocking. It was the way he looked that made me speechless. He looked...normal.

"Yes." He grinned. "Who did you expect to see?"

I shrugged. "I don't know...Chris Hemsworth?"

He laughed. "Yes, that would be a good package."

I couldn't stop staring at him. I'd only seen Logan without artifice once before and that had been three years ago at his grandmother's funeral.

He was dressed in blue jeans with a white shirt and black training shoes. His blond hair was combed back, and he was not wearing weird contact lenses either. Seeing his natural chocolate eyes still got to me.

"I... Did I forget we were supposed to meet?" I asked, letting him in.

He shook his head. "No, but for once I have a Saturday free and we are supposed to meet with Chago tonight." He shrugged. "I thought that maybe you and I could go to the mall."

I tried my best to hide my surprise. We never spent quality time, just the two of us. "Yeah, that would be fun!" I was actually pleased to go out for a little while. I usually cringed at the idea of shopping. It was probably one of my least favorite activities, but I was fed up with replaying a meaningless kiss with a guy who was everything that was wrong for me.

Logan looked at me with an eyebrow raised. "Really? There was no sarcasm in your voice, you know."

I chuckled. "Yes really. Just give me five minutes to change and we'll be good to go."

The afternoon at the mall was fun. I even managed to stop thinking for a little while. After getting a latte at Starbucks, we just sat there making fun of people walking up and down the mall.

"Is it your mother's birthday or something?" Logan asked as I stopped at a shop on our way out.

"No, why?" I asked, confused.

"You know what shop you are in, don't you? You are in an actual girly shop with makeup and crap like that and -" he pointed - "you are looking at lipsticks."

"So?" I asked, trying not to blush. "Maybe I want to start wearing makeup."

"Since when?" He frowned, crossing his arms on his chest.

"Since...Shut up! I'm just looking." I slammed the lipstick back on the table harder than expected. "Looking is not a crime, is it?"

"I...PMS?" he tried.

I rolled my eyes. "Let's go." I saw him glance toward the bookstore with longing in his eyes. I stopped, curious. People could look at a lot of stores with longing, but a bookstore was not one of them, especially when that person was named Logan Brier.

"What do you want us to do now?" he asked, looking at his watch. "We still have some time to kill before meeting el Hombre."

"Let's go to the bookstore." I tried to keep my voice nonchalant.

Logan, who was already naturally quite pale, managed to pale two shades. "Why? You are not even a bookstore fan."

I shrugged. "Why not? You said it yourself. We have time to kill and they might have some new political books that can interest me," I replied, already taking the direction of the store.

Logan grumbled, but followed me reluctantly.

We were in the shop for about two seconds when someone talked to us.

"Logan! Finally coming with someone? I was starting to think you were ashamed to bring your friends over."

I looked up and saw a very attractive young man smiling at me. He had jet black hair, deep brown eyes, and one of the brightest smiles I had ever seen.

The way Logan peeked at me with embarrassment made it clear he liked the guy. It was also clear that, based on how quickly the guy had come over to talk to us, he liked Logan too.

I smiled at him and extended my hand. "Hi. I'm Charlotte."

He took my hand in both of his. They were warm and dry, and his grip was frank. My mother always said that you could tell a lot about a person from the first greeting, and based on my observations, this guy seemed honest enough.

"Nice to finally meet you," he said, keeping his eyes on mine. "My name is Matt." He glanced at Logan after releasing my hand.

"Finally?" I asked, looking at Logan with wonder.

I could see poor Logan getting more and more uncomfortable, and it took a lot to embarrass him.

"Yes! You keep sending him to buy books. You're sending him almost every week. I was starting to wonder if you even existed."

"I… Yes, sorry." I nodded, trying to hide my surprise. "My schedule is so hectic and Logan enjoys coming to the mall so… Who better than my friend to do that?" I winked at Logan, seeing his muscles relax.

We stayed and talked a bit more with Matt. He was really nice, funny, and as far as I could tell, as 'normal' as can be - even if normal was overrated. I could also see that each guy was crushing on each other.

"I don't want to hear anything.," Logan threatened as we exited the mall.

"Oh honey, there is no way in hell that will ever happen."

He sighed. "I'm sorry I used you as an excuse."

I dismissed that with a gesture of the hand. "I don't care about that! That guy seems very nice and he is stunningly good looking."

"Yeah? I haven't noticed," Logan replied dryly.

"Sarcasm doesn't become you. That's my prerogative," I replied, sitting in the car. "And I wonder why you don't ask him out? It's clear that that's all he is waiting for."

"It's more complicated than that." He groaned, resting his forehead on the steering wheel.

"I don't see how it's complicated. You like him. He likes you…" I rubbed his back in soothing circles.

Logan remained silent.

"What are you afraid of Logan?"

He turned his head toward me after a while. "Probably the same thing you are afraid of. Getting hurt, giving a chance to someone who might actually get full access to your heart and hurt you beyond repair."

"Me? I'm not afraid!"

He gave a humorless laugh. "Right, and hiding behind Chago, letting people assume you guys are together just to keep them at arm's length?"

"I...don't do that," I denied, but I could hear the lack of conviction in my own voice.

"Sure, you don't," he simply replied, sitting straight on his seat and starting the car.

"You know, maybe I'm scared, but I'm pretty sure that if I ever met someone who seemed to be worth it, I would give him a chance."

"If people could get close enough to you," he commented. "You know I... I will think about it," he added, and I was pretty sure he was humoring me to stop this conversation.

<u>CHAPTER 11</u>

"Okay, wish me luck for this afternoon," Chago said as he took my hand just before the end of lunch.

"Good luck." I tried to figure out what he was talking about.

"You have no idea what I'm talking about, do you?"

I gave him my best sheepish grin.

He sighed, pulling me out of the lunch room. "I really wonder where you were last Friday. Probably on the moon." He shook his head. "You heard nothing I told you then, right?"

"No, not really…Sorry," I admitted. I hated how that kiss with Gabriel had shaken me so much. It'd been enough for me to put Chago aside, but it was better now. I understood it had all been a mistake, just a silly thing that had happened in the heat of the moment. I would never be a bad friend again.

I'd decided on how I was going to deal with the whole Gabriel situation. On Thursday, I would tell him he had no reason to be embarrassed and that it had meant nothing to me too. I knew it'd embarrassed him. It was clear every time our eyes met in the halls. His shame was so clear, I avoided his eyes because I didn't need the constant reminder of our moment of weakness.

"I'm taking the first tests this afternoon for the internship and the others next Friday all day." He looked thoughtful. "You'll be alright, won't you?"

I scoffed. "Of course! It's only one afternoon. What can go wrong in one afternoon?"

Chago cocked an eyebrow and I realized it was a stupid question. "With you? A lot!"

"I promise I will keep my mouth shut, no smartass moves all afternoon. I swear!!" Chago knew that when I swore, it was binding. I never went back on a swear, whatever it cost me.

He visibly relaxed. "No smartass moves? Even if someone provokes you?"

I shook my head. "I swear." I hugged him. "Buena Suerte."

"Yea, I'll need all the luck I can get." He hugged me back fiercely. It scared him, I knew that. He wanted this internship so bad; it was a whole future opening its arms to him and I knew he wouldn't forgive himself if he didn't get it.

"Come on. You better go now -" I let go of him - "if you don't want to be late." I reached for his hand again. "And you don't need luck, Chago. You are great. You will do great."

He smiled brightly before running down the stairs to his car. I stayed in the school square until I saw his car leave the school grounds.

I looked upward at the sky. "I don't know if you exist or not, but if you do, please help him get what he wants. He deserves this chance. Please don't let him down," I whispered to a god I was not sure was there.

When I turned around, the hall was almost empty except for Gabriel. He was standing by his locker, looking right at me.

I stayed where I was, not really knowing what to do. Had he come to talk to me or was it a coincidence?

He took a hesitant step in my direction, but then Doug came out of the cafeteria.

"Hey, dude! What's taking you so long?"

Gabriel waved a magazine in his direction. "Took me awhile. My locker is a mess."

I knew the bell was about to ring, so I decided to head in the direction of my next class. I couldn't help wondering how long Gabriel had stood there, looking at me and Chago.

I snorted, rolling my eyes. Even in my head, I sounded stupid.

Get a grip, woman. Why should you care anyway? I chastised myself.

The afternoon seemed to drag without Chago, and I couldn't help but stress for him. I kept wondering about him and how he was doing. Chago usually did well under pressure. I just hoped it would be the same today.

At the end of Advance Lit, Mr. Mulligan asked me to stay.

"I only have a couple of minutes before the editorial meeting, but I want to know how the assignment is going?" It was clear he was not talking about the assignment he had just given us, but about my tutoring of Gabriel.

I nodded. "It's going well."

"It surprised me to find out that you were continuing to help him after the first two papers." He bent down to put his stuff away, but I didn't miss the little smile edging at the corner of his mouth. It was the kind of smile that had always unnerved me.

"We have an agreement. He is helping me with chemistry and I'm helping him with literature. It's a win/win situation." I

111

shrugged dismissively. "Nothing more than that," I added a bit colder than intended.

Mulligan looked at me in surprise. It was true that I was never cold to him; he had quickly become my favorite teacher here. "I see," he said.

I sighed. "Everything is just fine. It works."

He nodded. "I'm glad to hear that."

"I still wonder why you did all this? Why did you help us?"

He laughed. "Not everyone has a reason to do things you know, Charlotte. I knew he needed help and I really like the way you express your way of thinking in your papers." He walked with me to the door. "I thought it was the perfect match."

I opened my mouth about to ask him what he'd meant by 'match,' but Logan caught my arm as soon as I'd exited the room.

"I'll see you tomorrow, Miss Miller." He glanced at Logan with an amused smile. "Don't be late, Mr. Brier."

"I won't!" Logan replied, but I could feel the excitement pouring from him. *What kind of gossip had he managed to get this time?* "Yes?" I asked, crossing the hall to my locker.

"You are one lucky chick, you know that, right?"

"Of course I do. What is the particular reason today?"

"When el hombre caliente is not here to take you home, you have the *super* caliente waiting for you in the car park."

I looked at him with confusion. As much as I hated it, I couldn't help but see Gabriel's face in my mind.

As soon as I had filled my backpack, Logan took my hand and pulled me toward the exit with long strides, forcing me to run.

"Short legs, Logan! Short legs!" I huffed, getting breathless as we reached the exit.

He snorted and stopped abruptly before pointing. It was Mateo, leaning carelessly against his car, his dark hair a curly mess in the wind. He was dressed in his usual faded blue jeans and white shirt, but based on the hungry looks the girls were throwing him, his style worked just fine.

I finally registered the car he was leaning on. It was the Corvette roadster and I couldn't help the little squeal escaping my mouth.

"See you later!" I shouted to Logan, rushing down the stairs. "Oh my God. You've finished it?!" I asked, standing in front of Mateo.

"Hello to you too," he chuckled with a wink, finally standing straighter. "I promised you the inauguration drive, didn't I?"

"Yes, but…" I looked down at the car before looking back at him. "Chago sent you, didn't he?"

"Can I at least get my hello hug before we get into accusations?"

I rolled my eyes, but hugged him tightly.

"You know most of the girls want to murder me right now?" I told him only half joking.

He shrugged. "That's the problem with being a machete. What can I say? It's a curse."

I snorted. "Sure it is. So did Chago send you?"

Mateo gave me his million-dollar smile, gesturing me toward the passenger side.

"Let's talk about it on your way home, shall we?"

I sighed. "Fine," I pouted, rounding the car. I looked up as I reached for the car's door. My eyes locked onto a group of jocks and particularly connected with Gabriel's eyes. There was something weird in the way he looked at me, in the way his jaw was locked. But he turned around almost immediately to talk to Doug again. It had all been too fast for me to register what it had been. If I had to guess though, it had seemed to be a mix of longing and jealousy.

"You are so hallucinating," I grumbled, sitting in the car.

"What?" Mateo asked, joining me in the car.

I shook my head. "Nothing. As for Chago sending you, honestly… Don't you think he is slightly overreacting?"

Mateo stayed silent for a second. "Well, you do have a temper, but actually, my little brother didn't have much to do with this. I knew he had his tests and I was done with the car." He shrugged. "I thought it would be nice, that you would be happy to see me." He sighed dramatically.

"Come on. You know I always enjoy seeing you."

"I know, but I still enjoy hearing you say it," he jested with his cheeky grin.

"And it's girls who are supposed to be needy." I rolled my eyes.

"So you like the car?" he asked out of the blue, parking in front of my house.

I looked at him in confusion. I was usually the random one, but right now I couldn't follow his train of thoughts.

"You like it or not?" he insisted.

"Of course, I do! You know it's a pure treasure," I marveled, stroking the dashboard.

"I will make you an offer." He looked so serious. "But it needs to stay between us. At least for now."

"Okay…" I trailed off, suspicious.

"If you accept driving lessons…"

I tensed up. "No, Mateo not that again." I looked away.

"I would let you drive this car," he continued like I hadn't interrupted him.

"What?!" I looked at him, taken aback.

He nodded, letting his hands go up and down the steering wheel. "I would teach you how to drive. I would teach you in this car and you could drive it whenever you wanted."

"Why would you do that?"

"I want you to drive."

I sighed. "Why is that so important? Many people don't drive…" I thought for a second. "Your mother doesn't drive, and I don't see you giving her shit about it."

Mateo let out a little groan. He didn't like when I swore, especially when his mother was in the sentence.

"It doesn't scare her," he commented, locking his eyes with mine.

"One more reason to leave me alone." I crossed my arms on my chest stubbornly.

"One more reason to try harder." He sighed again when he saw I was not going to answer. "I just want you to get past this. There is a part of you stuck in the past. I understand it had to be traumatic, but…" He reached over and placed a lock of hair gently behind my ear. "But I'm convinced that if you ever tried to drive a car, it would help heal the part of you that is still raw. Otherwise that will stay raw."

"There is nothing to fear except fear itself?" I asked sarcastically as he parked the car.

"You can laugh, but that's true."

"I'll think about it," I replied, reaching for the handle.

"No, you won't." He gave me a sad smile.

"Probably not," I admitted. "Want to come in?"

He shook his head. "No thanks. I need to go back to the garage. Some other time, si?"

114

"Sure." I kissed his cheek. "Have Chago call me when he comes home, please. And don't worry too much if he is all sullen, thinking he failed his tests." I rolled my eyes. "He most likely did not."

Mateo chuckled. "Duly noted."

As I took the mail, I couldn't help but snort at the letter from the school announcing the Christmas PTA meeting.

"Yes, she will totally go," I mumbled, throwing the blue flyer on top of the console.

I sat on the sofa, staring at the TV's black screen, rethinking about the events of the last few weeks. It felt like everything was changing and I wasn't sure if I liked it. Of course, I was happy for Chago. He deserved all the good things that might come his way, but it felt like nothing would ever be like it was before.

I grabbed my cell and started to go through my texts randomly.

When I reached Gabriel's texts, I thought about the way he'd looked at me back in the hall. He'd been guarded, almost angry. Had he been mad at himself for the stupid kiss? Did he feel guilty because of Darlene? He was probably thinking he'd spoiled our burgeoning friendship.

He needed to know we were okay. I would miss him, our chats, our fights... We were so different, but it was fun. Being his friend was better than nothing.

It didn't mean anything. Let's forget about it and go on. C, I wrote, but hesitated to press send. Was sending this text meaning I cared?

I decided to discard the message, but the sound of the kitchen door closing loudly made me jump and press the 'send' button at the same time.

"Damn it!" I swore loudly as the 'sent' appeared on my screen.

"Are you that displeased to see me?" my mother asked, walking into the living room. Her eyes went from me to the black TV screen and back to me. "Are you all right?"

I nodded. "What about you?" I asked, looking at my watch. "It's only 5:00 pm. I don't remember you getting home at that time in...forever."

She put her laptop bag in the armchair and just stood there looking at me as if she was trying to figure something out.

"We closed the first part of the negotiations this morning, I thought it would be nice to come home early." She shrugged dismissively. "I know I haven't been around for the last few months."

For the last few years! I thought, but decided that was a pointless argument I would never win. It was the kind of argument that was bound to end up with a *'You'll see when you grow up,'* or *'You'll understand eventually,'* or even my all-time favorite, *'You are not mature enough. You'll see that life is about responsibilities, not desires.'*

"It's okay," was all I could say.

"And I will be even busier in the coming weeks."

"Of course, you will," I couldn't help but let out.

Her eyes narrowed in a glare, but she ignored my comment. "So I was wondering if you wanted to go out and have a pizza or something with me tonight? You could tell me how things are for you at school."

"What about ordering in?" I tried. "I still have homework and I'm waiting on a call." *We will probably end up fighting over something stupid and I would rather be at a walking distance from my bedroom when that happens,* I added to myself.

Something flashed in her face. It looked a lot like sorrow and disappointment, but I couldn't be sure. My mother was the hardest person to read, probably because of her legal training.

"Of course." She turned toward the kitchen. "I'll call you when the food is delivered."

I went up to my room and finished the little homework I had left. I had barely put my pen down when my phone rang to Chago's familiar ringtone.

"How did it go?"

He chuckled. "Hi to you too."

"Yeah, yeah, so?" I asked, standing up and pacing the room. He seemed happy enough.

"I think it went well."

"Of course it did! You're made for the job."

He chuckled again. "You have so much confidence in me."

"It's what best friends are for." I made a silly face as if he was in front of me. "I know you well…maybe better than you know yourself."

"Charlotte, the food is here!" my mother shouted from downstairs.

"Is that your mom?"

"Yep," I said, popping the 'p'.

"At…" He'd probably looked at his watch. "Six thirty at night?"

"Yep."

"Wow…"

"I know."

"Charlotte!" my mom called again.

"I'm coming!" I shouted back. "Listen, guapo, I'll give you a call later. Mother is expecting me for a family dinner."

"What did you do?" he asked, only half joking.

I snorted. "I don't know, but I'll keep you posted. Love ya."

"Me too."

I hung up and threw the phone on my bed.

When I joined my mother in the kitchen, she was already sitting at the table with plastic plates and Chinese food.

We ate most of the meal in silence.

"So, Charlotte, how are things at school?" she finally asked.

"Fine, thanks for asking."

"Why didn't you want to go out? Do you have problems with your homework? Do you need help?"

I gave her a *'who are you and what did you do to my mother'* look. "No, I'm done."

"Are you still waiting for your call? Your boyfriend?" she asked, making me choke on my noodles.

"Excuse me?"

"The phone call you seem to be waiting for," she said before taking a sip of water. "Is it from your boyfriend?"

"Honestly Mom…what do you want?" I asked, leaning back in my chair. This was really starting to get freaky.

She sighed with annoyance. "I'm trying here, Charlotte, but you are acting out like always. Being rebellious."

Of all the things she could have said, that was the worst. It activated my angst-ridden teenager glands.

"Really?" I let go of my chopsticks, "You know what? You're right. Let me just ask you five very general questions and if you get them right, I'll apologize and answer all the questions you might have."

She let go of her own chopsticks and stapled her hands under her chin, looking at me in silent agreement.

I cleared my throat and a part of me wished she would get them right. I needed her to get them right, even if the rational part of me knew she wouldn't. "Okay… What is my favorite color, my favorite subject in school, my favorite movie, my favorite band, and my favorite pastime?"

My mother looked at me silently and for once I saw some shame in her face. She was trying to hide it, but I could see it in the hard lines of her mouth, the lines on her forehead. I also knew that we could stay here until next year and she would never get the answers right.

Her phone started to vibrate on the kitchen counter.

"I think you should get that. You've already messed up the relationship with your daughter, better not mess up the job you sacrificed almost everything for." I stood up. "Good night, Mother."

I sat on my bed after my dramatic exit. It was barely seven thirty. It was going to be a long, long evening.

I rolled my eyes, falling back heavily onto my bed before dialing Chago's number.

"Hey, guapo."

"Chula so, what was that dinner about?"

I sighed. "Whatever."

"I see." He realized it was my way of saying, 'leave it alone'

"Can I ask you questions?"

"Sure…" He trailed off.

"What's my favorite color, favorite subject in school, favorite movie, favorite band, and favorite pastime."

Chago laughed. "Really?"

"Guapo, please, just answer."

He sighed. "Fine. Red, literature, Back to the Future… Favorite band? That's a trick… You love two the same: The Script and Oasis. And your favorite pastime? Playing guitar."

I closed my eyes. Yes, it was official. Chago knew me better than my own mother.

I spent the rest of the evening talking to Chago and listening to music. It was not a surprise that my mother didn't interrupt. Maybe now she would know where she had failed. Maybe now she would actually try.

CHAPTER 12

"So tell me again. You had an essay and then a multiple-choice questionnaire?" I asked Chago as we sat in third Period PE. Today was the first day of dodge ball and our gym teacher, Ms. Burton, always spent at least two classes explaining the rules, origins, and all that crap whenever we started a new activity.

Could you even spend two hours talking about dodgeball? I doubted it was possible, but if anyone could, it was her. She loved the sound of her own voice. It was good for us though because she never noticed that some of us got lost in our own conversations.

He nodded. "Yes, and next week we have 'practice' whatever that means."

I reached for his hand and squeezed it. "You'll be fine."

He bumped me with his shoulder. "I owe you, you know that?"

I looked at him warily. Did he know what I'd done? No, it was impossible because if he did, he would have given me shit about it. "You owe me?"

He smiled cheekily and nodded. "Of course! If it wasn't for you, I don't think I would have even tried! But you have so much faith in me, I had to go and do my best. I have to believe I'm good enough because I don't want your effort to be wasted."

We usually didn't have a cheesy friendship, but my heart tightened in my chest and I had to look up for a minute to make sure tears wouldn't fill my eyes. It reminded me of what Cardenas Ruiz had told me at the party, *"Never underestimate your impact on his success, on his life. Having someone who trusts you fully, forces you to try to be as good as you can be."* Maybe he had been right. Maybe I did play a part in Chago's decisions.

"Dang, we're cheesy," he snorted, shaking his head.

I chuckled. "We are."

Chago was about to say something when the inside door of the gym opened and a little blond kid entered. He walked straight to Ms. Burton and gave her a piece of paper.

She sighed, skimming it. I was not sure if it was what she was reading or the fact that she'd been interrupted that annoyed her the most.

"Miss Miller, you are expected in the Principal's office," she announced, looking at me.

"Who?" I asked stupidly. Even in a million years, I wouldn't have expected this note to be about me. I hadn't done anything reprehensible these days - at least not anything that could be traced back to me.

"I'm pretty sure you are the only Miller in this gym," she added.

"What did you do?" Chago whispered and I could see the worry on his face.

"I have no idea," I whispered back. "Please listen carefully so you can tell me everything about dodge ball when I come back," I said loudly, knowing all my sarcasm were completely lost on Ms. Burton.

"Hey Kid, did the Principle look mad when he'd given you the note?" I asked when we exited the main gym.

He glanced at me, but kept on walking silently.

"Aren't you a little chatterbox?" I sighed. "Just tell me if you saw the vein on his neck throb. If you did, it means major trouble."

I growled as he kept ignoring me. We walked down the little corridor leading to the changing rooms, the equipment room, and the janitor closet.

Just as we reached the exit, I felt someone grab hold of my wrist and pull me into the janitor closet. I let out a little squeal.

"That was one hell of a scream," Gabriel chuckled with a playful smile as he closed the door of the closet with a kick.

I blushed. "Yeah, well… Sorry, but I'm not used to being kidnapped." I tried not to sound as if the proximity to him affected me, but it did… Boy, it did.

He grimaced, but didn't say anything. He kept looking down at me, and the way he eyed me made my stomach uneasy. It was doing all the flips it usually did whenever I was on a roller coaster, except that my feet were on solid ground. This was all so new to me.

"I…need to go." I pointed at the closed door, but could hear my own reluctance.

"Do you?" he asked, and his voice was teasing, teasing enough to make me question him.

I raised an eyebrow. "I'm not expected in the Principal's office, am I?"

He shook his head, his grin widening.

I was impressed. "Being a popular jock does have its perks, doesn't it?"

He laughed out loud. "It does. I can't deny that."

"What can I do for you?" I asked, reading the name of the cleaning products, trying to concentrate on something other than him.

When he didn't reply, I looked at him again. I could see a peculiar look in his eyes even in this dim light. "I…"

I didn't get a chance to finish my sentence as his lips were on mine, soft and warm, demanding and urgent.

All the warning bells in my head started to shriek full force. This was stupid, every kind of stupid. I knew what I had to do. I had to push him away, tell him to stop. But as I raised my hands on his chest to push him away, I felt numbed by his lips. I kept my hands on his chest for a little while, feeling the increased beating of his heart. I smiled as he kissed me with even more ardor; I was clearly having some effect on him too.

I let my hands slide up and wrapped my arms tightly around his neck, pulling him even closer.

Gabriel moaned, pushing me harder against the wooden shelves. *Damn, that was going to leave marks!* But then again, I didn't care.

When we finally parted breathlessly, Gabriel rested his hands on my shoulders and his forehead against mine. "I hope this one counts."

"Uh?" I asked laboriously, still trying to catch my breath.

He let his hands trail down my arms, intertwining our fingers. "The kiss… In your text you said it'd meant nothing. I hope this one does."

My heart started to beat even more furiously. "What does it mean?"

He kissed me again, but this time lightly, almost tentatively. "I don't know, but I would really like to find out."

It probably means we're morons, I thought, but simply let out a breathless, 'Yeah.'

He cocked his head to the side, clenching my hands. "You seem undecided."

I bit my bottom lip. The guy was good. Even in the darkness, he knew how I felt.

"Darlene," I whispered. Part of me regretted bursting that silly little bubble, but it had to be done. We had to go back to reality. How could I be okay with being 'that girl'?

He froze, muscles tensed. "We'll figure something."

Will we? I thought, but I was too chicken to press the issue. "I've got to go."

"I know… I just—" He stopped and looked up at the ceiling.

"Just?" I tried.

"Nothing." He let go of my hands and took a step back, sizing me up. I had to admit it made me self-conscious. He really made me feel things I had never experienced before and I was not sure if I liked it. He reached into his backpack and got out a yellow notepad.

"You've got an excuse pad?" I asked, surprised.

"Yes. I have many things." He winked as he scribbled something on the pad. "I'm a skilled guy."

"I know that," I answered, only realizing later the double meaning.

Gabriel didn't miss that and his smile turned playful again. "Glad to know you enjoyed it."

I rolled my eyes, trying to hide my discomfort, but I was not sure I'd fooled him.

"Here." He gave me the note folded in two.

I opened and read it, mouth wide open. "Are you kidding me?! I can't go back with this. *'Reason: was busy making out with a very skillful (her words not mine) soccer player.'* Briel come on!"

He chuckled. "Don't worry about it. I know Ms. Burton like the back of my hand. Just show her the paper folded. She will just gesture you to keep it."

"Yeah…I sure hope so." I sighed. "See you later."

"Still up for tomorrow, right?" he asked and I had to stop myself from doing my happy dance.

I nodded.

"I liked it," he added as I reached for the doorknob. It felt like he was trying to keep me with him.

"The kiss? Yes, me too."

"Well obviously, but I mean the way you called me. I liked it."

I tried to think of how I called him, but I couldn't remember. All I could remember of these twenty minutes was the way he'd kissed me.

"Briel," he said. "You called me Briel."

"Oh…" I blushed. That was what I called him in my head. I hadn't realized I'd said it out loud.

"Nobody's ever called me that, but I'm happy you do. I don't want you to call me like everyone else does… You're not like everyone else."

I wanted to ask him what that meant. Why did he want me to call him something else? But my time was running out and I really needed to go.

"See you," I whispered, rushing out. It took all my willpower not to look back as I walked to the gym.

As I walked in, Ms. Burton concentrated on me. I pretended to walk toward her with my yellow note very visible in my hand while praying Briel was right.

She shook her head negatively and gestured toward the benches.

I couldn't help but smile when I went to sit back beside Chago. Gabriel did know all the tricks.

"So what was that all about?" Chago whispered as I sat back beside him.

I looked at him for a second. I hated lying to him, but he would be ardently against what I'd done and what I was planning to do again. Hell, I was ardently against what I was doing! I knew it was stupid, reckless, and wrong, but when his lips touched mine, everything felt right. I knew Chago would tell me to stop. He would do everything to put this thing Briel and I had to an end. But the problem was, I didn't want it to end, at least not yet. So as much as it killed me, I had to lie…lie to my brother at heart.

"Nothing really," I tried to sound annoyed. "It was about the extracurricular activities, yet again." I sighed. "Silly, I tell you."

Chago looked at me and I saw his nostrils flare slightly. He knew I was lying. It was written all over his face. I expected him to get mad, to argue, but he simply turned his attention back to Ms. Burton. "Si, claro," he snapped.

The rest of the day was a bit edgy with Chago. I knew he was mad. It was radiating from him, but I also knew he wouldn't stay mad at me for long. That was the magic of our friendship. We loved each other too much to let anything come between us.

However, Karma was still one hell of a bitch. Ms. Burton caught me in the corridor just before my literature class.

"Ah Miss Miller." She stood in front of me in her famous gym teacher pose, which consisted of her hands on her hips and her legs slightly parted. "I just wanted to see your excuse note."

Where had this come from? I thought, trying to keep my poker face on. "Sorry, I threw it away. I thought--" I shrugged dismissively - "that I didn't need it."

She gave me a clearly overplayed sigh and I knew right then that I was pretty much screwed. "That is too bad..." She trailed off. "Because I was in the Principal's office earlier today and from the chat we had, he had no idea you'd been called in. Of course, I pretended I'd gotten it wrong because I preferred talking to you about it first. But if you want, we can go see him." She pointed behind her toward the Administration office.

I looked at her silently, tightening my hold on my backpack strap.

"Maybe if we can come up with some kind of agreement, I can forget you left for a little while?"

I forced a smile. "Sure, Ms. Burton. What can I do for you?"

She nodded, apparently pleased. "I'm glad we understand each other."

Yes, it was official. I was screwed and Karma was a bitch! I thought, waiting for her to tell me how I could 'help' her.

CHAPTER 13

"You should have let me talk to her," Gabriel insisted, sitting at the table and grabbing my chemistry notebook.

I shrugged, getting Cokes out of the fridge. When Gabriel had come over for our tutoring session, he'd pecked my lips as if it was a habit. It had been very intimate and I liked that. "It's alright. She thinks she is so smart, but I ended up negotiating something that was not really a pain."

"What did you negotiate?" he asked, taking one of the Cokes from my hand, letting his fingers linger on mine.

"Help organize and register what is in the equipment room for next year's order. Told you, nothing major."

"I can help you if you want."

I snorted and sat down. "Believe me. I managed to negotiate a sweet deal. I will give her thirty minutes twice a week after the Christmas break." I shook my head, taking a sip of my drink. "I don't mind. Chago has French anyways."

"Yeah…" He trailed off and I could see the muscles of his jaws bulge.

Was he jealous? I wanted to tell him the truth. There was no point in pretending anymore. "About Chago, I--"

He shook his head, turning the chemistry book toward me. "No, it's okay."

"What I mean-"

"No, really, Lottie. I don't want to hear it…please," he pleaded.

Hearing him call me Lottie again took my breath away. "You know, only my father called me that." I couldn't keep the nostalgia out of my voice.

"Oh…" He looked down for a second, gently running his fingers over my knuckles. "You want me to stop?"

"No," I replied and it surprised me. I liked it - him.

He smiled. "You are Lottie to me, not Charlie or Charlotte."

I looked down at the book, not really reading anything. I was not used to all this, to the romance, to having all these feelings rushing to the surface.

"Do you want to know what my favorite movie is?" he asked out of the blue.

"I… Sure, I would love to." I relaxed in the intimacy of the moment.

"It's Billy Elliot," he huffed as if it was a well-kept secret.

"Why is that?" I asked curiously. I loved Billy Elliot, but I would have never imagined it could be Gabriel's favorite.

He shrugged dismissively. "How that kid goes against his family wishes. He fought for his passion and managed to do what he wanted."

"Yes, a real role model." And I knew why he envied Billy. His family had been bankers for generations. They expected him to choose finance and go to Dartmouth as they all had, but he didn't want to. Deep down, he wanted to study architecture at Columbia. "Fight for what you feel is right deep in your bones."

"I wish it was that easy," he admitted, still stroking my hand gently, making my entire arm numb.

"Actually, it is Briel. You just have to stand up for yourself, for what you believe in…for what you feel is right."

Gabriel looked up and met my eyes silently. He stopped caressing my hand and took hold of it. "Do you really need to study chemistry today?"

I shook my head. "No, not really. I'm okay these days," I offered with a smile. It was an understatement. I was more than okay, but I didn't want to tell him that. I didn't want our study sessions to stop.

He stood up and extended his hand to me with a wide smile. "Come with me."

I arched my eyebrows in surprise before looking out the window. The sun was low in the sky and would set soon. "Where do you want to go?"

"Do you trust me?"

"In theory…" I trailed off, making him laugh.

"Come on, silly girl." He rested his hand on my shoulder. "I promise your honor is safe with me."

I snorted. "Okay, boy, let's go. But just so you know, I can kick your butt."

"Oh, I believe that!" he said without mockery, grabbing his keys.

His car was more beautiful inside than it was outside with windows so dark you couldn't see inside. It was all leather and expensive wood… *'This car smells like big bucks,'* Chago would have said.

"Nice car," I commented, padding the dashboard.

Gabriel shrugged like it didn't matter. "It's a Mercedes CLS Coupe."

I smiled. "I know."

"You know about cars?" he asked, throwing me a quick glance before concentrating on the road again.

I laughed. "Yeah, you could say that. Mateo owns a garage. When you almost live with the Valdez brothers, you are bound to become a pro. Sometimes, when I am there for the weekend, I even go to the garage and help Mateo with cars."

"You are close to them, aren't you?" he asked and I could hear the underlying questions.

"We're like a family, yes." I looked out of the window as he exited the city. *Where are we going?* "Life and circumstances brought us together."

We drove for about fifteen minutes. Gabriel kept giving me facts about himself. What he liked, what he disliked. He stopped talking as we reached a small dirt road surrounded by high trees. He stopped at the end of the lane by a cliff and I could see the sea in the horizon.

"It's beautiful here," I whispered truthfully. It was a forest and sea in one spot.

"It's even nicer from the outside. Come on, I need to show you something," he added, getting out of the car.

I met him by the trunk. "I knew it! People always need me to bury bodies. I wonder why that is?" I jested in a lame attempt to calm myself. I was nervous. I was in this remote spot with a hot guy I liked much more than I wanted to.

He looked down at me with a smile. "Funny." He kissed my forehead. "You said you wanted to know the real me, right?"

I nodded.

He opened the trunk, moved the carpet and the spare tire. I looked in and saw a black notebook. "Take it."

I was curious to see what was in it, but I tried to reign in my impatience.

Gabriel took a blanket out of the back and left the trunk open. "Come." He went to the front of the car, set the blanket on the floor, and sat on a corner of it. "Sit by me." He padded the spot beside him. "I won't bite."

I snorted, holding the notebook tightly against my chest. "That's one hell of a cheesy line," I replied, sitting beside him, our legs grazing.

"Sorry the space is limited, but I rarely have company when I come here, and this blanket is for one person only."

"You really think I'm going to believe that?" I blurted out before I could stop myself. He was one hot jock full of money, and we were in one of the most remote, romantic places I had seen around here. I might not have been very experienced, but I was neither naïve nor stupid.

"I just hope you do." He concentrated on the sea. "I've never lied to you." He looked at me again. "I wanted to share some of my most private things with you, Lottie." He smiled, nudging me gently. "This is my favorite place and this -" he pointed at the notebook - "is my best-kept secret."

I gently opened the notebook as if a snake would jump out of it. "Oh my!" I let out when I saw what was on the first page. It was a beautiful design of a beach house.

"These are my architectural designs." He looked away, fearing the way I would react. "You wanted to know me… You have me naked now." I could see the hint of a smile on his profile. "Metaphorically, of course."

I shook my head, but continued to turn the pages. His designs were too good for words. Each one was better than the previous ones. He could design houses, buildings, parks…everything. He had a gift and he was going to waste it all to gain his father's approval. I couldn't help the wave of anger toward a man I didn't even know.

"Briel this is…this is…you are so talented," I whispered, feeling like I was making the understatement of the year. "You can see and create beauty… I've never seen anything like it."

"I'm glad you like them." He turned a little toward me. The sunset playing shadows on his face took my breath away. His eyes looked greener on his tanned skin. I wished I could have taken a picture of him. There was no more doubt in his eyes, no more barriers and I understood that, for the first time, I was seeing the real Gabriel Johnson. It was also when I realized with unwavering certainty that I was way past being 'in like' with him… I was in love. Realizing that made me take a sharp breath. I was in love with Gabriel Johnson… It was going to hurt, hurt badly when he broke my heart.

"Are you alright?" he asked, concentrating on me again. "You are even paler than usual, and for you, that has to be a challenge."

"I…yes, I'm fine." I looked down at the notebook again. "Can I take one?"

"Sure," he replied, not even thinking about it. "Take the one you want."

I took the one of a beautiful four floors building with a small park at the back. "Thanks." For once I was the one reaching up for a kiss and he seemed to enjoy that.

He took the notebook and set it on the blanket before wrapping his arm around my waist, pulling me closer. I rested my head in the crook of his neck, skimming it with my nose. I closed my eyes and inhaled deeply. I loved the smell of his skin.

We stayed silent in each other's arms until the sun was fully set.

Gabriel sighed as he ran his long, strong fingers through my hair.

"What is it?" I asked, keeping my eyes closed as I enjoyed the closeness and warmth.

"I need to take you back. My parents are having a dinner tonight and I have to attend."

I nodded, but stayed where I was.

He chuckled. "I don't want to move either."

I sighed, finally moving from my spot. "Thanks."

"For what?" he asked, surprised.

"For showing me a bit more about yourself."

"You are welcome Lottie." He stood up and extended his hand to help me. "I love being myself with you."

Curiosity finally got the best of me. "How did you find out? About the Cure I mean," I asked as we drove back.

"Ah…once I got to know you, it was pretty obvious! You called me a fraud during our fight and when I read your comic, I saw I'd been called me a fraud, so I put two and two together. Why do you think I'm a fraud by the way?"

Note to self: next time kick self before talking. "It's just… I could see there was more to you than what you were showing, and it was frustrating me. There is the Gabriel you show the world and the one I see -the one you are willing to show me, bit by bit."

129

"And what do you think about that?"

"The Gabriel I see?"

He nodded.

"I like him...very much." *Too much,* I admitted, and I couldn't help the blush creeping across my cheeks.

"Can I ask you a favor?"

"Sure! What do you need?"

"You know I need to start sending my applications for college soon and I wanted to know if you could help me--"

"With the essays? Sure! Bring your applications on Saturday and we'll have a look."

"Thanks, Lottie." He parked in front of my house. "Have a good night."

"You too and thanks." I showed him the drawing he gave me. I reached to open the door.

"Wait." He reached for my arm. "Don't I get a kiss goodbye?"

"Shame on me!" I overplayed.

"It's okay... I can forgive you, but you have to make it good."

I leaned in to kiss him. As usual, it started soft and sweet before getting hot and passionate.

He groaned. "You better go now or I'll end up being late."

I chuckled. "Yeah...I think it's for the best. Bye, Briel."

"Bye, Lottie."

I ran back in the house with a huge smile on my face that I was pretty sure was still there the next morning.

<u>CHAPTER 14</u>

I was woken up by the doorbell. I looked at the clock through narrowed eyes. Who dared visit at barely nine on a Saturday? Someone with a death wish. I couldn't see anyone else.

I rolled out of bed and slid the curtain aside to see who was there.

"Really? This early?" I cursed, seeing Chago's car parked in the driveway.

I didn't even bother brushing my hair before going down. He deserved nothing more than my Medusa hair and morning breath.

I unlocked the door and I didn't even wait for him to walk in before taking the direction of the kitchen. "Really dude…" I grumbled when I heard him closing the door.

"It's nine!"

"So?" I asked, pouring myself a steamy cup of coffee. My mom had probably left it not so long ago.

"So? You are usually very awake by then, that's all."

I yawned. "Yeah, well…" I poured another cup and slid it toward him. It had been more than a week since my little escapade with Gabriel, but I've had trouble finding sleep since then. The stolen kisses, discreet touches, and the secret looks… It was not as fun as people thought. It was bothering me a lot more than I'd expected. The guilt and secrecy were taking a serious toll on me.

I was grateful Chago simply sat down, letting me sip my coffee in peace.

"Okay, I'm awake."

"I need a favor."

I rolled my eyes. "No, I told you before. I won't count your chest hair again."

His mouth popped open and I could see the faint blush on his tanned skin. "Come on, Chula! I thought you would have moved on by now. I was thirteen!"

"And I still haven't recovered from seeing those two hairs."

He threw me a dark look. "I need you to come with me to the Winter Ball."

He was lucky I was not drinking because I would have spat everything on him. "What? The Winter Ball?" I shook my head vehemently. "I prefer counting your chest hair, guapo."

He sighed. "Please Chula."

"Cha—Why?" I whined shamelessly. "I mean if there is anyone hating that stuff more than me…it's probably you!!"

"I need to show Eva I can do all that shit. That I can be more sociable."

I looked at him silently. He was getting to me and I hated it. "But if you want her to see that, why don't you invite her? I doubt the Winter Ball at her school is at the same time."

"She is already going to ours with Xavier," he sneered. "Who is called Xavier anyway?" He shook his head. "Preppy douche."

I tried my best not to smile. Jealous Chago was so fun.

"But what changed?" I asked seriously. "I've always disagreed with you, but you've always repeated that you'd only pull her down if you were to date her. Why have you decided to try? Why now?"

"Because of this" He took a folded piece of paper out of his back jeans' pocket. "I received this yesterday," he added, extending it to me

When I unfolded the letter, I couldn't help but squeal like a dolphin. I jumped out of my chair and pulled Chago into a bear hug.

"You got it!! I knew you would, but still. Chago, you have the internship!!"

"I know," he replied and even if I couldn't see his face, I could hear the smile in his voice.

I let go of him, but took hold of his hand. "So where do you want to study?" I grinned. "Now you can go anywhere you want."

"They need to accept me first." He sat down. "To be fair, I have no idea. I never thought I would have such an opportunity. I'll try Stanford for sure, but it's something we need to discuss you and I because I would like for us to keep on studying together."

I looked at him, so happy that my best friend was finally getting all he deserved. I knew he was one of the best people out there. Now we needed the world to see it too.

"Chula, please," he pleaded with his best sad puppy eyes.

"Oh, come on…" I whined again, but I was caving and he knew it. "I've never been that girl and…and I don't have a dress and you know I don't wear makeup or do nice things with my hair," I added, burying a hand in my crazy hair full of knots just to make my point.

"But mama said she has the perfect dress for you, and we can ask Maribel to do your makeup. Come on… I'll owe you one."

But I don't want to see Gabriel and Darlene being crowned King and Queen, I added to myself, so I could recall what a stupid mistake I was making. But Chago was the most important person in my life. The person I loved the most. "You really want to go?"

He nodded.

I sighed heavily, resting my forehead against the cool marble of the kitchen island. "Fine! But you know you'll be the death of me, right?" I looked up. "This might literally kill me," I added deadpanned.

He rolled his eyes, but pulled me into a hug. "Thanks," he whispered in my hair.

"Okay, but you'll need to promise me something."

"Let's hear it."

"I'm going to distract Xavier's attention for a little while and you will use that time to tell Eva how you feel."

"But—"

"*Promise me,* guapo," I added firmly. "We don't have time for these games anymore. You've got to fight for what you want." I was not sure I was talking about his relationship anymore.

"I promise."

I groaned, running my hands across my face. This was a stupid idea and I knew it. Nothing good could come out of this, at least not for me. "So, for the dress…"

He grinned. Boy, I really was a sucker for him. "Go get ready and I'll take you home. Mama will be ecstatic! This is the kind of thing she's always longed to do."

"Yeah, yeah, whatever. I'm going, but just so you know, I'll hate every minute of it!"

"That's the spirit."

I threw my hands up in surrender. "Okay, let me get ready before I change my mind."

The day was fun even if I had to cancel Gabriel's tutoring session and reorganize it for Sunday. We had been working hard on his College applications, so I'd put our so-called romance on the back burner for a little while. It was probably for the best because I was getting in too deep, too fast.

"I love this dress. It's very…unique," I admitted, touching the bodice of the dress on the mannequin.

Antonella smiled, visibly pleased. "I sure hope so, m'hija. I made it especially for you. Now please try it on so I can adjust it."

I nodded, taking the dress carefully off the mannequin. It was emerald green and I knew it would go perfectly with my skin tone and hair, but I also couldn't help but think that it was a perfect match to Gabriel's eyes.

Stop it! I thought, looking at myself in the mirror. I was impressed with Antonella's knowledge of my measurement. The dress just needed to be let out slightly at the hips and the bodice needed to be reduced a little...

I swirled and I really liked how the satin material followed my moves. The dress was long, stopping just below my ankles. The top was strapless and the bodice was embroidered with a very complicated and refined silver pattern.

"I'll need silver heels for this," I whispered, knowing I would have to take Logan shoe shopping. I grimaced. That was going to be painful.

When I walked into the living room, Antonella's face broke into a huge smile. She seemed to like what she saw.

"You are so beautiful." She gestured me toward the box she wanted me to step on, so she could make the alterations.

I had to take her word for everything because as soon as we'd walked into the house, Chago had disappeared to help Mateo at his garage.

"You can't have made this dress in two day." I noted as Antonella was busying herself on the dress, putting pins seemingly everywhere.

"Who said I did?"

"Well, Chago only decided to go to the Winter Ball on Friday, so...."

She laughed. "I made this dress before that. To be honest, I made it for your prom." She looked up with a smile. "I knew you would at least go to prom, but I never thought it would be with Chago."

"Who did you think I would be going with?" I asked curiously.

She shook her head. "It doesn't matter now. I'm just so happy you two will have fun."

I smiled, but remained silent. I remembered when I was younger and Antonella had taken me to church. I'd asked her why she believed in God and that if God existed, why did he hate me so much that he had to steal my father from me. She had smiled. What she had said then was still engraved in my mind so many years later.

'Carlotta, I believe everything happens for a reason. And how could I not believe in God when He brought such a sweet angel into our lives? You helped my sons in ways you can't even imagine.' She had kissed my nose. *'You will be fine, hija. Pain fades.'*

She had been right; the pain had faded along with the memories. But I wanted to believe in God. I just...couldn't.

"Carlotta?"

"What?" I blinked, coming back to reality.

"Where were you?" she asked, now standing in front of me.

"I'm not sure really. Just far, far away."

She nodded. "It's okay. I'm done with the marking. You can change now."

"Thank you." I squeezed her hand. "You have always been such a mother to me."

"Gracias." She hugged me tightly. "And you have always been so good to me, to us, but you have a mother and I know she loves you very much. She is just not that good at showing it, but please never doubt her love."

"K," I replied without conviction.

She helped me out of the dress. "Go on, go meet the boys. I know you're dying to."

I grinned, kissing her cheek loudly. "Gracias!" I replied before rushing out, hoping that Mateo would let me help on some cars.

I spent the rest of the day with the guys, joking and playing around with cars. It had been so long since I'd done this that I'd almost forgot how much I loved spending time here with my adoptive family.

****

As the Ball grew closer, things started to get weirder. I even enjoyed spending time with Logan to find the perfect pair of shoes for the Ball!

Things turned into a science fiction movie when Chago drove me home on Wednesday after we rented a tuxedo for the Ball.

'If I'm supposed to suffer to look stunning, believe me, you will too' I had said as we spent two hours looking for his tuxedo and dressing shoes.

He had glared the whole time but endured it silently.

When Chago parked, my mother's SUV was in the driveway. We sat there stupidly, watching it in silence.

"Want me to come in with you?" He finally asked. I nodded. I was freaking out too as my mother was never home before me.

"Mom?" I called as soon as we opened the door.

"Ah, Charlotte honey, I thought we were going to be late." She met me in the lobby. She seemed surprised to see Chago. "Santiago, hello."

I could see Chago tense. "Mrs. Miller, it's nice to see you." My mother had always intimidated Chago and I didn't really know why.

"What's up?" I asked her.

She glanced at her watch. "The PTA meeting, it starts in less than thirty minutes."

I laughed. "Nice one! No, seriously, why are you here?"

I saw her eyes narrow as she extended the blue flyer. "The PTA meeting," she repeated.

"You're joking, right?" I turned to Chago. "She is joking, right?"

Chago's face told me he was not about to reply, and he certainly didn't think she was joking. I also knew that he wished he could be anywhere but here.

"I'll see you tomorrow Chago." I gave him a way out.

He threw me a grateful glance. "Bye Mrs. Miller." He rushed out.

"Mom really, why do you want to go?"

She sighed and took her handbag. "You can leave your backpack here." She said ignoring my question.

I knew better than to add anything when she looked like that. "Here goes nothing." I stage whispered, following her to the car.

The PTA meeting was just as boring as I thought it would be. I just pretended I was not there, and my mom pretended I was not sulking…It was a great arrangement to be fair.

However, things took an interesting turn when we went into my lit class.

"Adam…" My mother whispered, and her tone made me look at her and Mr. Mulligan.

"Kate, it has been a long time. How are you doing?" He asked, trying to sound casual but there was something in his eyes too. Things that led me to think there was much more history between them than what he led me to believe.

"F-fine" she stuttered.

What? My mother stuttered, and my mom NEVER lost her cool. That was scary.

She sat down, and they started to talk about my grades, but I could see something was happening between them, something making me very uncomfortable and my mind kept screaming big loud '*Ewwww*'s. Did they share something? They seemed to be so much more than simple acquaintances.

"What was all that about?" I asked as we walked back to the car.

"What are you talking about?"

"Come on mother, don't play stupid." I snorted and regretted it when she threw me a dark glance.

"I'm still your mother, you owe me respect."

"And you owe me the truth. What was all that about?"

She sighed with annoyance as she sat in the car. She turned toward me so fast it made me recoil. "It all happened decades ago and since when do I owe you that? Are you honest with me? Are you talking to me about your life? Let's try again…I heard about you going to the ball, when did you decide that? Who are you going with?"

I turned toward the window, looking at the dark road as she drove off. She had a point; how could I ask her to share her past with me when I was not ready to share my present.

"Charlotte?" She asked coldly.

"It's fine, it doesn't matter…It's not like I need to get through your denial. You have so many years of practice." I snorted. "You almost succeeded to forget you had a daughter with David Miller."

"Charlotte!" She gasped as if I just punched her.

"Forget it." I added as she parked in front of the house. I knew it was childish to say that, even if I meant every word. I was not in the mood to hear her rant about how childish and rebellious I was.

"No, we need to talk about that." She added, locking the doors to stop me from getting out.

I turned toward her. "Sure, Mother! So, tell me why you didn't tell me you went to High School here? How did you meet Mr. Mulligan? There seems to be history here. So, mother, let's talk."

She looked at me challengingly for a minute before releasing the locks.

She looked straight ahead. "Some things are better left in the past. Good night Charlotte." She dismissed me.

As soon as I got out, she put the car in reverse and left me in the driveway without a look back.

I bit my bottom lip, maybe I pushed it too far. She was surely not as cold and strong as she was pretending to be.

I had been mean, I knew I had, and yet couldn't help it. It was my knee-jerk reaction. I kept seeing her trying to forget my father and consequently me, and it hurt more than I was ready to admit.

CHAPTER 15

I stared at my reflection in the mirror, not sure who I was looking at. Was this girl really me?

"Dios, I'm so proud of myself," Mariella marveled, clapping her hands. "Not that you were not pretty before, but now you are stunning, total *femme fatale*."

"Sure..." I trailed off, but it was true that I looked completely different. I was just not sure it was a good thing. I'd always thought people wearing a lot of makeup were trying to disguise themselves, but I guessed that for tonight that was the idea. Wasn't that what balls were all about?

"Don't you like it?" she asked, standing behind me, rearranging some of the loose curls she'd purposefully let out of the elegant bun she'd made.

"No, no! I promise I do. It's just very different. So...not me." I met her eyes in the mirror. "If you know what I mean."

She rested her hands on my bare shoulders, visibly relaxing. "I know, muneca, but it's just for one night."

I looked at myself again. She'd given me smokey eyes, but it was not making me look vulgar like some girls at school. It was elegant, and I realized for the first time how grey my eyes were; the makeup made them look eerie. I painted my lips deep red. Mariella had thought I needed to show my mouth as it was almost a perfect shape. She also added that the red on my pale skin would make it perfect. I looked, with the dress and hairdo, like a fifties' movie star.

"Chula, come on! We're losing daylight!" Chago shouted from the living room where Mateo and Antonella were waiting with, I could bet, the camera.

I sighed, sitting on the chair to put on my high heels. "Two minutes!" I shouted back.

"Yes, that's what you said fifteen minutes ago!"

"Honestly, the guy is lucky I'm not dating him." I stood up, not feeling so sure on the heels. Logan and I had settled on three inch heels. I'd even walked around the house with them just to make sure I would not embarrass myself in public.

"Okay, big girl, it's time to go." Mariella smiled encouragingly. "Let's show that idiot what we're made of."

I laughed. "Yes, let's do that."

When I walked into the living room, something that I had never witnessed before finally happened. The Valdez brothers were left speechless.

"See what we did?" Mariella whispered in my ear. "We managed to make them shut up and that's a miracle."

I smoothed my dress, meeting Chago's eyes.

"Wow, Chula, you are…wow," Chago whispered, burying his hands in his pockets.

"I second that," Mateo added before coming to stand beside Chago to get a better look.

"You look dashing too," I admitted sincerely.

"I know." Chago pulled at his collar making me burst into laughter, finally getting rid of the tension.

"Oh, you two are just so beautiful! Come on. Let me take pictures." Antonella beaconed us toward the staircase.

Chago and I posed for the next ten minutes, and for once I didn't mind the attention.

"Abrazame," Mateo requested, pulling me into a hug. "You are stunning; you'll be the most beautiful girl there," he whispered in my ear and Mateo didn't compliment easily. "You know it's not too late to change your mind," he added once we broke the hug. "If you think my little brother looks dashing in a tuxedo…it's because you've never seen me in one."

"I'll keep that in mind for prom." I winked.

We rode to the school gym in a comfortable silence, but no matter how much he wanted to hide it, I could see Chago was tense.

"It will be just fine; when she sees you there, she won't be able to keep her eyes off of you."

"Yeah…" He trailed off, apparently not convinced. He patted my knee. "And I don't think you'll have any problem distracting Xavier's attention. You are breathtaking; you know that, right?"

I grinned. "Plus, if my charms don't work, I can still beat the crap out of him. That will be distracting to him for sure."

"That's my girl!" He chuckled. "No, but seriously, it's okay, you know… No need to go in with all those tricks."

I snorted, which probably clashed big time with the glamorous image they'd tried to create. "Yes, right! After making me look like

Barbie Marylyn? I tell you…Xavier or not, you'll dance and talk with Eva tonight."

When we made it in the gymnasium, I still couldn't believe I was there surrounded by all the students.

"Come on, let's go have our picture taken." Chago pointed to the arch with fake snowflakes hanging around.

"You've got to be kidding me!"

He shook his head negatively, pulling me toward the couples queuing. "You agreed to come. Let's do things properly, the full experience."

"You'll pay for this," I muttered under my breath as we settled in front of the camera.

He pulled me to his chest, wrapping his arm around my waist. "I know, but it's totally worth it. Come on, Chula, smile for the camera," he added before settling for his cheeky grin.

Once the picture was taken, I couldn't help but scan the crowd, knowing only too well who I was looking for.

I found Gabriel in conversation with Doug. He was facing the group of cheerleaders and I couldn't stop the smile spreading on my face. He didn't seem to be so happy to be here... Just like me.

"Who are you looking for?" Chago asked, following my gaze.

I pointed at Logan who was making his way toward us.

"Who would have thought our Charlie was a real girl and a pin-up at that!" Logan commented with appreciation, taking in my outfit. "As for you, Hombre, I love the James Bond Vibe. Can I see your license to kill?" He wiggled his eyebrows suggestively.

Chago shook his head, but couldn't help smiling. "Any juicy story so far?"

Logan grinned, loving the subject change. "No, sadly I'm too busy being up there making sure all is fine." He pointed at the stage just as the deejay gestured to him. "See!" He rolled his eyes. "See you later and let me know if you find out something juicy," he added before going back on stage.

"Come on, let's go find Eva." I took Chago's arm, pulling him into the crowd.

We found Eva and Xavier by the punch bowl. She seemed bored, which was a good thing for Chago.

"Hey!" I exclaimed, probably way too cheerfully, because Eva looked at me like I had lost my mind.

"Hello…" Xavier replied, eyeing us warily. It was true that we didn't really know the guy. He was a senior, but quiet, not on the High School popular scene.

"I didn't think you would come to the ball. I always thought you hated these kinds of things." She was looking at me, but I knew I was not the one she was talking to.

"Yes, well, sometimes we have to make some efforts for the people we care about," I replied, hoping she would understand I was talking about Chago. Seeing the way her eyes lit up, I knew she'd understood the double meaning of my words.

"Let's dance," Xavier suggested, resting his hand on Eva's shoulder.

"Hey, chill bro," I whispered, squeezing Chago's arm as hard as I could. I saw murder in his eyes as he looked at Xavier's hand. "He is not doing anything wrong here; he doesn't know anything," I added as Xavier led Eva to the dance floor.

"Which side are you on?" he growled, his eyes following them on the dance floor.

"On yours, always. But boy you had years to do something about her and you didn't move. I think this little scene is a good return of karma."

"That's such a reply from a best friend," he replied sourly.

I shrugged slightly, looking around the dance floor. Some were dancing so terribly, I was pretty sure that if we turned off the music, it would look like they were having seizures.

"Ready?"

"Ready for what?" he asked cluelessly.

I sighed. "I'm about to give you your moment with her. Be ready," I replied as a series of slow songs started. I took his hand. "Come on, let's dance." I pulled him onto the dance floor before either of us could change our minds.

I could not even say what the song we danced to was though as I was too busy trying to dance toward Eva and Xavier as discreetly as I could. As soon as the song ended, I let go of Chago and did the rudest thing I could think of. I slid an arm between Eva and Xavier, facing him.

"Okay now, let's switch partners," I exclaimed, pulling Xavier away. He let out a surprised '*hey!*' but I ignored him and rested my hands on his shoulders with the most naïve smile I could manage.

This guy was so tall though, it was uncomfortable to stay looking up at his face.

Xavier looked down at me with incredulity, but, to my relief, he rested his hands on my waist and started to swing to the music.

"Why did you do that?" he asked as the first song ended, but surprisingly, he kept on dancing with me.

I turned my head to look at Chago and Eva. He was holding her tightly against him and she had her arms around his neck, playing idly with the short hair on the back of his head. The way they looked into each other's eyes, it was like they were the only people in the room.

I decided to play the honesty card. "Look at them, Xavier. I mean really look at them." I made us swirl around so he could have a good look at the couple.

Xavier looked up for a little while before looking down at me again, his brown eyes full of wonder. "But I thought that you and him…" He trailed off.

I chuckled, shaking my head. "Just like everybody else, but no. He is my best friend. I love him to death in a platonic way."

"Uh…" He tightened his hold around my waist; it seemed like my plan was backfiring. "I guess we are both dateless now," he commented with humor in his voice.

"You were not really into her, were you?"

He shrugged dismissively. "I like her, but it doesn't go further than that." He jerked his head toward Chago and Eva. "It's clear that I can't measure up. They're in love. Even I can see it. Maybe it's all for the best," he exhorted, looking back at me with what I presumed was his seductive smile. "You look so beautiful tonight."

Fuck my life… How could I get out of this one? I forced a smile. "I'm thirsty. I'm just going to get a drink. Why don't you just-" I looked around for an idea. "I don't know, go talk to your friends or something? You don't need to keep me company. I'm good…I promise." *Please, let me be,* I added to myself.

He shrugged. "I see my friends all the time. I don't mind keeping you company. I'm sure it will be fun."

"Peachy!" I exclaimed with sarcasm. I knew he didn't deserve that, but it was just who I was.

I looked back at Chago and Eva before they'd exited the dance floor. She had her head on his chest and he was resting his cheek

143

on the top of her head. They seemed to have forgotten they were even here.

I sighed. It was going to be a long, *long* night.

"Mr. Mulligan!" I exclaimed, sincerely happy to see my favorite teacher standing by the buffet table.

"Oh, hello, Charlotte. How are you doing tonight?" he asked before glancing curiously at Xavier who was standing too close for my liking. All my instincts wanted to push him away, to give me space, but I needed to be nice tonight…civil.

"I'm doing fine, thanks. How is your night as a chaperone?"

He looked heavenward wearily. "A lot more complicated and unnerving than I'd thought."

I chuckled. "Yes, teenagers can be a pain." That managed to get a smile out of him. I wanted to ask him about my mom, but with Xavier and all the students around I couldn't. I was also not even sure I really wanted to know.

"I need to stay by the punch bowl; you can't even imagine how many have tried to spike the punch."

"Actually, I can."

"And now I need more plastic cups, but I can't move from here and…"

It was like a miracle unfolding just before my eyes. This was my chance to get rid of Xavier for a little while. "I can do that for you!" I offered way too excitedly.

He looked at me, eyebrows furrowed. I knew he was about to say no, but I threw him the full force of my pleading eyes. Mulligan quickly glanced at Xavier, showing he understood my motives.

"Okay, you see the door by the stage?" He pointed toward it as I nodded. "Go down the small corridor, take the first right, and you will find them there. Be quick, okay?"

I nodded, taking the direction of the stage, closely followed by Xavier. "What are you doing?"

"Coming with you."

"No, you are not," I corrected a bit too coldly before trying to backpedal. "I mean, go talk to your friends for a little while; I need to see Logan for something too." I pointed at the stage where Logan was talking to the deejay. He was supposed to be up there. He was the head of the celebration committee after all. "But I'll find you as soon as I'm done okay?" It might have sounded like a question, but my tone hadn't given place for argumentation.

"I'll be waiting," he suggested with a wink.

"Yeah…" I gave him a thumbs up before entering the room. "I want that as much as a bullet through my skull," I added as soon as I was sure he was out of earshot.

The music was blaring in the room and it was creepy to be alone in here. I couldn't help but think about all those slasher movies I'd seen, which was certainly not the right thing to do in this situation.

Would anyone even hear me scream? Don't think about that, you idiot! I rolled my eyes, looking at the carton boxes and trying to figure out which one contained the plastic cups.

I stood on my toes, trying to catch the top box. Of course, it had to be the top box for my 5'2".

I had barely reached for the box when a hand touched my shoulder, making me jump and the box to fall forward. I closed my eyes tightly, waiting for the box to smash on my face.

When nothing happened, I opened my eyes and saw two manly arms keeping the box up.

I swirled around, facing Gabriel. "Are you really trying to kill me? My heart won't be able to take you creeping up on me for much longer."

He grinned, setting the box down before facing me again. "I called your name three times, Lottie, but the music—"

"Was too loud." I finished.

He nodded, "Yes, maybe I shouldn't have followed you here, but…" He shrugged, looking away.

"You were looking for me?" I asked, trying to sound like it was not a big deal; no, it was a *huge* deal.

"I could barely keep my eyes off of you tonight," he admitted, burying his hands deep into his dressing pants pockets.

My heart started to hammer in my chest. He was so beautiful in his black tuxedo with his broad chest, emerald eyes… It was like they had invented tuxedos for him.

He took a step closer and gently brushed my cheek with the back of his hand. "I have never been more jealous of someone in my entire life," he added now, cupping my cheek. I couldn't help but lean into his touch.

"Jealous of what?"

"Of the guy who got to take you here. The guy who is going to kiss you. I've never envied anyone's life more than I envy Chago's

145

right now." I was about to tell him the truth when he continued, "And he is messing it all up. I can't believe he is not realizing it."

I frowned. "Messing up?"

He sighed and I could see real pain in his eyes. "I... I think he wants someone else. He was dancing with that girl and---"

"Oh!" My eyes widened with understanding. "No, Briel, listen, it's all good." I smiled, resting my hand on top of his. "Chago is in love with Eva. He has been for years."

"But...I'm confused."

"Chago and I are not dating. We never were. I love him. He is my brother, but nothing more."

"My Lottie is single?" he asked, grinning. I nodded. "I like that...Very much."

I wanted to say that I wished I could say the same, that I was trying my best to forget he was with Darlene, and when we were together, I mostly succeeded.

He wrapped his arms around my waist. "You are breathtaking, Lottie," he whispered in my ear, brushing his soft lips against the shell of my ear.

I closed my eyes, burying my face in his neck, taking in his now so familiar and soothing scent.

"Please dance with me," he pleaded, pulling me even closer as if he wanted our bodies to become one. "I want to dance with you at least once," he whispered huskily.

I wrapped my arms around his neck and looked into his deep green eyes as Ryan Cabrera started to play.

I was lost in the moment. I wanted to freeze these four minutes forever. We were the only people in the world. In this moment, as our heartbeats were in perfect synchronization, we belonged to each other completely.

Gabriel leaned in. "I'm going to kiss you now," he rasped barely an inch from my lips.

I tightened my hold around his neck. "You better."

He kissed me slowly, softly... It was pure bliss.

"Hey, guys!" I heard Logan blare in the microphone, bursting our little bubble. "Now is the time to announce our Winter King and Queen."

"We have to go. You can't miss your crowning," I croaked, keeping my eyes closed.

"I'm good here," he whispered, pecking my lips.

I reluctantly got out of his grip. "Come on, go…" I pointed at the box. "I'll come out after you."

He sighed and nodded wearily. "I'll see you later."

"Later," I replied after he was gone.

Just as I walked out, I met Mr. Mulligan who was about to enter the room.

"What took you so long? I was worried. Took me forever to find another chaperon to cover the punch bowl."

"Sorry," I simply said, not wanting to lie about the reason for my lateness.

"Charlotte?" he questioned, trying to find something in my eyes.

"I…need to go." I pointed at Chago.

"I thought you forgot about me," Xavier whined, appearing as soon as I reached Chago and Eva.

"I wouldn't dream of it," I replied with heavy sarcasm. "How are you guys doing?"

Chago threw me a dark look, ignoring my question.

I frowned, but didn't get to ask any questions as unsurprisingly Gabriel and Darlene were elected King and Queen of the Winter Ball.

The rest of the night really dragged as Chago kept ignoring me and Xavier wouldn't let go.

"One more minute and I'll beat him dead," I whispered to Eva when she came back for a drink.

She chuckled. "Don't worry, he will have to drive me home soon. I came with him and I have to go back with him."

"What's wrong with him?" I asked, jerking my head toward a sulking Chago.

"No idea." She shrugged. "He got mad just like that."

I sighed. "I'll figure it out."

Eva went to Chago and gave him a goodnight kiss.

"Let's go," Chago barked coldly just after Eva left. He walked out without even a look back.

"We didn't say goodbye to Logan," I exclaimed, grabbing his sleeve.

"The hell with Logan!" he barked, jerking his arm out of my grip.

I was frozen, looking at his retreating back. Chago was never like this. He'd never talked to me in such a tone. I shook my head

147

and wrinkled my nose at the thought of being stuck in his car for the next fifteen minutes. It was going to be a long drive.

Chago drove silently and I could feel all the anger radiating off him. It made me very uncomfortable. He was holding the steering wheel so tightly, his knuckles were white.

"Are you okay?" I asked as we parked in front of my house.

He looked at me silently for a couple of seconds. "You know, if someone would have asked me who I trusted the most in this world, I would have said you in a heartbeat, no hesitation."

"I know I--"

"If anyone would have asked me who knew all my secrets, all my fears, I would have said 'Charlie does.'"

"Chago--"

"And if I thought I knew someone inside out, dark side and dirty secrets included, it would have been you. I could have bet my life on it."

"You know me better than anyone else Chago. I swear I--"

"*Chingaderas!*" he shouted, making me recoil. Chago had been mad at me before, but he had never shouted like this, never.

"I don't-"

"Tell me, Chula, are you hiding anything from me?" he asked darkly.

I looked at him silently, not trusting myself to talk.

"I saw you tonight…with him, dancing in that closet."

"That's nothing," I whispered.

"I saw your face when he touched you, Charlie. That was *not* nothing; it was everything,"

"I…" I looked down at my hands. "It's nothing serious."

"Chula," he sighed, and I could see he was not as angry anymore. He looked worried and worse of all, disappointed.

"This is not you. You're… you can't become a rompe hogares."

The insult stung because I often felt like a homewrecker. "They're not in love," I added stubbornly. It was one of my personal mantras.

Chago looked at me like I had just lost my mind. "Doesn't matter. They're committed."

I looked away as shame filled me yet again.

"How long has it been going on?"

"Not that long…"

He gave me a chastising glance. "Probably too long. You know it's wrong. If not, you would have told me."

"Maybe I didn't tell you because I knew it would lead to this."

Chago's eyes were shrewd into slits. "I'm worried about you, Chula. I--I don't want you to get hurt."

"We're just having fun. We're not serious." I shrugged.

"Arbol que crece torcido jamas su tronco endereza," he muttered wearily. "It's a proverb."

"I know it! I've been raised by your mother, remember? 'Tree which grows bent will never get straight again.'"

"Which means that what starts wrong will never get right," he added, turning slightly on his seat to face me.

"What do you want me to say?"

"You don't have to say anything. Just--" He shook his head. "Think about why you hadn't said anything, not even to your best friend. Try to figure out why he is happy to keep you a secret?"

"Let me figure it out." I looked out of the window.

He growled, resting his head on the headrest and closing his eyes. "I wish you would end this."

I looked back at him, deciding to be honest. "I won't."

He turned his head slightly to look at me. "I know…I just wish you would."

"I'm sorry for lying."

"Yeah…" He trailed off tiredly, running his hands over his face. "I think you're mainly sorry for getting caught."

He was partially right, so I decided to ignore that. "But I'm not sorry for being with him."

"Well, you already know what I think."

"You won't interfere?" I asked with incredulity.

He shook his head. "I don't need to. It's by falling that we learn, and I'll be here to catch you."

"I- I know we're not meant to last," I admitted, and it hurt me to acknowledge it out loud.

"Your mouth is saying one thing, but your eyes say otherwise." He ran his hands over his face. "If he hurts you Chula, if he makes you cry, I will not need your approbation. I will find him, and he will have a close and personal meeting with my crowbar."

"Chago, come on."

He looked at me, face set in stone. "It's non-negotiable. Nobody is allowed to make you cry."

149

I couldn't help but smile at his crazy protectiveness. "You won't be able to shield me from all the pain in the world."

"But I can sure as hell try," he replied firmly.

I kissed his cheek softly. I liked the idea of being protected that way even if he'd just made the most unrealistic statement.

CHAPTER 16

I couldn't help but feel giddy as I got ready for school. Even the start of my jail time with Ms. Burton didn't manage to sabotage my mood.

It had been a bit more than two weeks since I'd last seen Gabriel. He'd left the day after the ball to spend the holidays in Aspen with his family, while I'd spent my holidays on the Eastside with Chago's family. My mother, as per usual, managed to spend Christmas Eve and Christmas lunch with us and, as absurd as it seemed, she did have a pretty decent relationship with Antonella.

My relationship with Chago was better now even if it was still strained, but I knew time would take care of it. I was the one to blame, the one who had made all the mistakes…the one who had lied. I felt guilty; I regretted the way I'd handled things. However, no matter how much I should, I didn't regret doing them.

Chago was now officially dating Eva and that made me so happy, even if it didn't help my situation.

I knew the *'I'm happy for you. Can't you just be happy for me?'* argument would backfire because I knew he'd been right when he'd told me this could only end up with my heart being broken. So I'd decided to just give him time.

I met Gabriel's eyes as soon as Chago and I walked into the hall. It was like we knew where to look. We were magnets.

I saw his eyes light up and I knew he was as happy to see me as I was to see him. I threw him a small smile. When he smiled back, my heart started to flutter. I would never mock the silly teenagers I saw on stupid TV shows ever again. I was not better.

I let go of his eyes when Darlene appeared and hung on his arm like a piranha on a piece of meat.

I threw a glance at Chago as he glanced at Gabriel before looking back at me.

"Don't say anything…Please," I pleaded, sounding a lot more hurt than I'd expected.

He shook his head. "I wasn't going to. You know what I think. There is nothing left to add."

I kept looking at him. It felt like I'd lost parts of my best friend and it hurt…a lot. Chago probably noticed how much I was hurting because he sighed wrapping his arm around my shoulders.

"Come on, Chula." He kissed my forehead. "Let's go to my hell…Calculus."

I chuckled, resting my head on his shoulder. "Thank you." And those two words were full of meaning. *Thank you for loving me. Thank you for being here. Thank you for not judging. Thank you for supporting me even when you think I'm wrong.*

"De nada, I will always love you, I'm always here…Even when I'm mad."

The rest of the day was just like I'd expected - uneventful and boring. Except for lunch as Logan had some news. He had just started to date Matt from the bookstore and that was fantastic for him. Now I was the one in an unhealthy, secret, and condemned to crash and burn relationship…Lucky me.

At the end of school, I told Chago to go home as his French class was canceled and I owed Ms. Burton an hour of work. He didn't want to go, but when I played the Eva card, telling him that she was done with her classes too, he didn't argue anymore.

I met Ms. Burton in her office. She gave me a list of what was supposed to be in the equipment room. I had to do a full inventory first. Today kept getting better and better. Maybe I would get run over by a bus on my way home. One could only hope.

I was about fifteen minutes into the inventory check when I heard some muffled voices. I looked around, but the room was way too small for another person to be here unnoticed.

"I'm not crazy," I mumbled, still hearing people talk. I finally noticed the vent. As curiosity got the best of me, I grabbed a stepladder and stuck my ear to the vent to hear better.

"You didn't need to be so hard on us today; we're only human, not like, you know - robot or something." I recognized Brittany's annoying high pitch voice.

"If you weren't slackers, I wouldn't have to go so hard on you!" Darlene snapped angrily.

Oh, joy! I was eavesdropping on cheerleaders' talk in the changing room. So much for being interesting or educational, but at least it was bound to be full of drama.

"Is it because of Gabriel?" Brittany asked, getting my full attention.

"What does Gabriel have to do with your incapacity to coordinate your movements?" Darlene asked coldly.

"Maybe nothing, but it has to do with you being a bitch and right now you are in full mode." She sighed. "As your co-captain, it's my job to tell you that you went too far today. As your best friend? I need you to talk to me."

"He doesn't even touch me anymore," Darlene admitted with clear defeat in her voice.

"At all?"

"No, I should have known something was wrong when he refused to have sex, pretending he needed to keep his mojo for the soccer season." She snorted. "You are dating Doug and the football season doesn't stop him from being all over you."

"Do you think he knows about you and—"

"No!" Darlene growled, and I cussed her for cutting off Brittany. "No, if he knew - It would have been different. He is changing. I can see it. He is not the same and hasn't been for over three months."

I couldn't help the flush of pleasure creeping up my cheeks. Gabriel and I had started to work together four months ago. Maybe I'd had more of an impact on him than I'd thought.

"I can't even get him to kiss me," she whined.

"Maybe you two should break up. It's not like you love him."

"Are you kidding me?! We look perfect together! How would I be crowned Prom queen without him? Love's never been the point. We both know that."

I couldn't help but snort at that. I'd been starting to feel guilty. What an idiot! She didn't want to break up, not because she loved him, or even cared about him though; no, it was because they looked '*good*' together.

"Did you hear that?" Darlene asked, speaking much more quietly.

Damn it! They heard me. I got down and engrossed myself in the inventory, but I couldn't stop the smile spreading on my face.I knew it was going to stay in place until bedtime. I was getting through to him. I knew it now and maybe soon he would make the right choice.

I was just exiting the gym when I heard a car honking. I shook my head, rolling my eyes, I knew Chago would come back. However, as I scanned the cars in front of the gym, Chago's car was nowhere to be seen. Gabriel's Mercedes though was parked two spots from the door.

I frowned, looking around again. It could only be for me. As I approached the car, the passenger window scrolled down.

"Hi?" I tried, bending down. It wasn't supposed to be a question, but it came out that way.

He laughed his deep, throaty laugh, which I was addicted to. "Hi to you too."

I looked at him with questioning eyes.

"Since it's a bit, okay, totally my fault you are here. I thought maybe you could use a drive home."

"Oh…" It was guilt that had pushed him to offer me a lift. "No, it's c—"

"Also, I missed you very much and I wanted to find an excuse to spend time with you," he added with a lopsided grin that made me melt.

"I-" I was about to say 'I missed you too,' but I couldn't. The words just stayed stuck in my throat. "Are you sure?"

"That I missed you? Yeah, pretty sure," he replied with a cheeky grin.

"No, I mean for the drive. Are you sure?" I jerked my head toward the football field where Doug was chatting with another guy from the team.

"Just get in, Lottie," he said like he didn't care and maybe he really did not.

As we got out of the car park, Doug looked at the car and Gabriel didn't seem fazed by it.

"How were your holidays?"

"Small talk? Okay," he nodded. "It was decent. The skiing was neat, but the family?" He grimaced. "Not so fun. You?"

"Christmas at Chago's is always enjoyable." I chuckled. "Christmases in Mexican families are unique experiences."

"I bet they are."

I expected him to just drop me off, but he turned onto the side street and parked.

He probably saw my bewilderment as he kept his hand on the car key.

"I thought that maybe…" His cheeks turned pink, making him, if it was at all possible, even cuter. "I could come in?"

"Oh yes, of course, you can!" I smiled. "I thought you might have plans."

"Nope, the only plan I had was seeing you."

So if I am so important, why don't you let go of the pretense and just be with me for real? I thought, but knew it was pointless to say. It would have been unfair as I knew where I was going with him. He'd never made promises.

"You seem different," he noted as I joined him on the sofa after setting our drinks on the table.

"Different how?" I asked as he took my hand, lacing our fingers together.

He shrugged, looking down at our hands. "You seem…distant."

I remembered Darlene's word. He couldn't even kiss her anymore and he'd told me he missed me. He truly cared even if… I didn't want to think about all the things that were wrong in this relationship because if I did, it would remind me that we were on borrowed time.

He looked up at me when I remained silent, so I leaned in, to peck his lips. "I'm not distancing myself; I didn't expect to see you today, that's all." I smiled. "But it's a pleasant surprise."

He smiled back, visibly relaxing. "So what are we watching?" he asked, settling back on the sofa and pulling me closer to him.

"I don't care." I rested my head on his shoulder. If I was completely honest, as long as I was in his arms and feeling his warmth, I didn't mind much.

We settled on some random renovation show and I closed my eyes, drowsing off. It felt good to be beside him.

"Will you play for me?"

"Ummm?" I opened my eyes, but didn't move.

He pointed at the guitar on the armchair.

I chuckled. "Yeah…I don't play for people." Well, except for Chago, but I was not going to mention that.

"I'm not '*people.*' I'm Briel, remember? Please?" He tried the full force of his puppy eyes on me.

"Now?" I asked, sitting straighter.

"I would love that, yes."

"But I suck at it."

He chuckled, shaking his head. "I'm sure you don't, but even if you do, it's okay. I have to put up with my mother's crappy music. Believe me, I'm ready."

"Fine," I agreed. I thought for a while, I didn't want to play a song that could have a meaning for our relationship. I settled on *My Poor Old Heart* by Alison Krauss.

"Wow, that was good! It was more than good; it was excellent! Have you ever thought about playing in public? In an open mic night?"

"No."

"Too shy?" he asked with that cute little smile of his.

I shrugged dismissively. "Yeah, that's part of it, but I also want to play a song that means something to me. I want to feel the words in my heart as if they belong to me. If it ever happens, then I'll play in public."

"Fair enough, but I s—" Gabriel was stopped by the honk of a car in my driveway.

"It's Chago," I gasped.

"I better go," Gabriel replied, standing up, but everything in his body language showed how reluctant he was to leave.

"No, stay." I'd tried to sound much surer than I felt. "He knows about you, you know."

"I know, but—" Gabriel sighed. "Okay, but you'll have to protect me."

I chuckled. "I will." I had talked to Gabriel on the Sunday following the ball. I had told him that Chago had seen us. He hadn't seemed bothered by the fact Chago knew about our relationship, he was actually scared that Chago would kick his butt, which he probably could do without even breaking a sweat despite their five inch height difference.

Gabriel sat straighter on the sofa, his muscles tense. He looked like a boyfriend meeting the parents for the first time, and to a certain extent, that was the case. Chago was family for all intents and purposes. He was the overprotective slightly hot-blooded older brother.

I met Chago in the corridor as he walked in without knocking like he usually did.

"Be nice," was all I had time to say before he walked into the living room.

Chago stood straighter. He might not be as tall nor as wide as Gabriel, but all three of us knew he could kill him without working too hard.

They took each other silently. Green eyes stared into brown. I could feel the testosterone flying in the room, almost choking me.

Please, please be nice, I thought, holding my breath.

Chago took two steps toward the sofa as Gabriel stood up.

Chago extended his hand toward him. "Hi, we've never been properly introduced. I'm Chago."

Gabriel smiled, shaking his hand. "I'm Gabriel."

I let out a breath in a loud whooshing sound of relief, making Chago chuckle.

"Really, Chula, you need to give me more credit," he chided, turning toward me.

"Yeah…. It worked so well before" I rolled my eyes.

He grimaced slightly. "I just wanted to make sure you made it home alright, I can see you did. So I guess that's my cue." He gestured toward the door.

"No, stay!" I requested before even considering that Gabriel might not appreciate spending time with Chago when we already had so little alone time.

Chago was certainly smarter than I was because he shook his head. "No, Chula, thanks, but I really need to go. I'll see you tomorrow." He nudged me playfully, probably his way to show me we were 'cool'. "Don't need to show me to the door. I know it well," he added with a wink before nodding toward Gabriel. "See you, man."

"That went okay," Gabriel commented as I settled back beside him on the sofa. He seemed both surprised and relieved.

"Believe me," I chuckled. "I've known Chago my whole life and this went perfectly well."

"He is intense, isn't he?"

"It depends what you mean by intense," I replied, throwing him a sidelong look.

"He is very protective of you."

I nodded. "A bit like a pack of wolves."

"You mean like the alpha protecting his pack?"

I chuckled. "No, I mean Chago is a pack of wolves, alpha included."

Gabriel laughed loudly. "Yeah, I should have thought of that." He looked down at me, a seriousness replacing his good humor. "He doesn't like me, does he?"

I shrugged dismissively. "He accepts you." *For my sake,* I added to myself.

"I can't expect much more, can I?"

I grimaced. "In this particular situation? No, not really."

His cell phone on the coffee table started to blare *Don't Stay* by *Linkin Park*. As he reached for it, I saw Darlene's name flash on the screen. I looked away. I'd almost forgotten yet again that she existed, that Gabriel was not mine - at least not officially. She was probably getting impatient somewhere.

I started to hate this situation more and more. I'd never intended to get into this mess. Now I was not sure there was a way out. But if there was one, would I even want to take it?

He turned the phone off as I stood up.

"Where are you going?" he asked, frowning with clear displeasure.

"I thought you were going." I pointed in the direction of the door.

"Do you want me to go?" His frown deepened as hurt flashed in his eyes.

I shook my head. "No, but—"

He grinned, reaching for my hand and pulling me back onto the sofa and into his arms. "That's what I wanted to hear. But I do have a complaint though," he added, burying his face in my hair.

"What is it?"

"You don't kiss me enough," he pouted.

I laughed. "Let me remediate that immediately." I pulled back a little so I could reach his lips and brushed my lips against his.

"Much, *much* better." He smiled against my lips.

"Yeah, it's always better when you are here," I admitted out loud without even thinking.

Gabriel didn't say anything, but as he tightened his hold around me, I understood he felt the same.

I thought I was screwed, but I realized that we were both in a little too deep. We would both end up hurt in the end.

CHAPTER 17

When I woke up, a look at the calendar made my heart heavy with sorrow. It was a school day, but I knew Chago wouldn't show to pick me up and I wouldn't be showing up to school either.

"Happy birthday, dad," I whispered, closing my eyes. Today my dad would have turned thirty-eight. It hurt to realize I'd lost him eleven years ago. I never did anything special for his death anniversary because there was nothing to remember… Nothing I wanted to remember. I wanted to celebrate his life. I might have been only six when I'd lost him, but those years were still imprinted in my mind now that I was seventeen. His face, voice, and smell might have faded over time, but the way I had felt when I'd been with him would stay with me until the day I died.

I was not stupid. I had known for years my mother was trying to escape the memory of him particularly on this day. She'd always organized a trip around today. It was too convenient, too perfect to be a coincidence. This year she'd gone to Miami. However, I'd never understood why she acted the way she did, leaving me alone when this was when I needed her the most.

Maybe it's because you never bothered asking her to stay, I admitted reluctantly.

I usually ended up spending today at Chago's. This year, at my request, it was the first year I would be completely alone to deal with my grief. I was not a baby anymore; I could handle 'alone' just fine.

I started my day as I did every year with a visit to the small park three blocks from my house. I didn't have any memories of my father here, but I was going where I thought he would have taken me. He'd known how much I loved swings; I'd always asked him to make me 'fly'.

I'd like to think that, if we had been living here before he'd died, he would have taken me here after school. We would have laughed and joked. He would have cared, really cared.

I decided to leave my cell at home. Anyone who knew me, knew better than to bother me today. I walked to the park slowly, letting my face soak up the sun. I only stopped at a small coffee shop to order a latte to go.

The park was just as quiet as I'd expected. It was not popular with kids as the distractions were limited to a couple of swings and monkey bars.

I sat on a swing, going back and forth slowly while sipping on my drink.

I was imagining what my father and I would have been doing today. Would he be proud of me? Would he be present in my life or would he have been as self-absorbed as my mother was? I shook my head. No, he wouldn't have been, he loved me too much.

A shadow appeared in my line of vision.

"What are you doing here?" I snapped coldly before realizing who was sitting on the swing beside me.

"I…I'm sorry. It was a mistake. I shouldn't have come," Gabriel replied, standing up stiffly.

"Wait!" I shouted, jumping from my swing as he rushed away.

He stopped and turned around warily.

"I'm sorry. You…you just caught me off guards," I admitted.

"I probably shouldn't be here," he apologized, burying his hands in his jeans' pockets. "I thought it was a good idea," he added, looking down.

"I… How did you find me?"

He looked up with a small smile. "I can be very persuasive."

"Chago?" I asked, arching an eyebrow with incredulity.

"To his defense, I was really annoying and I'm pretty sure he knew I was genuinely worried about you."

"Why were you worried?" I asked, sitting back on the swing and gesturing for him to join me.

He shrugged dismissively. "You sounded off last night on the phone. I knew there was something going on." He sat and started to swing gently. "And then when I saw Chago arrive alone this morning, I realized I was right." He gave me a sideways glance. "I thought it would be good for me to be with you and Chago seemed to agree."

I stayed silent, not really knowing what to think of all that. We've known each other for only six months. Yet he seemed to already be so attuned to my feelings.

Gabriel sighed when I didn't reply. "Don't be mad at him. I think he just wanted to get rid of me."

I chuckled. "It is very unlikely. Nobody is more bull-headed than Chago. If he didn't want to tell you, nothing you could have said would have changed his mind."

"Maybe he is starting to think I might be good for you," he said finally, turning to meet my eyes.

Very unlikely. "Maybe."

A small smile spread across his lips. "I can see you're humoring me, but I appreciate the attention. So today…"

"Is my father's birthday? Yes," I confessed, looking straight ahead as the warm breeze played in the trees.

"Do you want me to go?" he asked and I didn't miss the hurt in his voice.

I shook my head. "No, I like you here."

His body visibly relaxed. "Do you want to stay here?"

I detailed him. "What do you mean?"

He reached for my hand holding the swing's rope and wrapped his long fingers around mine. "You were so sad, so lost in your thoughts, you didn't even see me come."

"Yeah…you are not really catching me on a good day, to be honest."

"I don't think you should be sad today of all days."

His comment displeased me. I had the right to feel the way I did. He didn't know what it felt like. I tried to remove my hand from his, but he held it tighter. "Why?" I asked, looking at him as if he had two heads.

"His death is a tragedy, but you've told me so many good stories about him." He squeezed my hand. "He seemed to love life, to enjoy every small thing."

"He really did," I admitted. "Well, at least as far as I was concerned."

Gabriel's smile changed to a tender kind of smile I had never seen before. "How could he not? He knew how lucky he was to have you as a daughter."

I looked away again, battling the tears stinging my eyes while hoping Gabriel was right.

"Obviously, I didn't know your father, but I don't think he would have wanted you to be sad today. You should celebrate the day he was born."

I knew he was right. "What's on your mind?"

He let go of my hand and stood up. "Let's spend the day together, have fun." He extended his hand toward me.

"What about school?"

"What about it?" He gave me a cheeky grin. "If you can take a day off, why can't I?"

I chuckled, rolling my eyes but took his hand anyway. "Where are we going?"

"Nope, I'm not telling you. You'll just have to trust me on this."

"I do trust you."

He bent down and kissed my forehead. "Thank you," he whispered, letting his lips linger on my skin.

We took the highway and drove for about forty minutes before taking the exit toward a huge mall I had never been to before.

"A mall? Did I miss something? Are you changing into a girl?"

He laughed the deep throaty laugh I loved so much. "No, you would be the first to know if I did, but there are many fun things to do here." He parked the car. "Come on."

I gave him a suspicious look, but followed him. He knew I hated shopping. To take me here, he had to have a good reason.

He was right. The day was fun. We went to the music store where I tried some guitars. Lunchtime came before I'd even realized it.

As we walked to the food court, Gabriel stopped in front of a photo booth.

He smiled down at me. "Are you up for some photos?"

"Sure, I'd love to," I replied, trying to sound more detached than I felt. I was squealing inside, knowing I would have pictures of us, a way to remind myself someday that we did happen, that it hadn't all been in my head.

We settled for black and white pictures. Gabriel held me close to him, cheek against cheek for picture one. Then he started to kiss my jawline softly in photo number two. By the last picture, we were kissing.

"That was the best photo booth experience I've ever had," he admitted breathlessly.

"Yeah, it was alright," I tried to tease, but I knew that my flushed cheeks and cracking voice gave me away.

"Alright?" he asked, cocking an eyebrow, playing along. "Let's try to make it better this time." He put some coins into the slot. "We both need a set, right?"

I smiled, pecking his lips. It touched me a lot more than he could imagine, knowing that he wanted a token of us too.

Once the pictures were ready, he gave me a set. Then he cautiously folded his strip in two before putting it in his wallet.

He reached for my hand and intertwined our fingers. We took the direction of the food court again, but this time I was the one that stopped. I nodded at a big comic book store.

"We're never going to eat, right?" he whined.

I laughed. "This one is huge. Just give me five minutes, okay? I want to see if they have the new Spiderman. I love Spiderman. Maybe I can also find Logan's birthday present."

Gabriel pulled me into the store. "You know there is nothing I wouldn't do for you Mary-Jane."

I laughed as I looked at the 'New Releases' stand.

Gabriel grimaced. "That was pretty cheesy, wasn't it?" he asked, turning a lovely shade of pink.

I chuckled. "It's okay. We are all allowed to be cheesy sometimes. Even the big baddies are occasionally," I added, still looking at the comic books.

"Oh really?" he asked, and I didn't need to look at him to know he had his trademark grin on his face.

"Sure, even Darth Vader had his moments and we're talking about the guy who built the death star."

"Darth...Vader?" he asked as if he couldn't believe I was making this reference.

"Of course," I reached for a Vader mask and played with it. "Well, we're talking when he was still Anakin, but it doesn't matter. That part was still in him." I put the mask in front of my face and turned toward Gabriel. I knew I was about to say something so cheesy, I didn't want him to see me.

"Scary," he jested, looking down at me.

"He sat with Padme and said: *'From the moment I met you all those years ago, not a day has gone by when I haven't thought of you. And now that I'm with you again...I'm in agony. The closer I get to you, the worse it gets. The thought of not being with you – I can't breathe. I'm haunted by that kiss you should never have given me. My heart is beating...hoping that kiss will not become a scar. You are in my very soul, tormenting me...what can I do? I'll do everything you ask.'*" I recited as I too hoped that our relationship wouldn't become a scar, or at least not a permanent one.

"You can quote Star Wars?" he asked reverently.

I nodded silently.

He chuckled. "See, that's also a reason why I love you," he admitted before freezing, eyes wide in shock.

I was just as shocked as he was. I'd never expected him to say those three words and, based on the look on his face, he hadn't expected to say them either.

I kept the mask in front of my face a little while longer, not knowing what to say or do.

He finally turned around as if nothing had happened, but I knew we had reached the point of no return. It was too late; the damage was done…for both of us.

I let go of the mask and reached for his hand. "Come on, let's go grab something to eat."

"Yes…let's do that." He squeezed my hand.

The rest of the afternoon was not as fun. I was sad about that, but I was just scared to reciprocate. What if it had been an impulse? What if he didn't mean it as much as I did?

It'd just started to rain lightly when we left the mall. By the time we reached home, it was raining buckets.

"I will leave you in front of your house." He sounded so distant.

"You don't need to. Rain won't make me melt, you know. I'm tougher than that," I tried in a failed attempt to joke. "Don't you want to stay a while? My mother is away and she won't be back before tomorrow afternoon," I added as he parked in the street adjacent to mine.

"Do you want me to?" he asked, and I didn't miss the much heavier underlying question in his voice.

I took a shaky breath. Now was the time to be honest. "Did you mean it?"

He looked at me silently and it was awkward with only the sound of the rain on the car. "Do I want to answer that question?"

"I would like you to, yes."

He looked away, running his hand through his hair. He took a deep breath before turning toward me again. "Yes, I meant it, I didn't know I did, but I do love you."

I nodded. "That's good because…I do too."

"You do too?" he asked and I knew he wanted to hear the words.

"Love you. I love you too."

He relaxed before my eyes, making me realize how tense he had been. He gave me a bright smile that lit up his eyes. It made my heart tighten in my chest.

"You know what I loved to do with my father too?" I asked, trying to change the subject. I didn't know where we would be going from this. It was all so new and scary.

"No, what did you like to do?" he asked, turning on his seat to face me completely.

"We used to live in Texas you know, and rain was rare especially in the summer, so when we were lucky enough to have a summer shower, I used to go out in the garden and run around." I smiled at the memory of my father running after me, pretending to chastise me as he tried to catch me. He never caught me though, even if he could have so easily. He'd just run around with me. I was pretty sure he'd enjoyed it almost as much as I had.

"Why don't we do it?" Gabriel asked, apparently excited by the idea.

"Do it?"

"Run in the rain!"

"Oh yeah…" I blushed furiously at the images that 'do it' had brought to my mind. "And let's take the long way!"

We got out of the car and started to run like kids, laughing. I felt good and it was all because of Gabriel. He helped me get through today and I was sure that from now on, my fathers' birthday would not be such a hardship anymore.

When we made it to the house, we were soaked to the bone, but laughing so much it was hard to breathe.

"We're lucky it's hot or we would have caught pneumonia," he breathed, taking his shoes off.

"Come on, let's go upstairs to get some towels before soaking the whole place." I opened the door and ran up, followed by his heavy footsteps.

As soon as we reached the closet, I grabbed two towels and threw him one.

"You can use this bathroom if you want." I pointed at the door across the closet. "I'll be in the one in my room."

When I stepped in front of the mirror, I couldn't help but laugh. My hair had a natural wave and now because of the rain, it was all frizzy. My tank top was like a second skin and I couldn't help but blush, thinking of all the parts of me Gabriel had seen.

I tried to brush my hair, but sighed and gave up. I stepped into my room to get a dry tank top, but stopped dead at Gabriel's naked back.

"Briel?"

He turned around with a little grin. "Yeah. Hi. I left my shirt to dry in the other bathroom."

My eyes shifted to his chest. I knew I was ogling, but I just couldn't help it. Would his skin be soft? How would his bare skin smell? I let my eyes trail up his abs, chest, throat, jawline and beautiful lips before meeting eyes that were a lot darker than usual.

"Lottie…" he croaked. He took two steps toward me and looked deep into my eyes. "You are so beautiful, Lottie. So, so beautiful."

I closed the distance between us, hooking my forefinger in one of the belt loops of his jeans. "You are not bad either."

He grinned, leaning down to kiss me. He let his lips roam to my jawline and down my neck. He gently moved the strap of my tank top, skimming my collarbone with his warm lips before kissing my shoulder and making me shiver.

I wrapped my arms around his neck, burying my hand in his hair, pulling him even closer.

When his hands roamed under my top, I didn't stop him. I knew I should have. The rational part of my brain told me I was taking a dangerous road. I also knew it was all kinds of wrong to let it go that far, but I loved him and I knew he loved me too.

"I love you, Lottie, I want to be with you," he whispered in my ear.

"Me too. I want to be with you," I replied, closing my eyes.

Gabriel pulled me to the bed and laid me down, gently breaking our kiss.

"Are you sure?" he asked, meeting my eyes.

I nodded and it was all the encouragement he needed. He crushed his lips to mine.

I didn't know what I was supposed to expect from my first time, but to me, it was perfect.

Gabriel was gentle and selfless. He kept repeating how much he loved me, how beautiful I was, how good I was making him feel.

Later, as I laid in his arms with him gently caressing my hair, I realized that even if we were to call it quits tomorrow, I wouldn't regret what we'd just shared. I couldn't imagine having lost my virginity any other way.

When I woke up, I was a bit sad to find the space beside me empty, but as I saw the note carefully folded on the pillow, a smile spread across my face.

How could you even doubt? I scowled, reaching for the note.

My dearest Lottie,

I wish I could have stayed with you all night and I'm very sorry you won't wake up in my arms, but we will one day spend the night together.

After today, after what we've shared, things will be different. We can't go on like this. I've spent the last two hours just listening to you breathe.

Looking at you breathing so peacefully hurt deep because I'm terrified that one day you will realize the best thing about me is you, and you will take yourself away from me.

I love you,

Briel.

I folded the paper and rested it on my chest, smiling even wider.

CHAPTER 18

I had been so sure that making love with Gabriel wouldn't change my expectations, but I couldn't have been more wrong. What we had shared had changed things and I was not sure it was for the best.

As soon as Chago and I walked into school the next day, I looked around and couldn't help the bright smile spreading across my face when I saw Gabriel by his locker. He smiled back, but my heart sank in my chest when he then turned around to talk to his friends, clearly dismissing me. I realized that deep down I had thought last night had changed everything. That today he would come up to me, letting go of all his pretenses. But we were not in a romantic comedy. This was life and it sucked. I understood in this moment that what we had shared hadn't meant as much to him as it did to me - at least not enough for him to leave the fake Gabriel and lies behind. Not enough for him to acknowledge to everyone what he'd kept saying last night - that he loved me.

I closed my eyes for a minute, trying my hardest to keep my face impassive. I wanted to convince myself that it didn't matter, that neither of us had expected to feel the way we did. I sure as hell hadn't planned on falling in love and letting things go as far as they had, but I hadn't tried to stop them either. I had no right to expect any more than what he gave me, and yet I couldn't help wanting more.

I looked at him walking away. The further he got from me, the more I could feel the first breaches forming in our relationship. I painfully started to understand that it was probably the beginning of the end for us.

For the next few days, I tried to rebuild some of my walls. Gabriel didn't comment, but I could see the confusion in his eyes when I tensed up every time he reached for me. I'd even started to space out during our moments together in the hope that a bit of distance would make me see things clearly, would make the thought of breaking it off a bit less painful.

"So you are coming tomorrow night, aren't you?" Eva asked as we sat on the beach with Chago after school.

"I…don't know…" I tried, throwing a confused look at Chago. It had been two weeks since my night with Gabriel, and Chago was the perfect excuse for keeping my distance. I was glad Eva liked me and that she didn't mind that I tagged along with them. I also appreciated they didn't make me feel like a third wheel.

"You didn't tell her, did you?" she asked Chago, slapping his arm playfully. "This guy has the memory of a goldfish."

"I agree to anything when I have my hands on you and you know that," Chago teased, taking her hand and intertwining their fingers.

She blushed slightly, but ignored the comment. "Chago told me you were a very gifted musician, and my father is organizing an open mic night tomorrow night." She smiled warmly. "He was supposed to do that Saturday night, but apparently there is a big sporting event, so it's been moved to tomorrow."

I nodded. "Yes, the soccer team made it to the finals. It's the last championship game." I looked away at the deep blue Pacific Ocean. "It's a big deal for our school," I added, remembering how excited Gabriel was about this game - so excited that he'd made me promise to go. I'd promised even if I'd known it would hurt me to see him wearing his perfect mask. I took a deep breath. "What about the open mic night?"

"I told her you wouldn't do it," Chago rushed out.

I ignored him and kept looking at Eva. "What do you need from me?"

She cocked her head to the side, detailing me. "Are you really that good?"

I shrugged. "That's what the Humber here is saying," I replied, pointing at Chago. "But he is a bit biased."

"See, the thing is that…" She cleared her throat. "Well it was not as popular as we thought it would be and we really could use another performer."

"Oh!" I bit the inside of my cheek, thinking. Was I ready to play in public? I'd lived so much in the last few months. I knew I could find a song that really spoke to me. It would also be in a small coffee shop that was not popular with the people from our school. What was the risk?

I nodded, "Okay."

"Okay?!" Chago gasped. "I…Really? Madre de Dios, what happened to you?"

I chuckled. "I think it's time and Eva needs my help, so why not?"

"Why not?" he repeated and I could hear the incredulity in his voice.

Eva flashed a grateful smile. "Tomorrow, 7:00 pm?"

I nodded. "I'll be there. For once we'll be doing something different on a Friday night."

I spent the rest of the evening trying to figure out what song I should play, what feelings I wanted to convey.

The next day I was surprised to find Mateo in the driveway.

"What are you doing here?" I asked, opening the passenger door.

"Nice to see you too and please jump in. I'll be your driver for the evening, Miss Daisy. My brother is busy helping his girlfriend setting up," he winked. "And do you really think I would have missed the first time you were going to sing in public?" He flashed me his big, goofy grin. "You better think again."

"It's no big deal," I replied, cradling my guitar.

"Claro, no big deal."

I looked at the list of participants as soon as we arrived. There were twelve people registered; I was number five.

"Not a bad spot," Mateo commented as we sat at the table reserved for us. It was good to be friends with the boss' daughter.

"Aren't you going to perform?" I asked Logan who was already seated.

Logan shook his head, scanning the café. "I don't think this café is ready for a dramatic reading of Poe."

"I don't think the world is ready for that," Chago muttered in jest.

Logan rolled his eyes, but otherwise ignored the comment. "And I wouldn't want to steal your sunshine."

Chago snorted. "Sure, *that's* what it is about…." He concentrated on me. "So what are you going to sing?"

"That's a surprise, my friend." Truth be told, I had a selection of three songs and it would all depend on the way I felt sitting on the stool with my guitar.

I was relaxed enough when my turn came because the four before me were terrible.

"At least you can't be worse than him," Mateo encouraged after the guy with his harmonica had left the stage.

I took my guitar and quickly scanned the room as I sat on the stool. I stopped dead when my eyes connected with the table at the back, meeting those green eyes I knew only too well.

What was Gabriel doing here? It was not even Gabriel that bothered me so much. It was his 'court' formed by Doug and his girl Brittany as well as the precious Darlene. The two girls were clearly bored out of their skulls.

I threw a dark look at Chago, knowing he had to be the reason why Gabriel was here tonight. *Café Latino* was certainly not a place where the 'in' crowd from school visited by accident.

I dropped the three songs I wanted to sing. Gabriel was here with his 'official' friends, so only one song came to mind. I closed my eyes and started to sing *Forever and Almost Always* by Kate Voegele.

The chatter died as soon as I started to sing. Maybe I was not half bad, after all. I opened my eyes and looked at Chago, Mateo, Logan, and Eva. Their pride was obvious. I smiled at them before looking down at my guitar.

When I finished, the room exploded into applause, but I ignored it. I only wanted to see the emotions in Gabriel's eyes. He looked at me for a second before looking down at his phone, and I could feel the breaches in our relationship grow a little deeper, probably just deep enough not to be mendable anymore.

I whispered a thank you before going back to my table.

"You were fantastic!" Mateo beamed, wrapping an arm around my shoulders, pulling me to him.

I forced a smile. "Yeah…thanks."

I pretended to concentrate on the girl playing on her keyboard.

"Are you sure you're okay? You seem hurt," Mateo whispered at my ear.

I looked at Chago across the table. He was looking at me, his eyebrows knitted in wonder.

"I'm tired. Can you please drive me home?" I asked Mateo.

"Sure!" He stood, extending his hand to help me up.

"Want me to drive you?" Chago asked and I knew he meant 'do you need to talk?'

I shook my head. "Nah, you stay here. I'll see you tomorrow."

"Thank you for doing that, Charlie. You are very talented." Eva extended her hand to squeeze mine.

"It's true honey. You're almost as good as me," Logan joked, pulling me into a hug.

"One can only dream." I kissed his cheek soundly. "It was fun. Thanks for thinking of me. I'm just tired," I added in an attempt to reassure Chago.

"Sure," he replied, but I could see he didn't buy it.

"Do you mind if we walk back?" I asked Mateo as he took the direction of the car park. "It's not far and the night is great. I really need some air."

"Are you sure you don't want to drive? It would be good practice, night driving and all."

I shook my head. It has been about a month now since Mateo had started giving me secret driving lessons. I'd decided I needed to learn after telling Gabriel repeatedly how he needed to face his fears, including his fear of rejection. I'd felt like a fraud because I had not even been trying to face my irrational fear of driving, so I'd gone to see Mateo, knowing he would let me do it at my own pace. Surprisingly, it had been going a lot better than I'd expected, and he was not making a world about it, not like Chago would have done. This was why I hadn't told anyone yet, not until I knew I could face it.

"I just want to relax and enjoy the walk," I insisted.

"Sure." He put his keys back in his pocket. "Let's walk." He reached for my hand, intertwining our fingers.

We walked silently for five minutes before he finally decided to ask. "What happened in there?"

"Umm?" I pretended not to understand.

"You were fine. You were having a blast and then you just flipped."

"I'm an idiot."

He chuckled lightly, squeezing my hand tighter. "Where does that come from?"

"You know I never expected for things to go that far between us."

"Us?" he asked, dumbfounded. "As in 'you and I'?"

"As in 'him and I'." I took a deep breath. "It was not supposed to happen. I know…knew we were doomed from the start, that I had no right to hope for anything, but I did hope. I started to hope we…he could be more, but I've realized recently that we can never be more."

172

Mateo remained silent and I was grateful for that.

"Want me to stay for a while?"

"No, it's okay, thanks." I stood on my toes and kissed his cheek. "I love you, Mateo."

He gently pulled on my ponytail. "Love you too, Carlotta."

I had barely walked into the house when my phone started ringing to the now very familiar sound of Gabriel's ringtone.

I sighed, not even bothering to check my phone. I walked up with heavy steps. I just wanted to throw on my PJs and crawl into bed.

In the time it took me to change, my phone rang five more times to the same music. Gabriel was persistent, I had to give him that much.

The phone rang again when I went to close my curtains. I saw Gabriel's car parked under the streetlamp across the street.

I rolled my eyes, but picked up the phone before he could come and ring the doorbell.

"I was about to give up and come to your door," he announced as soon as I'd answered.

"Sorry, I was changing, and I'd put my phone on mute at the café," I muttered. It was only half a lie.

"How are you?" he asked and I could hear he was sheepish.

"Where are your friends?" I asked, ignoring the question.

"I didn't want to take them, Lottie, but Chago had left the flyer on my car this morning and they saw it. What was I supposed to do?"

You could have told them you didn't want them to tag along. You could have sat at our table and rooted for me as any guy who pretended to love me should have done, I thought. "It's cool. I don't care."

He sighed and I didn't need to see him to know he was leaning on the headrest, eyes closed and pinching the bridge of his nose as he did every time something was frustrating him. "You were fantastic."

I kept looking at his car, not saying anything.

"Can - Can I come in?" he asked tentatively.

"Not tonight," I replied, even surprising myself for being that strong. "I'm tired and my mother will probably be home soon."

Gabriel stayed silent for so long, I almost thought he'd hung up. "I will see you at the game tomorrow, right?" he asked, uncertainty in his voice.

I closed my curtains. "Sure. Okay, I better get off now."

"Yeah, you need your rest. Good night, Lottie. I love you."

"Good night, Gabe," I replied before hanging up, purposely not calling him Briel.

I looked down at my phone, knowing I had done the right thing, but that didn't stop it from hurting. Far from it. I felt in the pit of my stomach that things were about to change - for better or worse, I didn't know yet, but it was too late to back down now.

The next morning, I woke up to the same lingering feeling. It was not overwhelming. It was just a discreet weight upon my heart, making it just a little harder to breathe, a reminder that things were unraveling.

I already knew that Chago would not go to the game. He had told me, '*Are you serious, Chula? Spending more time with those cabrones would hurt my soul…really.*' So when he asked me later today if I really wanted him to go with me, I dismissed it with a laugh. But the truth was, I didn't feel like going by myself. I didn't belong there and there were only so many pretenses I could take from Gabriel. I knew we were close to breaking. I was just not ready to say goodbye.

My mother was still here when I came down. For once she wasn't dressed for the office. She looked casual even by my standards.

I was about to tell her that I didn't even know she owned a pair of jeans when she smiled. That smile took me back; it seemed so…real.

"Charlotte! I - I thought you were staying at Santiago's last night."

I gave her a suspicious look. *Why, mother, do you have something to hide?* I thought, but I really didn't feel like bringing her wrath upon me, especially today. I simply shrugged. "Nah, there was a change of program."

"Oh…" She nodded, concentrating on her cup of coffee.

"Do you have plans today?" I asked, looking pointedly at her jeans.

"I'm going out with some colleagues. Casual day, office bonding, nothing exciting."

At that moment, the doorbell rang and she almost jumped from her stool to go open the door.

"That's new," I mumbled, taking a sip of coffee.

Logan walked into the kitchen a minute later. "Hey, your mom told me to tell you goodbye. Her colleague was waiting for her in the driveway."

"The woman was spooky. She was almost human this morning."

Logan chuckled. "Scary thought for sure."

"Something else is scary." I pointed my spoon at him. "What's up with the clothing? Did someone challenge you or something?"

"Oh." He grimaced, looking down to his 'Go Vikings!' grey sweatshirt. "Yes, as the Editor-in-Chief of our well-respected newspaper, I have to show my support! It has been like forever since our soccer team was in the finals. 1972 I believe." He snorted. "I will even go to the game, can you believe it?"

I chuckled, concentrating on my cereal again.

Logan sighed dramatically, sitting across from me. "Tell me what's up."

"Uh?"

He rolled his eyes. "Come on, sweets. You've been different for a while. Before you seemed much happier, so I decided not to pry. But now..." He tried to find my eyes. "I don't know. You've been off for a week or two. It's like you're having a problem you can't solve."

I stopped playing with my cereal and met his concerned eyes. "Have you already done something stupid?"

He burst into laughter. "Oh my! I do stupid every day! You need to be far more specific here."

"What if you were doing something stupid and you knew it was stupid and only good to hurt you; what would you do?"

"Is the hurt inevitable?"

I nodded. "I'm afraid so."

Logan opened his mouth to answer when his phone vibrated on the table. "Damn organizing committee!" he grumbled after reading the text. "Believe me. These guys are completely lost without me."

"You should go. It's silly anyway. I'll see you later. I promise."

"I'll see you later, sweetie, and please don't worry too much. What should happen will happen." He turned around before reaching the door. "And if you're hesitating, maybe you should wait a bit before making a rash decision. I'm sure something will come up to help you make that choice."

"Yeah." I smiled again. "Thanks."

"Anytime."

I spent the rest of the day wandering around the house, not sure what I wanted to do. I didn't feel like drawing or playing music. I didn't want to bother Chago, who knew only too well that something was wrong. I didn't know how long he was going to rein in his horses before asking what was up with me.

I still wasn't sure what I wanted to do when I took the bus to go to the game. It was crowded,and people were excited, shouting and singing awfully off key. I couldn't help but curse at my inability to drive myself. I would have to ask Mateo to make me drive more.

When I made it to the stadium, people rushed to get to the best seats. I stopped in the middle of the way, getting cursed at.

Somebody bumped into me. "Hey, girl! Walk or move away!"

I turned around to see a freshman and frowned. "Do you have a ticket?"

"I…what?" he asked, taken aback.

"Do you have a ticket?"

He sighed. "No, and if you stay in the way, I'm not going to."

I could feel my own ticket in the back of my jeans' pocket, a reminder of the silliness of the situation. I reached for my ticket before thinking. "Here, take mine."

"You…You don't want it?" he asked, reaching for it tentatively.

"No, I'm not going."

"That's a great seat! Are you sure?"

I nodded. I knew it was a great seat, first row. "Have fun tonight." I left before he could add anything or before I could change my mind.

I went to the rear of the soccer field. The view was not the best, but at least I could see the game without being seen. I didn't want to be a spectator of my own stupidity. I always knew we didn't belong, that he would never leave his world for mine. He was not brave enough to be who he really was or maybe I was just not worth it in his eyes. Either way, we were taking our last breath.

As I watched the game from afar, Chago's words from the ball kept playing in my head. *Arbol que crece torcido jamas su tronco endereza.* He had been right…so, *so* right. It had been a mistake from the start. Briel probably knew that I was the only one who had been too blind to see it or maybe I had just refused to acknowledge it. Delusion was a powerful thing.

I stayed the full ninety minutes, but it was clear from the beginning of the second half that the Vikings would win.

When I heard the whistle at the end of the game, I saw the fans run onto the field. I couldn't stop a little sigh of relief from escaping me. He had done it! He had told me this was his last chance to bring his team to victory and he had done it.

I saw Gabriel scan the benches before turning around. Was he looking for me? He finally turned toward me and I almost thought he saw me. I raised my hand to wave, but Darlene appeared and jumped into his arms, kissing him.

I looked down, feeling my heart break a little more, a little deeper, but it reinforced my decision not to go to the game.

I walked home, lost in thought. This was for the best. Briel would realize now too that we didn't make any sense. I let out a humorless laugh. I'd become one of those stupid girls who believed chick flicks could be true. But I was not the geeky star who stole the heart of the most popular boy at school. I had just been a weakness, a temporary answer to Gabriel's secret personality, a guilty pleasure, not worth enough in his eyes. I was just not enough for him to walk away from the fake self he'd been living as for the past ten years. Or maybe he was just not as strong as I thought he was.

CHAPTER 19

I was not surprised that Gabriel hadn't tried to call during the weekend. I'd let him down and I knew it. It had not been an easy decision to make, but I'd known I wouldn't be strong enough to stay away from him. I needed help. I needed *his* help.

I was like the moth flying too close to the flame, in the end, it always ended up being burned.

"How was the game?" Chago asked Monday morning when he picked me up for school.

"I don't know. I didn't go," I replied, looking out of the window. It was a white lie, my way to let Chago know Briel and I were done without saying the words.

"Claro… Do I need the crowbar?" he asked seriously.

I couldn't help the small smile forming on my face. My best friend was really my angel. "No, guapo, you don't need the crowbar, but thank you," I added, turning toward him.

Chago nodded. "I just wanted to put it out there."

"I'll see you in Calculus," I promised with a quick wave, taking the direction of the girls' washrooms. I didn't want to see Gabriel, not yet.

When I walked in, Darlene and Brittany were chatting. *God, why do you hate me so much?*

They looked at me up and down before turning toward the mirror again.

"You were saying?" Brittany asked, reapplying her lipstick.

Darlene threw me a glance in the mirror, but I ignored it and got into a stall.

"You know the problem I had."

"With the sex thing?"

"Shut up!" Darlene hissed.

God, Brittany was dumb for real.

"What?"

Darlene sighed. "Well, yes, that problem was settled on Saturday." She chuckled. "Twice."

I had to sit down on the toilet. It felt like I'd just gotten punched in the stomach. Thinking of Gabriel with her made me nauseated even if it had no right to.

I left the toilet in a hurry, not even pretending I'd done anything.

I was rushing down the corridor, looking at the discolored lino, when I was pushed forcefully into a room. I swirled around as the door slammed behind me.

"Why didn't you go?" Gabriel asked and there was a cold edge to his voice I had never heard before.

"Does it matter?" I crossed my arms over my chest.

He was standing tall in front of the door. I was not sure if it was to stop others from coming in. Or me from getting out.

"It mattered to me," he replied and I could see his stance relax a bit. He was letting go of his pretenses.

"It didn't stop you from sleeping with Darlene." I jerked my chin toward him, challenging him to try to explain that one.

He paled and I knew Darlene hadn't been lying.

"That's -that's not what I'm talking about," he stuttered, trying to regain his composure.

"I think it's important."

He shook his head. "No, it's not. It all happened because you were not there. Because of you-"

"Oh, come on, that's bullshit!" I threw my hands up in exasperation. "Why? Why did you do-"

"*She* is my girlfriend!" he shouted and I didn't think it could have hurt more if he had slapped me.

I recoiled as the first bell rang. He was right. As much as I wanted him to be wrong, it was when he was with me that he was a cheater. I kept pretending I was in the right, but I was the bad one, the side girl…The cheater.

I pursed my lips to stop them from quivering.

"Oh, Lottie, I didn't mean that." He took a step toward me. "Shit." He ran his hand through his hair. "Sometimes-"

I raised my hand to stop him. "I'm sorry," I uttered, voice breaking.

"You--What?"

I forced a smile and sighed. "You're right. I'm sorry. I have no right to say anything."

"No, I'm not. Lottie, please." He took another step, extending his shaky hand toward me. "Let's talk…Please."

The second bell rang. *Saved by the bell,* literally.

"I can't be late." I managed to dodge him as he took another step toward me.

"But we need to talk."

"Later," I replied, getting out of the room.

I made it to class breathlessly under Chago's questioning look. I mumbled a quick apology before sitting down.

I faked a small smile to calm Chago.

I needed to get out of here, but I didn't want to get Chago into trouble. He had his internship to worry about and I couldn't jeopardize that.

I felt the weight on my chest during the whole class. Briel's words were true. Darlene might have been an unfaithful, despicable person, but I was no better. I was a liar and a cheater just like she was.

I pretended to look at my notebook while texting Mateo. I looked at the clock, twenty minutes left before the bell.

Need to get out of here. Don't tell guapo...Pick me up in thirty?

I'll b there, he replied not even five seconds later.

"See you at lunch?" Chago asked as we exited the room.

I nodded, not trusting my voice. I wouldn't be there at lunch, but if I told him I was leaving, he would have wanted to come with me and he couldn't afford to ditch class.

I went to my locker, looking for the photo booth pictures I'd taken with Gabriel. I ripped them in half, before putting them in an envelope with the simple words 'we're done' scrawled on the back.

The corridor was mostly empty except for the few students hurrying to their next classes. I slid the envelope in Gabriel's locker before walking outside, praying that nobody would stop me.

Mateo was parked at the bottom of the stairs, casually leaning on the driver's door. I ran to him, burying my face in his chest. I loved his scent, the mix of woodsy cologne and car. It was the odor of safety, the odor of someone who would never hurt me.

He rested his chin on top of my head, rubbing my back.

"We don't want to talk about it, do we?" he asked gently.

I shook my head against his chest.

He held me closer, "We will need to, eventually." He rested his hands on my shoulders, pushing me back gently. "Do you want to drive?"

I shook my head again.

He kissed my forehead. "Get in the car, mi reina, before someone sees you. I'm going to text Chago before he goes crazy when he realizes you're gone."

We drove in comfortable silence until we reached the house.

"Mama is not here and I need to go back to the garage for a little while. You want to come with me or stay here?"

I chewed on my bottom lip, unsure of what to do. I didn't really feel like being alone, but being in a garage surrounded by loud Latino men full of hormones seemed even more unpleasant.

"I think I'll stay here."

"Claro." Mateo turned to me. "I'll be back as soon as possible. If you need anything, just call me. I'll be five minutes away."

"I know…"

"I love you"

I faked a smile. "I love you too."

I had to admit daytime television sucked. I didn't understand how people could spend their days watching this crap. I had been watching for less than an hour and I wanted to destroy the TV.

I decided to go in the garden for a while. The sun was out and getting some vitamin D seemed as good an idea as any. I settled on the lounge chair under the tree and closed my eyes, but inevitably every thought kept bringing me back to Gabriel. All the warning signs I'd decided to ignore. How could I have been so stupid and clueless? Why did I refuse to see that he and I couldn't work? He should have broken up with Darlene as soon as we'd kissed or at least as soon, as he'd told me he loved me. I'd never believed he could be so deceptive and yet, here I was, heartbroken, knowing that no matter how I wanted to tell this story, I was one of the bad guys. It was not okay for him to just love me when he wanted to.

My phone vibrated in my pocket. I'd expected it to be Chago making sure I was okay, but the screen was flashing to the painful "G". He'd gone to his locker earlier than I'd thought he would. I ignored the call. I didn't see why he was so obstinate. I'd just given him a way out. He'd managed to sleep with the stupid girl. We were over without him having to go through the painful break-up speech.

I received a text a couple of minutes later.

We're not over! We need to talk. Where r u?

I deleted the text before putting the phone on the floor. I closed my eyes, trying to escape to my happy place, but the phone kept vibrating.

When I looked at my phone, I was at thirty-one missed calls and twelve voicemails.

"Leave me be!" I screamed, looking at the phone screen. "There is nothing left to take!" I threw the phone as hard as I could, hoping it would shatter on the concrete patio, but it was caught by Mateo.

"I think it will be way more effective and less expensive to do this." He turned it off before sitting beside me. "You need to talk to me. I've never seen you so....so irrational. This is not you."

I buried my face in my hands trying to hide the treacherous tears filling my eyes. I never wanted him to see me like this. I'd never thought I would be the kind of girl that cried over a boy.

Mateo stayed silently beside me, rubbing my back in soothing circles. I let go of my face and leaned on him, resting my head in the crook of his neck.

"No man deserves your tears, angel. You know that, right?" He kissed the top of my head.

"I made a mistake," I confessed barely louder than a whisper.

"We all make mistakes. It's human nature, but all that matters is that we learn and do our best not to make them again."

"It's just that—" I sighed, moving from my position on his neck, looking straight ahead.

"It's just that what?" he encouraged, grabbing my hand in his.

"I knew it couldn't work between us, you know?" I quickly glanced at him, but I was grateful that he was looking straight ahead too. "It's like when you are on the road and you see a violent accident. You know it's going to be ugly with blood and guts and yet you look and end up having nightmares for a week. Every time I saw him, I got deeper into this relationship. I had warning bells going crazy in my head." I shook my head. "I seriously don't like what I've become. There was a voice in my head telling me to run and I ran alright." I snorted. "I ran in his arms."

"It's okay. It's over, now right? You did listen to that little voice. It just took you longer than expected." He squeezed my hand.

"I did the right thing. It had to end." I nodded, still trying to convince myself. "I know that and I'm sure he knows that too, but it seems that he is not ready to let me go without a fight and I feel so weak when I think of him. I'm just - just so torn inside. I used to think that love was black and white, but with him, it was so wrong and yet it felt so right." I pursed my lips to stop them from trembling.

Mateo slid closer to me and wrapped his arm around my shoulders. "At least you gave it a try. Believe me, it's better to have remorse than regrets." He leaned down, resting his forehead against my temple. "You'll be okay. You will mend. I know it doesn't seem real right now, but it's true. At least you didn't do what I did. You didn't let the chance pass you by just because you were too scared of what it could have been."

I turned toward him in surprise and met his troubled eyes. "But you are not scared of anything."

He gave me a tired smile. "I always love the way you see me - like I'm a superhero."

"But you are my superhero."

Mateo brought his wide hands to my face, resting them on my cheeks and gently drying my tears with his thumbs. "Believe me, I've been spending the past few months being eaten by regrets."

"Tell me." I needed a distraction so badly. Anything that would stop my heart from aching for at least five minutes was good to take.

"Mas vale tarde que nunca," he whispered, letting go of my face before looking away. "It's the story of a boy who met a girl a long time ago..."

His voice was quivering a little with nervousness and that was the biggest surprise of all. I knew Mateo inside out and he was never nervous when he was talking to me. I rested my hand on his forearm, encouraging him silently.

"She was much younger than him, five years to be exact, so he'd always seen her as a baby sister, an annoying baby sister, but he loved her to death."

My breath caught in my throat, wondering if he was talking about him and me. No, it was impossible.

"The years passed. She grew up to become a beautiful young woman and he hated the lustful way some boys were looking at her. He tried to convince himself it was because he wanted to protect her, but he was a fool. He just couldn't imagine someone else's hands on her."

My heart was beating so hard it was painful. I wanted him to stop. He had to stop, but I was unable to speak.

"He kept thinking he had to wait for her to be legal, that she needed to experience life, that it wouldn't be fair of him to drop that bomb on her before she even knew what love was." Mateo laughed humorlessly. "He was foolish enough to want to let her graduate high school and choose a university. He promised himself that if she decided to stay around, he would tell her how much she meant to me---him. He would tell her that he knew her inside out, flaws and crazy quirks included, but that he loved her anyways. He would tell her that he knew she wasn't perfect, but that you--she was perfect for him."

My heart was weeping even more now - once for the man I had been foolish enough to love and once for the man foolish enough to love me. A man who had been cowardly enough to simply watch from the sidelines.

I tried to talk, but it came out as a squeak. I cleared my throat. "When did he realize how he felt?"

"Almost two years ago at her Quinceanera. She was breathtaking in her dress…he just wanted to steal her away."

"He should have told her. She deserved to know."

Mateo turned to me, looking deep into my eyes and making me self-conscious. "Does it matter now?"

"Do you really love her?"

"You mean more to me than anyone I ever loved at all."

"Oh, Mateo…" I closed my eyes, hoping we could go back in time and forget everything he'd just told me.

"Te quiero sin saber como, ni cuando, ni de donde."

"Pablo Neruda…" I opened my eyes. "It's too late now. I'm different."

"And I wanted that. I wanted you to experiment. I never thought you would meet your perfect match. He was a fool, whatever he did to mess it up. He doesn't deserve you."

"He has a girlfriend." I admitted

"He. Has. A."

"Yup."

"And you knew that?"

"Uh huh"

He pursed his lips, scrunching his nose in disapproval. "What were you-"

"Thinking? Nothing. I wasn't thinking about anything. That's the problem."

"And he didn't break up with her for you?"

I shook my head.

Mateo swore under his breath. "If it was me -"

"Mateo stop…This is not helping."

He took my hand, intertwining our fingers. "I just wanted to put it out there. You have options. You shouldn't be anybody's second choice. You will always be my first choice."

It was like I was seeing him for the first time. "Thanks…" It was horrible to say that. He'd just told me he loved me and all I had to say was 'thanks'.

Mateo leaned slowly toward me and kissed me. His lips were soft and warm. He was very skilled and yet I didn't feel anything.

"So?"

"Nothing."

He sighed, kissing my temple. "Come on, let's go for a ride and don't worry about everything I've just told you. You are still my little Carlotta. I'll be here for you no matter what. It doesn't change anything."

"Would it have made a difference?" he asked as I parked in front of my house.

I looked at him with puzzlement.

"You and I —" He ran his hand through his hair. "If I had spoken before, would you be mine now?" His voice was deeper, raspier than usual.

I bit my bottom lip, pondering his question. I'd crushed on him for years; I'd wanted him to like me for so long. "Do you really want to know?"

"I think I am a masochist like that."

I took a deep breath. "Maybe – Yes, it would have."

Mateo exhaled, closed his eyes, and rested his head on the headrest. "Yeah, it doesn't help."

"I'm sorry, Mateo. If I could just-"

He turned toward me, resting his fingers on my lips. "Don't, please. Never apologize for what you feel or don't feel. You better go now. It is getting late."

I knew he needed time. Rejection, voluntary or not, hurt like a bitch.

I got out of the car and looked at him as he took the driver's seat. I kept my eyes on his car until it disappeared down the street.

When I turned around, I saw Chago standing there. The look of pure anguish on his face took my breath away.

"Chago?" I tried breathlessly, my heart in my throat. "Eva?"

"I don't know how to tell you. I know it's better coming from me, I just…There was an accident, Chula, it's bad. It's really bad."

My knees buckled from under me. I didn't realize I'd fallen until my knees hit the hard concrete of the driveway. Chago didn't need to say more. I knew – I just knew. He was now kneeling beside me, but I could barely hear him as my blood pounded in my ears. I heard the words 'hospital', 'Gabriel', 'car crash'.

I couldn't breathe. I tried to get air in my lungs, but it was like my chest was in a metal vise, stopping my lungs from expanding.

Chago grabbed my face, forcing me to lock eyes with him. "You're having a panic attack."

I shook my head. "Can't. Breathe."

Chago grabbed my freezing hand and rested it on his heart. "Inhale, Chula. Follow my lead." He took a deep breath. "Exhale…"

I forced myself to follow his lead. The only thing I was trying to think about was his gentle heartbeat, his deep breathing which I was trying to mimic. After a few seconds, the pain in my chest started to ease, allowing me to breathe a little easier.

"I need – I have to." I shook my head.

"I know." Chago stood up, wrapping his arms around me to pull me from the floor. "But not tonight, there is no point, Chula."

"But- Chago, not again." I leaned heavily on him, feeling suddenly drained.

"You need to sleep." He caressed my hair soothingly. "Let's go to bed. Tomorrow we will go."

"You are staying, right?" I asked hopefully as he half carried me back to the house.

"There is no getting rid of me, Chula. It's you and I forever remember."

"Forever…" I whispered as the stupor of the news kept me numb.

CHAPTER 20

As we drove to the hospital in silence, I went over all the scenarios of what could have happened. I'd barely slept last night, too busy following the updates on Darlene's Twitter feed. Darlene's Twitter... But least I knew he was alive. That was all that mattered.

"Just leave me here. Go park." I didn't even give Chago a chance to reply as I exited the car and ran to the intensive care unit.

Breathlessly, I arrived in the waiting room. I realized my mistake as soon as my eyes locked onto an older woman who I assumed was Gabriel's mother and a crying Darlene who was being comforted by Doug.

When Darlene looked up, I saw her sadness switch to pure anger. "What are you doing here?" she spat, straightening in her seat.

"Darlene!" Gabriel's mom chastised before eyeing me curiously.

"She is nobody!" Darlene pointed an accusing finger at me. "She doesn't even know Gabe! She is probably here to get some juicy info for her friend at the newspaper. Aren't you?"

If looks could kill, I would be lying on the floor. "No, I –" I stopped, detailing the four people in front of me. His mother was looking at me curiously. His father hadn't even looked up from his phone. Darlene was throwing daggers at me, but strangely enough, Doug was looking at me with something that looked a lot like pity, which didn't make sense.

"You what?" Darlene insisted.

"Stop it, D," Doug breathed, reaching for her hand, which she removed sharply.

"I'm just. I'm just –" My eyes filled up with tears. There was literally nothing I could do or say now to make the situation any less awkward and yet, I would have given anything just to know if he was going to be okay.

"Come, Chula, this is the wrong floor." Chago reached for my hand.

I looked down at our joined hands. When had he even gotten here? I looked up and met his concerned eyes. "What?"

"Marco. He is in trauma downstairs." He said slowly, keeping his eyes locked with mine.

"Oh…" I turned to Gabriel's mother. *Just tell me if he is going to be okay. It can't end like this – We were a love story. We can't become a tragedy.* But I nodded, still numb.

"I'm sorry for the intrusion. my cousin got into an accident at work and Charlie came to the wrong place." He sounded so calm, so serious – so unlike him. He nudged me in a failed attempt to make me move or talk or do anything to show these people I hadn't completely lost it. "I will pray for your son," He added, pulling me a bit harder as he turned around.

Turning with the pull, I followed him to the elevator, trying to clear my head. Just before the door closed on us, I heard Doug call Darlene a bitch.

"I don't know if he is going to be fine." I sighed with defeat.

Chago pulled me into a hug. "He'll be fine, Chula. We'll speak to Maria. She will let you know."

"They don't know him the way I do and yet-" I turned to him. "I need to go see my mom, Chago. Can you drive me there?"

He looked at me like I'd lost my mind. "Chula, we're supposed to be in class and you're an emotional wreck. I don't think facing your mother's tough love is the best for you right now. Why don't we go to my house? Mama knows. She will take good care of you."

I tried to smile at him, knowing it looked more like a pathetic grimace of pain than a smile. "No, I just- I need to save what's left of him."

Sadness clouded his features, but he didn't get a chance to speak.

"Hey!"

I turned around to see that Doug had followed us to the car park.

"Hey?" I leaned against the car, trying to look a little less mentally unhinged as I had in the waiting room.

Doug looked around, rubbing his neck uncomfortably.

"Can we help you, gringo?"

Doug looked back at me, ignoring the barely veiled threat in Chago's voice.

"They brought him in with multiple injuries and some internal bleeding. They-" He stopped, frowning in concentration, probably trying to remember everything that was said to him. "Last nigh, they managed to stop the bleeding and he's responding well to the meds. He is now in surgery. His prognostic is still engaged, but the doctors have good hope. And you know better than anyone else how stubborn the mofo can be." He gave me a rueful smile. "He will be fine."

I knew what I was supposed to say. That it didn't matter, that I was not here for him, that I didn't know him, but Doug's look was enough to let me know he knew much more than I'd thought he had. "Thank you." I finally let go of my pretenses.

He shrugged and looked away. He growled, shaking his head as if he was having an internal debate. After a few seconds, he sighed and got his phone out of his pocket. "What's your digits?"

"My digits?"

"Your phone number. I'll text you when there is news."

"Why?" I couldn't help but wonder. I was grateful, but at the same time Doug and I had never been on speaking terms, pretty freaking far from it.

He looked heavenward with exasperation before throwing a wistful look toward the hospital. I knew that he just wanted to go back and support Gabriel's family. "Because I am not as clueless as people think I am, because I know you matter, and because I know you care."

My voice broke as I gave him my number. It was a relief knowing I was not completely out of place. "Thank you from the bottom of my heart…Thank you."

"Yeah, it's okay." He turned around and jogged back to the hospital.

I kept my eyes trained on him until he disappeared into the building. Then I turned to Chago, puzzled.

"No, sabo Chula." He sat in the car. "Is there anything I can say that will stop you from going to see your mother?"

"Sadly no. Believe me, if there was any other way…but she is the only one who can help me."

I couldn't let the only part of him we had shared disappear, no matter what. I needed to fight for who he really was and his beautiful drawings were a big part of him.

I barged into my mother's office, knowing I was about to do something I'd sworn to myself I would never do. I was going to beg for her help.

My mother jumped from her chair. "Charlotte, what are you doing here?" She glanced at her watch. "Why aren't you at school?" she added angrily.

I just stood there in silence, trying to catch my breath. Running up all her floors had really taken a toll on me.

As my mom stared at me, I saw her features morph from anger to concern. She noticed the dark circles, the bloodshot eyes, and the more than disheveled appearance.

She took a tentative step toward me. "Tell me what's happening." There was even a hint of fear in her voice.

I fell to my knees. "I need you to help me, mom. Please, I need you." I couldn't help my voice from breaking.

My mother took another step toward me, lifting her hand to comfort me before letting it fall to her side, having thought better of it.

If I was not already so broken, I would have laughed at that. The only person who was supposed to be able to soothe me had no idea how to make me feel better.

"What do you need?"

"He is hurt, Mom. He might not –" The lump of unshed tears in my throat, formed by the idea of Gabriel dying, made it impossible to continue. I winced, trying to swallow through those tears.

"Are you talking about Gabriel Johnson?"

I nodded wordlessly.

"You- I didn't know you were friends." She detailed my face, her amazing lawyer talent in full force. She was trying to see past my words, past my silences.

"We were-" I took a shaky breath as my heart constricted even harder in my chest. "I can't let this beautiful part of him disappear, Mom. I have to – I need to," I finished rather lamely.

My mother crouched in front of me, removing some hair from my face in such a gentle gesture it took me aback. My mother was not a loving woman. "What do you need?"

"I need to get something from Gabriel's car, something nobody will know where to find. It's nothing illegal, Mom, I promise."

My mom went behind her desk and looked at me for a few seconds before reaching for her phone. "I need you to talk to me," she said, her voice full of weariness.

I nodded, drying my tears with the back of my hand. "I will. I promise I will, but not now – I don't have time to open up now. If I do..." I took a deep, shaky breath, trying to give myself some much-needed composure. "If I do, I don't think I will ever be able to breathe again."

My mother's face crumpled with grief and strange recognition. Was my pain and helplessness a reflection of the pain she'd felt when she'd lost my father?

She shook her head, as if to will her painful memories away, then picked up the phone. "Detective Russel? Katrina Miller. I think now is the time to call on one of the favors you owe me," she said, keeping her eyes locked on mine.

****

The taxi dropped me in front of the car's depot less than fifteen minutes after my mother's call. Who I assumed was Detective Russel was waiting for me in front of a giant metal door.

"Charlotte?" He asked, taking a step toward me.

I nodded, meeting him by the door. He looked much younger than I'd imagined, but the sternness of his features let me know he was older than he looked.

"It had to take a lot for Katrina to call on this favor." He showed his badge to the officer sitting at the front desk. "She is with me," he added, jerking his head toward me without even looking. "Where is the black Mercedes that was brought in yesterday?"

The officer typed on his computer. "Forensic finished with it a few hours ago. It's still in lot B."

Russel let out an annoyed sigh. "Follow me." He started to walk briskly down a corridor.

He was tall and I had to take at least three steps to match one of his. By the time we reached the door leading to lot B, I was both breathless and sweaty.

"Not sure what you expect to find in this car. Forensic went through everything."

"Not through this," I insisted as I scanned the lot for Gabriel's car.

I froze when I finally found it. It was hardly recognizable. I wouldn't have known this scrap of metal was his if it hadn't been for the soccer team logo hanging from the rear-view mirror. The front of the car was completely pushed in. *His legs….* I bit my lip as I fought back tears. It was not the time nor the place to break down. I had something to do; I would have time to hurt later – in the privacy of my room.

I took a few slow steps toward the car and shivered as a wave of nausea hit me. There was blood on the steering wheel as well as on the windshield's busted glass. *Had he gone through the windshield?*

I turned around and looked at the detective helplessly, not knowing how much closer I could get without falling apart.

He sized me up, his eyebrows knitted with concern. "You're not about to break down on me, are you?"

I wanted to shake my head negatively, but I turned back to look at the car. The splatters of blood. The destroyed windshield...

"You know, usually the cars look way worse than the actual accident," he explained.

Was this his attempt to make me feel any better? I had to look like a real mess to convey such an attempt.

He took a deep breath. "Why don't you go stand by the door and let me know what you're looking for?"

"In the trunk under the spare wheel, there is a leather-bound notebook." I couldn't recognize my own voice.

"All thIS for a notebook?" He asked with incredulity.

"It's not just a notebook. it's who he is."

He looked like he wanted to ask more, but simply shrugged and went for the notebook.

Once he came back and handed me an undamaged notebook, I couldn't help but let out a sigh of pure relief. At least what Gabriel had been was not lost to the world. I clasped it to my chest, closing my eyes as if I was attempting to let his art heal me.

"Do- Would you like me to give you a ride somewhere? Home perhaps?"

I opened my eyes and met his weary gaze. Did he think I would break down?

I nodded. "I need to go to Central Bank headquarters. Can you take me there?"

"Are you sure it's wise?"

Yep, he definitely thought I was crumbling down. "I have something I can't miss." I was crumbling down, but it was slow, slow enough to let me do everything I had to do before I started to cry and never stopped.

He nodded reluctantly, but he seemed to think twice about it when he stopped in front of the bank.

"You seem very upset – I believe it would be best-"

"I know what I'm doing," I interrupted him. I was angry and in pain, but I needed to keep hold of this anger to do what I had to do. I knew if I let the pain take over, I would crumble, and I couldn't let that happen yet.

I exited the car. Before entering the building, I turned around and saw him on his phone. I was certain he was calling my mother. I needed to act fast.

I looked at the listing on the wall.William R Johnson - Twenty-seventh Floor. Of course, it was. The more important you were, the higher up your office was.

When I arrived upstairs, I scanned the listed names, trying to find his because I knew the receptionist would never let me through. You couldn't just barge into the office of the VP of a major bank and yet, I was about to do just that.

"May I help you?"

I looked at the receptionist, hoping that what I'd learned in the episodes of the *Mentalist* would help me.

"I would like to speak with Mister Johnson."

She glanced left and I guessed that his office was that way.

"Do you have an appointment?"

I shook my head. "No, but I need to talk to him about his son, Gabriel. It's important." I tightened the hold I had on the notebook.

She pursed her lips, frowning with disapproval. She obviously knew Gabriel was at the hospital. "Mr. Johnson has been in the hospital and he is very busy and now is not the time for-"

I didn't give her a chance to finish as I rushed down the corridor. I heard her shout for me to come back, but I didn't turn around as I skimmed each door, trying to find his office.

When I saw his name on the last door, I didn't think twice before barging in.

Gabriel's father let go of the phone he was holding and glared when he realized the person who had just rudely interrupted, was not a threat, but a half-demented teenage girl.

"Mr. Johnson, I tried to stop her," the receptionist exclaimed with a high-pitched voice. "Let me call security."

"I'm here to talk to you about Gabriel. You know, the son who is in the hospital while you are picking up calls," I spat with as much anger as I could muster.

He kept glaring, but dismissed the person on the phone. "It's okay, Gladys. This young lady will have five minutes to tell me what she fought so hard to say. Call security and have them on standby because done or not, she will be escorted out of the building in exactly five minutes."

"I don't need five minutes." My voice was calm, almost eerily so, despite the turmoil of emotions. I tried to keep ahold of the anger, ignite it and let it consume me. Anger would help me keep the rationality I needed.

"May I at least get your name?" he asked, leaning back on his chair after his assistant had left.

"Charlotte Miller," I replied before letting Gabriel's notebook fall heavily onto his desk.

"Miller?" He frowned, looking at the notebook. "Katrina Miller's daughter? I'd believed any child of Katrina Miller would have better control over their temper."

I glared at him, opening the notebook. "I only have five minutes. I'm sorry I can't indulge in a simulacrum of politeness."

"What is this?" He pointed at one of the buildings drawn by Gabriel.

"This is your son Gabriel." I looked at the drawings fondly. "This is who he is. He is not like you. Gabriel – he is not a banker." I kept on turning the pages slowly as he kept his eyes on it. "Gabriel can see the beauty in this world. He is an artist – a dreamer."

His father rested his hand on the notebook, stopping me from turning the page. It was the drawing of a cabin lodge and when he looked up at me with confusion written all over his face, I knew it was touching him.

"He's never said anything," he admitted, looking down at the drawing again.

"Of course, he didn't." I shook my head. "Gabriel wants you to be proud of him. It's the only thing he wants, even if it is in spite of his own happiness. But there is something he never realized, something that was clear from the day I met him." I let out a weary laugh.

"And what is that?" Gabriel's father asked, tightening the hand resting on the notebook into a tight a fist.

"You will never be proud of him. He will never do enough, be enough. But he didn't understand that that is not a reflection of who he is; it's the reflection of who you are. How you feel about your own miserable life," I spat.

His father jumped from his seat, pointing his finger at me. "How dare you judge me on how I deal with my son who is lying in a hospital bed?"

"And yet here you are!" I exclaimed, gesturing at the office.

"But who are you?" he asked, resting his hands flat on the desk, leaning toward me in a threatening gesture. "My son never even mentioned you before."

His words stung, but I tried my best not to flinch at the coldness of his words.

"I am nobody. I don't matter, but he does. This does." I pointed to the notebook again. "I am not here for your ego. I'm not here for you to like me. I'm here to ask you to change. When he wakes up, you will need to show him that you will love him no matter what, that you will be proud of him no matter what he decides to become. He is exceptional, your son. He deserves to know this." I felt exhausted now that I had said what I needed to say.

Mr. Johnson looked at me silently, his jaws locked with bottled up anger. After a few seconds, he pressed the intercom button on his phone.

"Gladys, Miss Miller is going to leave now. Please have security escort her out of the building. Miss Miller, I can't say it was a pleasure."

I shrugged. "Likewise." I looked achingly at the notebook resting on his desk, knowing I would not have it again. I started to regret not keeping a few pages for myself.

The security had been ready for me. There was even a taxi waiting in front of the building to drive me home. Talk about premium service.

I knew he was going to call my mother. I knew there was going to be hell to pay, but the reaction I'd gotten from that cold man was worth any punishment I would be facing.

CHAPTER 21

I looked at the book I was trying to read, reading the same page for the fifth time. I couldn't concentrate on schoolwork, not with Gabriel in the ICU, but the school would not be lenient, not like they would be with Darlene, Doug, or even the rest of the soccer team.

Publicly, I had no reason to be upset. What would they see me as? An attention seeker? A slacker? Some conniving bitch who would do anything to get out of assignments? I couldn't blame them. As far as everybody knew, I'd never even said a word to Gabriel Johnson.

I growled before looking at my phone, making sure it was on and the battery full. *Please ring—Chago, Maria…Doug—anyone.* I needed to know he was going to be okay. I just needed to see him once, if only to make sure he was still here with us.

I was about to pick up the book to give it another try when I heard a faint rasp at my door.

I frowned, "Yeah?"

To my surprise, my mom walked into my room still dressed in her suit. She crossed her arms on her chest, looking around my room as if she was seeing it for the first time, and I realized it had been years since she'd come into my room.

"I received a call in the office this afternoon—William Johnson." She looked into my eyes. "He informed me you'd caused a scene."

I waved my hand dismissively. "Mom, I know you think I was out of line, but please, not today. I can't, please," I begged, rubbing my hand against my forehead. "I would honestly appreciate it if we could keep the lecture for another day." I was too exhausted for this.

She sighed, sitting at the bottom of my bed. "I told him I would talk to you, but truth be told, that man has always been a pompous ass. He probably deserved everything you'd told him."

I let out a surprised snort. That was so not my mother. It was much more like…well, like me.

She looked at me with a tired smile. "I need you to talk to me, Charlotte. I know I didn't do anything to deserve it, but I don't want you to hurt." She shook her head, her eyes full of sadness. "I realize it is hard to open to someone who never opened up to you."

I looked at her in stunned silence. I was not sure I could open up about Gabriel and all of the mistakes that had followed our meeting, but I wanted to tell her. I realized I needed my mother— the person who was supposed to love me unconditionally, so I told her as much as I was ready to tell her. The tutoring, the falling in love, the heartbreak, and my faults. Of course, I left out some details, especially our night together.

"You ran away?"

I nodded, looking at the Led Zeppelin poster on my wall. I wanted to look anywhere but at her. I was not ready for the disappointment I was bound to find in her eyes.

"Of course, you did. You're doing what you've seen me do all these years."

I looked up, astonished. "You? You're probably the strongest woman I know."

She let out a humorless laugh. "I am a real tiger at work, but in my life,,," she said, shaking her head. "I did nothing but run every time it could have hurt and I've taught you to do the same."

She reached into her pocket to retrieve a laminated photo and extended it to me. It was a Polaroid shot of a young Katrina, her hair just as unruly and crazy as mine, but her smile, however, constricted my heart. It was the brightest smile I had ever seen, and it was only matched by the one on the tall, young man standing beside her. A young man I knew only too well as my father. He had his arm wrapped around her shoulders, pulling her to him. They were posing in front of my high school, and based on their looks, they couldn't have been much older than I was now.

"It was our last year of high school," she said, confirming my unspoken assumption. "This photo goes with me everywhere. This was when we'd both realized with unwavering certainty, that we were meant to be together and that—" She sighed. "Adam took that picture."

I frowned at the change of subject. "Adam? Who the hell was—" My eyes widened as I connected the dots. "Mulligan?"

She nodded. "Adam and I—we were dating. We were supposed to date. Our parents were friends. We were both popular, smart." She smiled, but it lacked conviction. "It was just easy, you know? Who needs complications?" She looked away, her eyes glazed in her moment of reflection. "And then your father entered our life like a hurricane. He was beautiful, confident, talented, and so smart. You know he wrote a song about my eyes within a week of meeting me?" She smiled at me, her voice soft with affection. "I never stood a chance. Even Adam was seduced, although very differently. I understood then what real love was and I didn't mind leaving everything behind to be with him. It wasn't a sacrifice; it never was a sacrifice if it meant being with him. You came along before we'd expected. I was just twenty and I panicked. I was still at university, but your father, he was ecstatic. He made it all okay. He made sure my studies didn't suffer and he loved you. Oh, Charlotte." She reached for me and squeezed my hand. "You were the love of his life."

"Knowing what you know now, would-would you do things differently?"

"Are you asking if I would have picked the easy way?"

I nodded, praying she would give me the answer I was hoping for.

She shook her head, straightening with determination. "No, never. I only had him for ten years, but it was ten amazing years. I loved—I still love him, but I didn't do right by you, and for that I'm sorry."

I looked away, not sure of what to say.

My mother took a deep breath, looking down at her hands wrapped neatly on her lap. "His death was sudden and unexpected. I'd walked out that morning as a fulfilled wife and mother after a kiss goodbye, and I'd come back a widow and a single mother. I watched his casket being lowered into the ground and the lower it went, the more I was engulfed in the fog of grief and guilt. It was an emptiness that filled my heart, my lungs, making each breath laborious. It was making it hard to think, to know that the reason he was dead was me. Because he put my needs, my dreams before his own."

"It was a medical condition. Nothing was your fault," I forced out as silent tears streamed down my face. My heart ached for her, for him, for Gabriel, and for myself. For once, I could understand her more than I ever had. I was grieving in my own way. I was always running from the pain and guilt, and she did just the same. She ran from her feelings.

She reached for my hand and clasped it. "I've learned about the deepness of pain and the viciousness of loss. I've let life suck me under and I lost you in the process." She took a shaky breath, pressing her lips tightly together most likely to stop her tears. "I thought if I could keep on going, stop myself from feeling— I was so terrified that if I let myself cry, I would never stop, and I thought that you needed me to be that rock, but it wasn't what you needed." She let go of my hand, quickly wiping her eyes. "I have learned sadly too late that the easy days would always be easy, but it is in the face of pain and adversity that you discover who you really are."

"Mom…" I whispered as her pain was hurting me.

She pointed at my vinyl records, the drawings on the walls. "This is all your dad. You only had a few short years with him, but you are so much like him, and I can't help but think it would have been so much easier for him to get through to you." She gave me a sad smile and stood up to go through the records. "Sometimes I can't help but regret that, for your sake, it was him instead of me."

This had the effect of a slap; how could she ever think that? "Mom, no, don't say that. We might have our problems, but I wouldn't trade you. I just wished you would have been more open. I've always thought you rejected me because of what I represented - a painful past, and losing someone you loved."

She choked back a sob. "No, it made me love you even more! I was just trying to make you harder, stronger than I was. I didn't want you to ever have to suffer. I am very good with words. I can charm a room full of people and yet when it really matters like now, I am at a loss." I could see this admission surprised her just as much as it surprised me. "But you see, daughter of mine, I am going to try to be like your father by letting the music express the things I cannot say, but wish I could." She took one of my vinyls and I recognized the music as soon as it started to play. It was *"Father and Son"* by Cat Stevens, and all my bottled-up feelings just submerged me like a tidal wave. I didn't want to break down. I didn't have the time to break down and yet, I couldn't stop it anymore.

My mom laid on the bed behind me and held me. As I sobbed, she gently whispered the words of the song to me.

"It hurts, Ma. It hurts so bad," I gasped in between sobs. "It feels like it will never get better."

She brought a hand to my hair and caressed it soothingly. "I know it does, but it will get better. That boy is going to wake up, and whatever you decide to do, don't do it out of fear or guilt. Just do it because it's right for you and because it makes you happy."

I grabbed her hand resting on my waist. I let her hold me until the sobbing subsided. Then I fell into an exhausted slumber.

I woke up with a banging headache and winced when I turned around and faced the blaring sun. I was alone in my bed and based on how high the sun was in the sky, it had to be late.

I reached for my phone, but there was a note where it should have been.

Your phone is in the kitchen. I thought you needed some sleep. I called the school and told them you were sick. Just take the day and feel— Don't bottle up.

When I finally went downstairs, I had two texts. One from Doug telling me the second surgery had gone well, and a second from Maria telling me she was doing the night shift at the ICU and to be there at 9:00 pm sharp.

Just thinking about seeing Gabriel made me both happy and terrified. Doug had told me Gabriel was responding well to the surgery and treatments, but I needed to see it with my own eyes.

CHAPTER 22

I went to the ICU using the back door. A, and as soon as I walked into the corridor, Maria pulled me into the staff room.

"Just wear that." She pointed to the nursing assistant uniform resting on the table. "We don't want to raise more attention than necessary."

I nodded, trying to fit into the much too-tight uniform she had given me.

"Sorry, that's all we had." She looked up and down the corridor before rushing to the left.

"Maria, I don't want you to get into trouble—"

She waved her empty hand. "No te preocupes, es familia."

I smiled gratefully just as she opened a door, gesturing me in.

My breath caught in my throat when I looked around the room, at all the machines hooked to Gabriel's still lifeless body.

"It looks much worse than it is." Maria squeezed my shoulder. My eyes burned with unshed tears as I walked toward him. Seeing him covered in bandages and, so fragile, made my heart ache even more. I gripped the cold metal of his bedframe to stop my knees from giving up under me, as I looked at the tube in his mouth, breathing for him.

"The machine is not permanent,." Maria tried to reassure me. "He has swellings in his brain. I, it's why they've had him in a coma. The medication is working well. I, it's resorbing."

I nodded; I was not sure what it all meant. "Will he-will he recover?" I asked, sitting by his bed and, reaching for his hand.

Don't ask a question you're not sure you want the answer to. Id always believed this, but today I needed to know no matter how painful the answer might be.

"We can't be sure. His body is healing, but he needs to want it. He needs to fight."

I squeezed his still hand. "He will fight, won't you, Gabriel?"

"I can only give you ten minutes tonight. I'm sorry. It's just that tonight's supervisor is a Nazi, but tomorrow I can give you more time."

I forced a smile and looked at her. "It is more than enough, more than I'd expected. I am not family." I raised my hand, brushing his cheek. "I am nothing."

His usually tanned skin was so pale, unnaturally so, much like a wax figurine. I looked at the heart monitor to somehow reassure myself that my Gabriel was still here with us.

"Come on, Briel, you win. Wake up, please," I begged, kissing his cold hand. "You have so much to live for." I took a deep breath and took out the Romeo and Juliet book I had in my bag. "To find your Juliet, you need to wake up," I whispered as I wrote those words in the book. After sliding it under his pillow, I ran my hand in his silky hair, removing it from his face. "It's not time to say goodbye, Briel. We can't part like this. You taught me so much. You changed me for the better and I can't believe you will not do everything to come back. No matter what happens, I love you, Gabriel Miller, and I believe love is much stronger than death. I saw love in you, so much love, too much love for letting this take you away. What about your dreams? Your dreams are worth fighting for and I—"

A sharp knock at the door reminded me that my time was up.

I stood up and brought my lips to his forehead. "Please come back because even if I never was to see you again, I just can't imagine living in a world where you're not."

As promised, for the next four days, I came to see Gabriel at night for thirty minutes - thirty minutes I was looking forward to, especially since by day three, he could breathe by himself.

The book I had placed under his pillow was now resting on his side table. I wondered what his family thought about it, what Darlene might have thought about that book.

"You look better," I told him as I arranged his hair in the style I was used to seeing him wear. "I have been told you're healing well and that you should wake up any day." I sighed, sitting on the chair beside him. "At least this horrible situation had a good thing. My mom and I are getting closer. She comes with me every night, letting me do the night driving." I looked down at his hand and ran my fingertips back and forth on his knuckles. "She is not nagging me or anything. She waits in the cafeteria downstairs, drinking their dreadful coffee, and then we drive home, and she silently listens to what I am ready to share. We bonded over grief and ill-placed guilt. I guess it's good to have someone understand how I feel without having to explain all the time."

I looked at the clock and shook my head. I only had five minutes left. How did time just pass so fast when I was with

Gabriel? It felt like I only had time for a quick hello before my time was up.

"I miss you," I admitted, holding his hand just a little tighter. "I never thought I would miss your stupid grin or your all-knowing eyes and yet, I miss them more than anything. My mom says that missing someone is a way to say that you love them – I love you so much." I felt better letting those words out, knowing there would be no consequences.

On the fifth day, as I was getting ready for school, I received the text I had been waiting for, a text that made the now permanent weight on my chest ease just a little. Three little words sent by Doug. Three little insignificant words which meant everything to me. *"He is awake,"* it had said, nothing more.

I spent most of my day thinking of what to do with this information. He was going to be okay now, but what was I supposed to do? Was he angry at me? Would he blame me? Would he be upset if I went to see him? Or would we fall back into the same unhealthy pattern?

"Is your mother taking you to the hospital tonight?" Chago whispered as we sat down for lunch.

I shook my head and looked around the room as I assumed both Darlene and Doug were absent.

He frowned with confusion, leaning closer. "What happened?"

"He is awake," I answered, sliding my phone toward him and showing him Doug's text.

Chago jerked his head back in surprise. "That's great!" he exclaimed.

I nodded, biting into my sandwich. "Yes, fantastic."

Chago slid closer to me on the bench, crowding my space. "If I didn't know any better, I would say you couldn't care less, but I know you, Chula. I know how you feel, so you can let go of your 'fake it till you make it' with me; it's beyond insulting."

I sighed, putting my sandwich back on the table. "I am not sure of what to say to you, guapo. Am I happy he is awake? I am beyond happy, but what now? I can't go see him. I've seen his scars—scars which will remind him forever of the mistake we made, of the fact that when he asked me to wait, I ran and—" I shook my head, looking away. "What if I go and he doesn't want to see me? What if I go there and he is—no. I can't go."

Chago wrapped his arm around my neck and pulled my head to his. "I don't know how many times I will need to say this, but I will repeat it over and over again until you believe it. You are not to blame. You didn't do anything wrong. This is not your fault and you don't owe him or them anything."

I looked at his earnest face. "I will need to see him one day."

He kissed my forehead. "Yes, you do, but not before you're ready. Not before you feel the time is right."

I wondered if the time would ever be right.

CHAPTER 23

I opened my locker, my heart tightening yet again at the view of the discarded version of the Romeo and Juliet book Gabriel and I had exchanged.

I found it in my locker about a week after Gabriel had woken up. The only difference was that under my Juliet comment, there was an answer. The letters were a bit shaky, but I could still recognize Gabriel's handwriting. "*What if I've already found her?*" he had replied, and it took all my willpower not to go to the hospital.

He is lost and confused. He doesn't know where he stands. Let him heal and see how things are afterward, I kept repeating myself.

I knew I should have given the book back to Doug or gotten rid of it, but I couldn't, at least not yet. It was a reminder of our story. I was doing penance, paying for my many sins.

I hadn't had a real update on Gabriel's health since he had been discharged and sent home a week ago. Doug had told me that since Gabriel was not at the hospital anymore, I would have to go see him if I wanted to have some news. The problem was, I was not ready to face what my cowardice had caused. If only I had waited, if only I had answered that damned phone, he would never have tried to come to the Eastside and he would have never crossed the path of the—

A sharp knock on my locker's door brought me back to reality.

I closed it wearily and turned to face a pissed-off Doug.

"Yeah?" I asked, not sure why he looked so pissed.

"Are you ever going to go see him?" he hissed.

"Gabriel?"

"Who else?" he asked, pursing his lips.

I looked around, so used to being careful every time someone mentioned Gabriel. "I-I don't think I'll be welcome," I admitted, which was only half the truth. But after the scene I'd pulled at his father's office and everything that had happened to his family, I was sure I wouldn't be welcomed with open arms.

"He is not walking, but he could if he tried," Doug replied, completely ignoring my previous comment.

"What do you mean?"

"I mean he is wallowing in self-pity. He is in a dark place and nothing seems to reach him. But I'm sure you could. If anybody could reach him, it is you," he added, and I didn't miss the hope in his voice. Hope was only good to make you fall harder.

"And how do you know that?" I asked challengingly. "For all we know, he could hate me for involuntarily causing his accident and I wouldn't blame him for it."

"Because his mother said your name was the first thing he said when he got out of the coma. Because for the first few days I went to see him at the hospital, he asked me to take you along. Because—" He leaned against the locker beside mine with a weary sigh. "Because no matter what might have happened, he loves you."

I looked at him, mouth slightly agape with surprise.

He snorted. "I thought you loved him too. I guess I was wrong."

I slammed my locker shut and pointed an accusing finger at him. I didn't even mind the curious looks we were getting. "How dare you presume to know what I feel or not?! You know nothing!" I poked him in the shoulder with my finger. "There are many, *many* reasons I am not going, and you have no place—"

Doug caught my finger in his fist. "I don't care." He shook his head, keeping my finger in his grip. "I. Don't. Care," he repeated slowly and so calmly it was more concerning than if WHAT. "You are hurt?" He shrugged dismissively. "He is hurting more, so suck it up and just go… You owe him that much, don't you think?"

I opened my mouth to answer, but I was speechless at the harshness of his words. It was true what they said: nothing hurt more than the truth.

Doug looked at me for a couple of seconds before shaking his head and raising his hands up in surrender. "You know what? Do whatever the fuck you like."

He left me there, frozen in the corridor, trying to register all that happened.

It took a hard nudge from Chago to bring me back to reality. I looked around the now empty corridor. How long had I just stood here?

"Are you okay, Chula?" He took the textbook I was holding and put it in my bag.

"I need you to drive me somewhere." I turned around, looking at the exit. I had to do it before I changed my mind. "I need to go see Gabriel."

"I thought you were not ready." His voice was full of concern.

I smiled, but I knew it didn't reach my eyes. "I will never be ready, Guapo. We both know that." I took a deep breath. "Can you take me? I can call an uber if you don't want to miss class. I under—"

Chago raised his hand to stop me from speaking. "Nothing is more important than you, Chula." He picked up my bag from the floor before grabbing my hand. "Let's go."

As Chago parked his car in front of Gabriel's house, I took a deep, shaky breath before reaching for the handle.

"You don't have to do it if you don't want to." Chago shook his head, meeting my eyes. "You don't owe him—owe them—anything."

The harshness in his voice surprised me. I couldn't say he had been supportive of this relationship or whatever it had been, but in this situation, knowing what he knew… How could he be so cold?

Chago reached for my hand. "I don't," he growled. "You are my only concern, Chula, and I see how this is eating you up. You are obviously exhausted and worried. You don't deserve this guilt." He shook his head. "You've done nothing wrong."

I grimaced, looking out of the window. "I'm sure Darlene would not agree with that statement." I wiped my clammy palms on my jeans before finally opening the car door. "I have to do this. I need to do this for him and for me."

Chago nodded as if that made sense, but I was not even sure I was making sense to myself. "I'll wait for you."

I shook my head, reaching for my bag on the floor. "No, I am not sure how long I will be here for." I looked at the house before turning toward him again. "Go back to school. I'll be fine."

Chago looked at me, eyebrows knotted with uncertainty, hands tight around the steering wheel. "Chula, you don't have to do this alone."

I tried to smile. "Actually, yes I do." I walked to the door, head high, trying to muster as much confidence as I could for Chago's benefit.

I took a deep breath as I stood in front of Gabriel's door, trying to command my hands to stop shaking.

You can do it. It's not about you. He needs it. I rang the bell before thinking any longer than necessary out of fear of losing the little courage I had managed to muster.

Gabriel's mother opened the door, a slight frown of puzzlement settling on her face. I realized she didn't know who I was, not really. I had seen her quickly in the hospital the day Gabriel had had his accident, but she wouldn't remember me.

"I'm sorry to bother you. I'm Charlotte Miller and—"

Her face brightened with recognition. "You're his Lottie." She beamed, opening the door wider and inviting me in. "I hoped you would come."

I opened my mouth to correct her; I was not his Lottie—not anymore. I was not even sure I ever was.

I took the direction of the stairs, but her mother stopped me, resting a gentle hand on my arm.

"No, his—" She shook her head. "It would be too difficult for him to go upstairs." She pointed at the door down the corridor. "We've temporarily transformed my office into a room for him."

I nodded. I took a few steps toward the door, but stopped as my heart was hammering in my chest. I turned and met his mother's concerned eyes. "How is he doing?"

"He is in a dark place, and it looks like everything we do just angers him even more. He is my son and I don't know how to help him. I feel so helpless. Please, bring him back."

If I'd ever thought about changing my mind and walking away, the trembling of her voice and the weariness in her face stopped me from even considering it.

I gave a quick knock at the door.

"If you're waiting for an answer, you will stay outside a while." His mother jerked her head toward the door. "You better go in."

I walked in to find Gabriel in his wheelchair, his back to me as he stared aimlessly out of the window.

I waited a few seconds for him to turn around, but he didn't.

"Briel?" I called, taking a tentative step toward him.

He stiffened in his chair, his head jerking back ever so slightly— the only sign of his surprise.

"Have you finally decided to visit the crippled?" he asked, keeping his back to me.

"I came to see you at the hospital." I looked down at my clammy, shaky hands. I felt guilty for everything, but it was not the time to apologize. "But I was not welcome there. I was neither family or friend... I was nobody."

Gabriel turned slowly in his wheelchair. He looked the same and yet so different.

His hair was longer, curling on his collar; he was sporting the beginning of a beard partially hiding the angry red scar on his left cheek. His eyes had lost their usual spark. There was nothing there and the emptiness scared me much more than anything else.

"Why are you here? Did you come because you feel sorry for me?" He tried to sound angry, but the pain in his voice was unmistakable.

"No, I don't feel sorry for you. This is not what prevented me coming." I stopped, fearing I had already revealed too much.

His eyebrows shot up as his eyes widened in understanding.

"You feel guilty! You—" He moved his chair toward me.

I looked down at my hands, the guilt of putting him in this wheelchair wrapping its nefarious hands around my heart.

"Please tell me you don't actually think you've got anything to do with this? Please tell me it's not the reason you're here now," he begged and the despair in his voice made me lose the battle against my emotions.

I looked up, but my vision of Gabriel was blurry from tears. "The guilt is not what brought me here, Briel. It's what kept me away." I choked on my unshed tears. "It's hard to see one of the people who means the most to you being hurt because of you." I took a shaky breath as the ache in my chest made every breath challenging. "I understand why you're angry, why you would hate me. I—"

"I just—" He threw his head back, running his hands down his face. "No, Lottie, no! I could never hate you! I could never be mad at you – at least not for this." His voice was hoarse, his face a turmoil of emotions, which I suspected were mirroring mine. "It was that man's fault. He was drunk and he went through the red light. You had no hand in what happened."

I shook my head. He shouldn't be the one consoling me. "You wouldn't have been on that road if I had not been my usual cowardly self. If I had answered your calls instead of running away. If I'd just-"

"You are not a coward. You're a fighter." He rolled to his desk and retrieved a brown manila envelope from the first drawer. "You fight for everything and for others. You fight for people to have their dreams when they are just too weak to reach for them." He turned the envelope so I could see it was from Columbia.

I tried to keep my face blank as some excitement surged through me. The envelope was thick enough to be an acceptance letter.

"They have accepted me in their architecture curriculum."

"Why do you sound surprised?" I asked, sitting on the foot of his bed. "You are extremely talented. Columbia will be lucky to have you."

"I'm surprised because I didn't apply and also because-" He opened the envelope and retrieved the drawing he'd given me. "This was not in my possession anymore."

Applying for him had been easy, especially since I'd helped him with his other applications. "I believe in you, Briel. I've always believed in you even when you didn't believe in yourself. I wanted you to have the option; I wanted you to have the choice." I took a deep, shaky breath, looking at the drawing he was holding. "I didn't know the choice would be taken away from you and for that, I'm sorry."

A small smile tucked at his lips. "You're making it so hard to be angry with you!" he muttered with exasperation.

I looked at him in puzzlement. He'd said he didn't blame me for the way I'd acted when I'd bailed on him after I had promised to stay. "I don't understand." I chewed on my bottom lip, trying to put some order to my thoughts.

"You never came," he murmured before looking away, seemingly fascinated by what was happening outside.

"Came? Came where?" I stood up and walked around the bed to see his face better even if it was only his profile.

His eyes were shut, his jaws clenched, a deep furrow of concentration between his eyebrows.

"Gabriel?"

He opened his eyes, startled to hear me so close to him. He turned his face toward me, unable to hide the glistering in his eyes.

"See me. I waited, waited but you never came. Of all the people, you were the one I wanted to see the most," he admitted before clearing his throat and running his finger over his scarred cheek. "Don't you love me anymore? Is it because of this?" He pointed at his legs, his eyes full of anguish.

"I came!" I exclaimed, somehow offended by his assumption. How could he imagine I would be that shallow? The scars and the wheelchair didn't make me love him any less. "I was there the first day, but I was sent away by Darlene." I shook my head with a humorless laugh. "Not sure what I was expecting there to be fair. I was insignificant and – I believed it would be better to avoid any unnecessary drama. But I came," I admitted. "At night, I had a nurse smuggle me into your room. I came every night until you were out of the coma. Once I knew you would live…" I sat on the bed so close to him I could feel his body heat – boy did I miss this.

Gabriel looked at me in a sort of awe, making me self-conscious. "You still love me," he marveled.

"I what?" I cocked my head to the side, taken aback by his surprise. *When did this become a point of discussion?*

"You still love me," he repeated and the hope in his voice made me regret sitting so close.

"Love." I took a shaky breath. "Love has never been our problem."

Gabriel leaned in and I didn't realize what he was doing until his lips were on mine.

I jerked back quickly, resting my fingertips on my tingling lips. "No-" I croaked as my heart was hammering so hard in my chest it was physically painful. "This can't happen, not anymore, not ever."

"Is it Darlene?" he asked. "Because we're done. The day I woke up, I told her I was in love with someone else. I know I should have done it before and I'm sorry, but I'm yours now, Lottie." He grabbed my hand. "All yours."

"No," I whispered, removing my hand from his.

Gabriel's face distorted with pain and rejection. "Are you trying to punish me for what I did? Because I'm sorry, Lottie, sorrier than you think."

"I am not trying to punish you for anything." I shook my head. "You need to find out who you are, who you want to be. You've spent so much time being what you thought people wanted you to be, what you thought you were supposed to be, I don't think you know who you really are."

Gabriel sneered. "You've become a therapist too now?"

"No, but I see you're lost and confused. I had glimpses of the real Gabriel and all I can say is that he is spectacular!" I pointed to the sketchbook on his desk. "The passion you've put in your drawings, that shows your capacity to see the greatness in the world, to see the beauty." I reached to grab his hand before thinking better of it. He was still hurt about my earlier rejection. "Go to Physio. Don't give yourself excuses not to shine. I know it's scary."

"How would you know? You're not the one crippled on this chair!" he spat. "Is this why you don't want me anymore? Because I am a weight?"

I recoiled as if he had slapped me. I knew he couldn't think that, not really. But he wanted to hurt me as I'd hurt him, and I was ready to take it as long as it made him do the right thing. "Don't be stupid, Gabriel. This chair is irrelevant!" I replied coldly. "As for being crippled on that chair? No, I am not, and neither should you! I spoke with Doug. You've got about an eighty-five percent chance to walk again without help! Eighty-five percent! Do you know how many people in the hospital right now would kill for those odds? Do you know how many kids are fighting like warriors for their lives with much lesser odds?!"

"What if I give it all I have and it doesn't work? What if – What if..." I saw all the anger drain from his face, leaving an exhaustion well beyond his years.

"Then you will adapt. You will still be you, but you need to try. You won't be able to regret anything. If you give all you have, it's all you can. I can assure you, if you don't do it, you will wake up one day regretting not trying, and on that day, it will be too late."

"Regret it?" He looked down at the sketch resting on his knees and drew the pattern with the tip of his forefinger. "Regret it as I regret letting you walk out of the classroom that day? Regret it as I regret not owning my love for you? I love you, Lottie, maybe more today than I did before. I've realized how painful it is to lose you and I will never make the same mistake again."

His words hurt, hurt more than anything because they were words I had wanted to hear. But I knew that at this stage, we wouldn't be healthy for each other. He needed to heal, both physically and mentally, and I needed to let go.

"Just try, please. Just..." I ran a shaky hand through my hair. "You need to try."

Gabriel looked up and met my eyes, he just stared and strangely enough that silence was not awkward but somehow soothing. He was thinking, I could almost see the cogs turning and suddenly, the look in his eyes switched, from dreary weariness to sheer determination.

"Okay, I will try." He nodded as if he was still trying to convince himself. "But there will be a couple of conditions."

"Gabriel," I sighed resignedly. I couldn't let myself be sucked into this again.

"No, it's nothing like that," he reassured. And I realized it was still there, the connection. He could still read me like an open book. "Just promise you'll do it and I will go to physio, starting with my session today."

"Okay, I promise."

"I will go to the sessions only if you drive me there."

"But-"

Gabriel raised a finger to stop me. "And if I manage to walk in the next six weeks, you will come with me to senior prom and you will dance with me... as friends," he added quickly, but the excitation in his eyes illustrated his ulterior motives.

You don't owe him anything. I could hear Chago so clearly in my head and yet, I felt like I owed Gabriel that much. No matter what he said, what they all said – he had been on that road because of me, because of my ineptitude to face my bad choices. *The tragedy of us.*

"I don't have a car," I argued rather lamely. I didn't even need to mention that I'd just gotten my driving license and that his accident was a real setback for my anxiety issues.

Gabriel raised his voice ever so slightly. "I'm sure my mother will lend you one of the cars. Won't you mother?"

Confused, I turned toward the closed door. The room was silent for a moment and I was about to ask Gabriel why he'd spoken so loudly when his mother spoke.

"Yes, any car, any time," she replied.

I turned back to Gabriel, flushed with embarrassment as I realized his mother had been listening this whole time. "Was she there the whole time?"

Gabriel rolled his eyes. "I've lost all privacy when this happened. I think she is terrified I will try to kill myself or something."

213

"Will you?"

He shook his head, meeting my eyes. "So, Charlotte Miller, do we have a deal? We've always been good at making deals, don't you agree?"

I couldn't believe he'd done that to me – put me in charge, so I was liable for his health. I was somehow angry at him for putting me in this position, but I knew that, no matter what Chago or anyone would say, I had to deal with the consequences of my actions. I took a deep breath. I knew how to drive and the hospital was less than two miles away.

"Okay, I'll do it." I looked at my watch. "What time is your session today?"

"In thirty minutes," he replied and the victory in this face didn't predict anything good, but I owed it to the both of us to at least try.

"Okay." I stood up and wheeled him out of the room before I could chicken out.

His mother followed us to the driveway and mouthed a thank you as she handed me the keys to their Volvo.

"No," Gabriel growled as his mother leaned down to help him in the car. "I can do it and Lottie can help."

She took a step back, throwing me an apologetic glance. I wasn't sure what had happened between them, but I was not sure it was my place to investigate.

Gabriel wrapped his arm around my shoulders as I wrapped mine around his waist. I tried to concentrate on every gesture, the mechanics of it, and not on how warm his body felt against me or on how his stubble felt against the side of my face. I helped him up from his chair and into the car.

I folded the chair in the trunk and took my place in the driver's seat. I took a deep breath before inserting the keys in the ignition.

"You're going to do well, Lottie. I trust you," he encouraged as he adjusted himself in the seat.

"Maybe you shouldn't – I'm just –"

"Not confident?" he tried.

"Understatement of the year."

"You've passed the test. You can do it. The hospital is close by and if this –" he patted his leg - "can help you get over your fear, it will be something."

I didn't talk all the way to the hospital, concentrating too much on the road. My knuckles were white from grasping the steering wheel so hard. I knew I was driving painfully slow as what should have taken less than ten minutes, took over fifteen.

"We made it," I huffed once I parked close to the physio entrance.

Gabriel turned toward me and smiled. "I never doubted it."

"Don't worry. I doubted for both of us."

"Why were you so mean to her?" I asked after helping him in his chair.

Gabriel knew exactly whom I was talking about. "She is smothering me."

"She is trying to help you," I defended as we sat in the waiting room.

"I don't like it," he replied and the edge in his voice told me not to push it, but I decided to ignore it. If I had to be here with him, I wanted to shake things up.

"I'm helping you and you don't seem to mind," I insisted.

"It's because it's you, Lottie. You've always seen who I really was and I see that behind the guilt, you can still see me."

"Gabriel Johnson," someone called.

Gabriel raised his hand and started to wheel himself in the direction of the door as I followed him.

The young physio looked at him with his eyebrows arched in surprise. "Well, holy shit balls, you came!" he exclaimed with a half-smile which made me like him instantaneously. "I was losing hope man! Nine sessions you missed."

I scowled silently at Gabriel.

The physio concentrated on me. "Is it your doing?" He looked genuinely impressed. "Lots have tried, but I've rarely met someone as pig-headed and as hell-bent on self-destruction. What's your magical power?"

Gabriel twisted his head and met my eyes. I was not sure what he'd expected me to say. "I think I am good at showing him parts of himself he is not very good at uncovering alone."

The physio snorted, but moved from his spot in front of the door, silently inviting us into the room.

Gabriel started to go forward, but stopped and half turned toward me with an apologetic look on his face.

"Lottie, I-" He twisted his mouth into an uncertain grimace. "Would you mind waiting for me here, please? I just – I don't want you to see this."

I took a step forward and leaned down. "You know I won't think any less of you, don't you?" I whispered, somehow hurt by his lack of confidence.

"I know, but I will – Please, Lottie."

I sighed, straightening up. "Of course." I pointed at the chair just across the door. "I will be right here waiting for you."

"It has nothing to do with who you are, my Lottie, and everything to do with me," he insisted, probably seeing the hurt on my face.

I nodded, forcing a smile. "As long as you are here."

He nodded his gratitude and wheeled himself into the room.

I read a magazine for about twenty minutes before the physio came out and sat beside me.

"Gabriel?" I asked, not able to conceal the dread in my voice.

"He is fine. He is in the pool now with the other physio." He smiled at me. "I wanted to have a quick word with you about what happened before."

"I don't-"

"He didn't reject you when he went in alone, you know that, right?"

I shrugged. "It doesn't matter."

"It does though," he pressed, keeping his eyes locked with mine. "I've been trying to get through to him since he woke up from the coma. Everybody tried to get through to him and yet, you're the one who got him here. You know in there -" the physio pointed at the door - "it's painful, it's hard, and it makes him feel weak. That boy used to be all-powerful, an athlete. It's hard for him… When something he used to consider easy looks impossible. You know, everyone has, or will, experience something that will change them in such a way that they could never go back to the person they once were. Gabriel experienced that when he had this accident."

"He will walk again," I assured him. I knew Gabriel maybe better than he knew himself. He needed to acknowledge the fact of what had happened and own it. I shrugged. "He needed to have a purpose bigger than himself."

"And what is that purpose?" he asked curiously.

"That I can't really say." 'Me' was the most logical answer, but it would have been the most narcissistic and destructive answer I could have given. Destructive for the both of us. I didn't want to be the main character in his story. I couldn't afford to lose myself in him again.

"He has the drive; I can see the determination in his eyes. Whatever you did or said, it worked."

"Thank you," I replied, not sure it could truly convey the pure relief and hope that settled into my chest in this moment.

I waited another twenty minutes for Gabriel. When he came out, his face was tight with tiredness and pain. I decided it was better to be a silent supporter and just be here if he wanted to talk.

Gabriel was silent the entire drive back, keeping his eyes on the road. I glanced at him every time we stopped at a traffic light. I could see his jaw clench and unclench at the rhythm of his dark thoughts.

I knew I should have just let him deal with whatever was bothering him, but no matter what I said or wanted to do, his pain was my pain. "You can't expect to succeed at the first try, you know."

He didn't answer, but his jaw relaxed. I was spot on.

"It will take time and effort, but it will be much more rewarding."

"It's more painful than I thought it would be," he admitted, brows furrowed while he subconsciously rubbed his left leg.

"I can't even imagine, but I would do anything to make you feel better. But not everything in life comes easy, Briel. I know you are strong enough to face it. You never know how strong you can be until being strong is the only choice left."

"You should work for Hallmark, you know." I knew he wanted to be sarcastic, but his remark lacked bite. He knew I was right.

And for the next three weeks, four times a week, I drove Gabriel to physio, waited for an hour, and drove him back home. We talked about a lot of things, but stayed away from the subject of us. Gabriel had accepted his spot at Columbia and I couldn't help the little pinch of sorrow that seized me when he told me.

It was what was supposed to happen. It was what I'd wanted and yet, knowing I wouldn't see him any more hurt deeply.

At the end of the third week, when Dan the physio opened the door, I expected him to come to chat with me for a few minutes and give me a quick update on Gabriel's progress. Instead, he smiled brightly, victory written all over his face as he gestured me in.

"There is someone who wants to ask you something," he joked as I walked into the room.

I glanced around the room and stopped when I saw Gabriel standing in the back of the room with only a crutch to help him stand.

I brought a hand to my chest as my breath caught in my throat. I took a quick step toward him.

"No." He shook his head, stopping me in my tracks. "I am coming to you," he added with his brows furrowed in determination.

His steps were slow, calculated, and a bit choppy, but he was walking. At that moment, it was probably the most beautiful thing I had ever seen, and I could not contain the tearless sob from escaping as he stopped in front of me.

"I am so very proud of you, Gabriel," I whispered with emotion. I had to use all my willpower to stop myself from pulling him into a hug.

He smiled brightly, towering over me. "I kept my part of the deal, so now, Charlotte Miller, will you come to prom with me?"

Did he even know the pain that question put me in? Had he even guessed that I loved him just as much as before – maybe even more so? I sucked in my bottom lip while thinking of all the reasons why this was one of the worst ideas. I looked up and saw that his eyes were darkening as he stared at my lips. *'Don't bite that lip. Let me do it for you. It will be much more enjoyable for the both of us, I promise,'* he had said to me once, and I could see in his eyes that it was exactly what he was thinking now.

I nodded. "Of course, I would love to go with you."

He smiled even brighter and before I could think better of it, I pulled him into a hug.

Gabriel pulled me even tighter against him, resting his cheek on top of my head. "Also, don't worry. Dan said that if I continue this way, the crutch will be gone by prom."

"I don't mind the crutch. I don't mind it at all." I closed my eyes for a few seconds, enjoying the moment - being in his strong arms and forgetting what had happened and where he was going. Just being here with him now was everything.

He turned his face and kissed the top of my head. "I love you so much, Lottie," he whispered so low I could have almost imagined it. My only answer was to hug him just a little tighter.

CHAPTER 24

"This is so stupid!" I shouted with exasperation, scowling at my reflection in the mirror.

I turned around, almost twisting my ankle in the stupidly high heels and looked at my mother and Chago sitting on my bed. "No, but seriously?!" I pointed at the dress I was wearing.

My mother looked puzzled as Chago shrugged.

"Don't see the problem here, Chula… This dress is spectacular." He turned toward my mother. "You picked well."

My mom smiled at him. "I've been told you can never go wrong when you pick a Madison James dress."

Chago nodded as if he knew what she meant.

I rolled my eyes, huffing in frustration. When had these two decided to become best friends and gang up on me?

I turned to the mirror again, detailing the purple scoop neck A-line long sleeveless prom dress with a beaded waist that my mother had brought home yesterday. "This is really…. really…. promlike." I grimaced at the stupidity of this statement.

"Okay…." My mother trailed off. "I thought it was where you were going tonight."

"No, I'm, yes." I turned around again to face them. "It's not like that. It's not my prom. It's senior prom. It's a promise to a friend. It's not a date. It's not a date," I repeated, trying to convince myself as much as I was trying to convince them.

My mother's face softened with understanding as Chago's smile disappeared from his face.

"It still counts, honey. You still have to make it count." She stood up and came to stand behind me to work on my hairdo.

"It's his first big return to school, Chula, and it's not like they'll be surprised to see you walk in with him."

I pursed my lips, remembering the rumor that had spread around school a little over two weeks ago. It seemed that one student had seen Gabriel and I in the hospital when I'd taken him to physio, looking cozy. Even though he didn't need the cane anymore, I still had to give Gabriel my arm for support as we walked. Part of me wasn't sure he needed it, but I'd enjoyed the contact too much to say anything.

When I'd arrived at school the next day, I hadn't missed the sidelong glances, the 'hellos' and smiles of people I had never even spoken to before. It had all become clear when Doug had come to my locker, telling me that my relationship with Gabriel had been outed.

I'd wanted to deny it, but what would have been the point? People were not interested in the truth and part of it was true. Only the timeline was flawed, but at least with this rumor, I was not a homewrecker.

What had surprised me the most was that Darlene had never confronted me, had never tried to get revenge. She hadn't even looked at me and I hadn't complained.

I took a deep breath, fumbling with the necklace I was wearing.

"I'll be at the café down the road with Eva. I'll be a phone call away, Chula. If it gets too much for you or for him, just call, si?"

I nodded, giving him a grateful smile. I glanced up at the clock. We had to pick up Gabriel in less than thirty minutes.

"Okay, let's go before I change my mind," I growled, reaching for my shawl and bag.

"Give us a minute, please, Santiago," my mother requested, adjusting the shawl on my shoulders.

"No problem. Chula, I'll be in the car. Take your time."

"You know it's not my actual prom, right? You are a year too early for the whole 'my baby grew up so fast' speech."

She rested her hands on my shoulders and squeezed ever so lightly with a sad smile on her face. "But you did grow up too fast. You've grieved much more than you should have." She shook her head, forcing a smile. "You're so pretty, Charlotte. So driven by this sense of right and wrong, but you've learned that life is not always that way."

"What are you trying to say?" I asked, getting restless.

"I am trying to say that no matter what you think should be done, what you think is right – You have to do what makes you happy. Don't be afraid to be who you are, to feel what you feel." She squeezed my shoulders a bit harder and kissed my forehead. "Love as you want to be loved," she simply added before letting go of me and putting away her make up as if nothing had happened.

I leaned down and took my shoes off. "Health hazard these, let me tell you," I joked, trying to ease the sadness I saw in my mother's face despite her trying to hide it.

"But honey, they're Louboutin!" she teased, playing along.

When I made it to the car, Chago was on the phone with Eva.

"Okay, ready to go pick up Prince Charming?" he asked as soon as I sat beside him. "Don't you think the Mexican driver is a bit cliché?"

I gave him a withering look, making him laugh out loud. "It's too easy to wind you up. I love it!"

"We'll see if you still love it with my high heel shoved up your ass!"

He winked, but reached for my hand. "I love you, Chula."

"I love you too…. most days," I admitted begrudgingly. My heart started to race in my chest the closer we got to Gabriel's house.

"It's only one night, Chula, you know that, right?" Chago said as we turned onto Gabriel's street.

"But it isn't, not really. It's not just a night between two friends. It doesn't matter how much I've tried to convince myself that it is. There is too much love to be innocent."

Chago quickly glanced at the clock before parking a couple of houses down from Gabriel's. "We have a few minutes to spare." He turned on his seat to face me. "If there is that much love and if not being with him makes you miserable, why don't you give in? We both know you just have to say the word and he will be yours again. I don't even know the guy well, but the couple of times I've seen him recently, there's longing in his eyes every time he looks at you when you are not looking. He is desperately in love with you."

"It's not that simple." I shook my head stubbornly.

"Actually, it kind of is," he insisted.

I shook my head again.

Chago let out an exasperated sighed. "Eres tan obstinada!"

"Look who's talking! I'm not more pig-headed than you are!" I cleared my throat. "You want the truth?"

"Yes!" he exclaimed, throwing his hands up in relief. "Well, at least as much truth as you can give me in -" he glanced at the clock on the dashboard - "seven minutes."

I took a deep breath, ready to unleash the Kraken of my confused mind. "Tell me what changed, guapo? From the moment I found out he'd slept with his girlfriend after sleeping with me? Tell me what is different from the moment he wrote me his love note the morning after and yet, didn't even acknowledge me in the school corridors on the same day?"

Chago's jaw locked, his lips pursed in a fine line, his nostrils flaring. I knew he was pissed as he was finding out, for the first time, the extent of our screwed-up relationship.

"Now can you tell me without a shadow of a doubt, that if he'd managed to drive to your house to discuss things or if I hadn't run away and instead waited until our discussion, that I would still be the one he would be taking to prom? That he would be following his dream and going to Columbia? Or would it have been the more sordid and more likely scenario, where he would have told me that once the year was over, once he was at college, that things would be different and that we would be free to be together? Can you tell me he wouldn't be in a car with Darlene, while I would be wallowing in self-pity with an extra-large tube of ice cream? Tell me Chago...can you?" I challenged.

Chago twisted on his seat, facing the road again. "No," he growled.

I nodded, not surprised by his answer. "I have been trying to convince myself otherwise from the moment I'd taken him to the hospital, but I can't. And doubt like this weight of uncertainty?" I shrugged. "It would destroy us even more. It will get ugly and I don't want this to happen. I'd rather keep it as a sweet memory."

Chago gave a sharp nod before putting the car into gear. He stopped in Gabriel's driveway less than a minute later.

"So, Cinderella, are you going to look for Prince Charming or should I?" he sneered pointing at the door.

"Chago, not now," I sighed with weariness, regretting opening up to him today.

"Do you really expect me not to react after telling me what you told me?" he asked, glowering.

"No, but not today. You can argue tomorrow. You can be mad tomorrow, but not today, Guapo, please. Not today."

Chago growled, rubbing his jaw. He still glowered at Gabriel's door, but I assumed his silence was a reluctant agreement.

I took a deep breath as I walked to Gabriel's door, but I didn't have time to overthink anything as the door opened to Gabriel's mother's squeals.

"Oh, Charlotte you look stunning!" she marveled, resting her hand on her heart.

"Thank you, Mrs. Johnson." I couldn't help but blush at her compliment.

"I really think it's time for you to call me Samantha! Please, come in. I want to take a few photos of the two of you." She gestured me in, her wide smile still plastered on her face.

I glanced at Chago who still had a scowl on his face, but he was now on the phone. I was pretty sure it was to Eva. If anyone was able to smooth that scowl, it had to be her.

As I walked in, Gabriel was coming down the stairs, his steps only ever so slightly stiffer than they ought to be. When he looked up and met my eyes, we both froze. He was absolutely stunning in his tuxedo.

His hair was slicked and parted at the side in a hairdo that seemed to be out of a fifties movie. He was clean shaven and the scar on his cheek made him even more beautiful than he ever was.

He looked me up and down, and my pulse quickened under the appreciation in his eyes.

"Lottie, you are…" He shook his head before pulling me into a hug and holding me tighter than friendship should allow. "You are the most beautiful thing I have ever seen," he whispered, quickly kissing the hollow behind my ear before letting me go.

"You're not bad yourself," I whispered breathlessly as his kiss overtook all my senses. I tried to avoid his eyes, not wanting him to see how he affected me. I looked at his bow tie, which was the exact same shade as my dress.

I tucked at it gently. "We're matching… How did you know?"

"That's a secret I'll never tell." He nudged me before wrapping his arm around me and twirling me around to face his mother's camera.

Gabriel's father was standing behind his mother, his usual stern look on his face. I held his eyes even if part of me was mortified over the breakdown I'd had in his office.

He gave me a quick nod and I didn't miss the respect in his eyes. Maybe fighting for his son had helped me gain some respect.

Gabriel's mother took so many photos, I was sure I would never see properly again.

"Come on, Mother. It's time to let us go now." He reached for my hand and intertwined our fingers. "We can't be allowed to be fashionably late." He turned toward me with such a bright smile, his green eyes shining with such happiness my heart tightened almost painfully in my chest. "And I think my Lottie is going blind."

I nodded mutely, not trusting my voice right now. This had been a mistake. I was so sure it had been the right decision, that he had to go find himself, and that if I ever wanted us to be together, I would have to let go of my doubts. But right now, I was just so close to kissing him senseless and destroying every painful choice I had made in the last few months.

"But you two are just so beautiful together. Just one more!" She snapped one more shot as I was looking up at Gabriel's profile. I wondered what that photo would show? My love? My pain? My doubts? Maybe all of them mixed in one.

"Sorry, I couldn't drive us," he apologized as we walked to the car. "I'm taking short drives with the driving instructor, but sadly my reflexes are not yet good enough for me to risk it – to risk you."

I shrugged dismissively. "I think it's much better to be chauffeured anyway. Come on, lets both sit in the back."

I opened the door, but before I had time to step in, Gabriel pulled me toward him. Wrapping his arm around my waist, he kept his eyes locked with mine. "I meant it, you know. You look stunning. Lottie, I lo-"

Chago honked twice. "Vamonos!" he shouted and I rolled my eyes, but I was grateful he'd stopped Gabriel because I would have told Gabriel I loved him too.

"How are you, Chago?" Gabriel asked with a smile as he settled in beside me.

Chago glared at him through the rear-view mirror. "Si supiera entonces lo que sé ahora ... habría cortado los frenos de tu coche," he growled.

"You know, I don't speak Spanish, but if his tone and glare are any indications, I don't think he said, 'Hi Gabriel, it's good to see you.'"

I chuckled and shook my hand dismissively. *No, he said 'If I knew then what I know now, I would have cut the brakes on your car'.*

"He is just playing the role of the angry driver. Aren't you, guapo?" I met his glare with one of my own. "We wouldn't want anybody regretting opening up now, would we?" I asked pointedly, pursing my lips with disapproval.

Chago sighed and broke the glaring match first. I had won. "We're going to pick up Eva on our way, si? We're going to the movies and then will go for some food at Denny's. Just text me when you need a ride home."

<u>CHAPTER 25</u>

Gabriel asked Chago to leave us by the main entrance of the school instead of the gym.

"Why did you want him to leave us here?" I asked, straightening his bow tie.

He looked down and seemed to notice my impossibly high heels for the first time. "I'm so sorry, Lottie! I didn't think about your feet. Are you going to be okay?" he asked with genuine concern.

I turned around and looked at the gym's door about three hundred yards away before turning toward him with an amused smile. "Well, one way to find out." I gripped his hand. "No, but seriously, why?"

He grabbed my other hand and we stood there silently facing each other for what seemed like an eternity even if it couldn't have been more than a few seconds. "Because I'm not quite ready to go in yet," he admitted. "Because I haven't seen most of them in almost three months, because no matter what, I'm different – much more different than a few scars will ever show, and because I know that once we will walk through those doors, it will be the beginning of the end for us. You made me a promise and you are keeping it, but after tonight…. There is no certainty." He squeezed my hands as the anguish he felt was reflected in the curve of his mouth, the darkening of his eyes. "I'm just not ready to say goodbye."

I could tell him that nobody knew what tomorrow was made of. Give him hope we were not on borrowed time, but that wouldn't have been fair, even for one night. "You can't delay the future, Briel. Time doesn't stand still and neither can we." I let go of one of his hands and tugged at the other. "Come on, Gabriel Johnson, the seniors are waiting for their Prom King."

As we approached the gym, a couple of students who were outside rushed in, probably to announce our arrival.

Gabriel stopped in front of the door and took a deep breath before gripping my hand tighter. "Here goes nothing."

As soon as we walked into the gym, the chatter died and the silence was overwhelming. Gabriel smiled, but his grip on my hand tightened painfully, the only sign of his discomfort.

The crowd broke into applause and cheers. I tried to take a step back, to let him enjoy the moment, but he pulled me even closer and I had no other choice but to plaster a fake smile on my face and be there for him.

I scanned the room and saw Darlene beside one of the football players. He looked down with clear guilt on his face. I guess we now knew who Darlene's side man was.

Gabriel accepted all the nice words, the taps on the back. I felt like Jackie O during the election campaign.

I got bored after a few minutes and tuned out the conversation, looking around the room for Logan. After a few minutes, I found him by the deejay table. I was happy to see Matt with him. He'd finally stepped away from self-destruction. Logan turned at that moment and we shared a smile, a smile which said we were okay and that he was not angry anymore that I had hidden my involvement with Gabriel from him.

Gabriel probably noticed my boredom because he pulled me closer. "Let's dance," he whispered against the shell of my ear.

"Are you sure?" I asked, glancing at his legs with concern.

"With you? I could dance forever. Come on, Lottie."

By the third song, Gabriel got a little stiffer. I looked up and saw a small frown between his eyebrows.

"Are you hurting?" I asked, stopping in the middle of the dance floor.

He shrugged, pulling me closer to him. "I just want to enjoy this a little longer."

I raised my hand, patting his chest. "I need a little break anyway and your teammates are looking at us like kicked puppies. Go talk to them for a while. I will be back in a bit, okay?" I pointed toward the hall. "I need to go to the bathroom."

Gabriel nodded with a small smile. "You'll know where to find me." He brought his hand up and brushed my cheekbone with his knuckles. "Don't be too long."

"I promise." I forced a smile as my cheek tingled from his touch. I couldn't help but wonder if his touch would ever stop affecting me.

The queue for the women's restroom was enormous. Thanks to my earlier community work imposed by Ms. Burton though, I knew there was another bathroom in the back of the gym.

I let out a little yelp of victory when I found the small two cubicles restroom empty.

I was washing my hands when Darlene entered and rested her back on the door.

I straightened up, squaring my shoulders, showing her I was neither impressed nor scared and that I would be able to take her down if I needed to.

I was actually surprised it had taken her so long to come and confront me about Gabriel. After the rumors had started about Gabriel and I, I'd expected drama, but she had remained suspiciously silent.

"I am not here to fight," she admitted, raising her hands. "I know being cornered like this doesn't look good, but Doug and your Mexican friend did an excellent job keeping me away from you until now."

I relaxed a little, but kept a defensive stance.

She looked down at her red nails before looking up at me with resignation on her face. "He looks well."

I nodded mutely, trying to figure out where she was going with this.

"He-" She twisted her mouth to the side. "He looks at you in ways he never looked at me," she admitted reluctantly. "Never…" She took a deep breath and shook her head as if she was having some internal debate. "I knew it was you…I always knew."

I cocked my head to the side, still not sure what I could say to her. "I am not sure I understand."

She rolled her eyes. "Please. I knew you were the girl he loved. I knew it from the night he'd won the championship."

The night he slept with you. The pain of that discovery was just as overwhelming today as it has been on the first day.

"I knew who you were when you came to the hospital. I wanted to humiliate you just the way he'd humiliated me when he'd decided to love you instead of me."

"How?"

"At least you're not insulting me further by denying it." She took a deep breath, resting her hands on her hips. "We had an after-game party at my house and Gabriel just disappeared. I'd found him in one of the guest rooms sitting on the floor, leaning against the bed and looking out of the window. He was holding a half-empty bottle of whiskey." She rolled her eyes. "He was so drunk when I found him. He'd kept repeating he had been waiting for his Lottie, that the only person he'd wanted to witness his win hadn't been there. He'd told me how much he loved his Lottie, and how both angry and sad he was that she didn't care." She snorted, rolling her eyes again. "Lottie, Lottie, Lottie…"

"Why are you telling me all this?" It didn't fit her character; she was basically telling me that someone preferred me to her.

"Because he never looked at me the way he looks at you, because I realized I never really knew him, and because Doug told me that my lie broke you up, and maybe caused the accident."

I frowned. "What lie?"

She let out a humorless laugh. "Gabriel never slept with me that night. He only thinks he did. He was just so drunk, I got him naked and when the party was over, I joined him in bed." She shrugged. "I thought it would maybe help him stay with me until prom." She glared, pointing an accusing finger at me. "Hey, don't look at me all judgy on your high horse! You're just as much of a cheating bitch as I am."

I tried to smooth my features. My facial expressions had the habit to get me into trouble.

"But he'd started to freak out, like he'd done something horrible and then when you walked into the restroom at school, it all made sense. I realized it was you, so I told Bethany what I'd told Gabriel. I wanted you to hear, to feel pain."

"Thank you." I knew it had to cost her to admit that and I didn't want to rub it in.

She shrugged again, adjusting the bow on her dress. "Karma points, you know." She moved from the door. "Now you better go before he sends the swat team to find you. I need to freshen up my make-up before being crowned Prom Queen."

She turned toward the mirror, opening her clutch bag and just like that, I had vanished from her universe.

When I went back into the room, I found Gabriel looking around. It was an advantage to be with someone who was tall.

"Are you okay?" He rested his hands on my shoulders, idly rubbing them with his thumbs.

"Yes, why?"

"You've been gone long. I missed you." He kissed my forehead before reaching for my hand. "Come on, let's go dance some more. My legs are okay now."

"I was there." I blurted out as we started to dance.

He pulled back a little, keeping his hold around my waist. "Where?"

I looked up, meeting his curious eyes, which seemed even greener under the light. We were swaying softly at the sound of the music. I was not sure we were in rhythm, but I knew neither of us cared.

"At your game. I was there. I saw you win and score that beautiful goal."

His hand tightened, his fingers digging into my back almost painfully. "I never knew." His voice broke and I could barely hear him over the music. "Why didn't you show yourself? Things would have been different," he stammered, pulling me even closer. "I wouldn't have lost you."

I cocked my head to the side, not able to stop a tender smile from spreading across my face. Hadn't he realized that our relationship had been fizzling for a while? I knew he had not been the only one to blame; I had been burying my head in the sand, pretending we were okay. "I couldn't stay away. I needed to see you win."

He took a deep breath. "I love you so damn fucking much, Lottie."

"I love you too," I admitted and surprise lit up his face.

He bent down to kiss me and I knew I would have let him do it, but my saving grace came when the Principal took his place on stage to announce the prom king and queen.

Without surprise, Gabriel and Darlene won. Gabriel squeezed my hand, giving me a longing look before walking to the stage.

I kept my eyes on his retreating back, finally realizing that this was really the end. I was leaving in two days with my mother on a family holiday. It was the first time in more than five years that we'd vacationed together. I also suspected she was taking me away for another reason. When we got back, he would be gone, and then what?

"You look like your heart is breaking in your chest."

I looked up, startled to see Mulligan standing beside me. He looked down, giving me a sad smile.

I shrugged, looking ahead. "My mom asked you to keep an eye on me tonight, didn't she?"

"She loves you, and she is worried. Can you blame her?"

I shook my head as I looked at Gabriel getting his crown. "No, I can't but it's life... young love. It's supposed to end." I almost wanted to add that he should have known that better than anyone as my mother had left him for my father.

"It doesn't have to be. You don't have to let him go."

I let out a humorless laugh. "Come on, aren't you supposed to say that we're only teenagers? That we don't really know what love is and that we all think that our first love is the only love we'll ever have?"

"But sometimes it is true. Sometimes, your first love is the only love you'll ever have."

I looked up at his profile. As he kept staring at the stage, I realized that he was talking about my mother. No matter how much my mother had loved my father, Mulligan had always loved her.

I grabbed his hand and gave it a quick squeeze. "If it's supposed to ever happen, we will get a second chance." I took a deep breath as Gabriel smiled at Darlene as she received her own crown. "Please tell my mother she doesn't need to be afraid to tell me you two are dating. I am happy for both of you and she has every right to start living again. I know she is forgetting my father by being with you." All this talk was getting to me and I felt myself caving. I could see myself changing my mind, asking Gabriel to stay or wait for me. I shook my head. Mulligan was trying to help, but he was giving me a hope that couldn't be... *Arbol que nace torcido jamas su rama endereza.* "If you'll excuse me."

Mulligan just stood there, probably frozen by the shock of my revelation.

I found Doug in the crowd as Gabriel and Darlene were dancing the traditional prom couple dance.

I grabbed his shirt and pulled him down so his ear was leveled with my mouth. "I have to go. Can I trust you to get him home safely?"

Doug pulled back, scrutinizing my face as he nodded his agreement.

"Don't look for something that is not there. Just – See you around."

I got my phone out and texted Chago as I tried to walk efficiently to the main entrance on killer heels.

"Lottie, stop!" Gabriel shouted just as I reached the main entrance.

I turned around and saw him hurrying toward me, limping much more than usual. Yeah, this evening had really taken a toll on him.

"This is how you were going to leave it?" he asked with incredulity. He winced as he rubbed his thigh.

"You better sit down." I pointed at the wooden bench by the entrance. "You really overdid yourself tonight."

He threw his hand up, tightening his lips in both pain and anger. "You were just going to leave me? You said you loved me and you just – leave?."

"I promised you an evening and the evening is ending, Gabriel. You have your future and I have mine."

"Why can't it be ours? Why-" He looked up at the sky for a second, taking a deep breath. "Why don't you stop being scared and – Why is it hurting so fucking much if we're actually doing the right thing?"

His eyes were glistening as he took a step closer to the light.I realized that he was trying to fight tears.

"Donde hay amor, hay dolor," I whispered, not able to stop the quiet tears from falling. "Where there is love, there is pain. Sometimes you just have to love people enough to let them go no matter how much it hurts."

Chago stopped the car beside me and I was pleased that Eva was not in it. I was on the verge of breaking down and I didn't need an unnecessary witness.

I quickly pulled Gabriel toward me and kissed him. "Never be ashamed to shine, Gabriel Johnson, never be afraid to show the world your greatness. Never be afraid to be the amazing man you are becoming."

"I will get you back, Charlotte Miller. One day you will be mine and when that day comes, I will never, ever let you go again."

I gave him a last look before getting into the car. I watched his retreating form in the side mirror, hoping that he was right - that one day I could get past the poison of doubt and that he would still want me then. I wished that one day I would not be scared. I would let him have me back and that, true to his words…he would never let me go.

EPILOGUE – 1 year later

Gabriel's POV

I sighed, sitting on the window bench of the loft I was living in. My father had kept his word and had bought me this loft close to Columbia.

Charlotte had been right. Some things had just needed to be said to him. He needed to understand what I was all about in order to not repeat the mistakes of the past all over again.

Well, this confrontation would have never happened if it wasn't for Lottie. She'd stood straight and proud in front of him, pleading my case and doing all the things I should have done, saying all the things I should have said. She had always been so much stronger than I. It was not obvious when people looked at us… If only they knew. If only she knew how much I needed her, how much I loved her… How the feelings she'd told me would fade had kept on growing.

"Lottie…" I whispered, closing my eyes and resting my forehead against the glass. It had been almost a year since I'd last seen her. It seemed like she was a fragment of my imagination, a beautiful dream I'd had and refused to let go.

I opened my eyes and looked down at the row of black and white photos we'd taken, what seemed to be, a lifetime ago. I couldn't help but smile despite the aching in my chest as I looked at our happy faces. It was one of the only tokens that proved the relationship had been real, that she had chosen to be with me for a time. A time when I'd still been her superhero, a time when she'd looked at me not as the man I was pretending to be, but as the man she knew I could become.

I'd truly thought that with time, I would start missing her less, but truth be told, I missed her even more. Some simple things would just come up and the pain would be back just as real as when she'd left me on the curb at prom. I felt like an exposed nerve that some little things could just inflame. Just last week I'd gone out with some other freshmen and a song from Kate Voegele had started to play. It had taken me back to the open mic night when I still hadn't realized how lucky I was to have her in my life.

If I'd known then what I knew now, I would have run on that stage and kissed her senseless. It had hurt me so deeply to hear just a simple song, I'd gone back to my loft. My love for her hadn't faded. It had grown. I guessed it's true what they say: *we only realize what we had, once we lose it.*

My mind often wandered back home, thinking of her, what she was doing, how she was feeling, if she was letting go of me or falling in love with someone else.

Thinking of her being in love with someone else made me physically sick. I would eventually go back. I would see her again. How could I ever see her happy with another man? Watching from the sidelines? I shook my head, trying to get the ugly picture of her wrapped in Chago's brother's arms out of my head. I wouldn't be able to bear it. I knew I wouldn't.

I growled with frustration, getting up from my spot on the window sill and walking to the desk where the '*Congratulations for your Graduation*' card I'd bought for her, but had never sent was resting.

She'd graduated two days ago. I'd wanted to go, wanted to see that so badly, but there was no need to remind her of me. If she had let go, I couldn't blame her. That was also why I'd accepted the summer-long internship at the best architects office in town.

I loved her enough to let her go. I loved her enough to not torment her with my feelings.

Since I'd left for New York last August, I'd only run into her once. It had been at the end of my Christmas holidays, and I had seen that, back then, it had hurt her as much as it had hurt me. I had seen in her grey eyes the love she was trying so hard to hide.

I was not stupid. I knew she had been avoiding me. Or maybe it was a way for life to show us we were better apart.

When I went home for Thanksgiving, I tried to '*run*' into her from day one. I had prepared everything I wanted to tell her: how much I missed her, that parting was a bad idea, that I was willing to make this work even if we were three thousand miles apart, that none of it really mattered, and if she wanted me, I would transfer to the college of her choice. But unfortunately, I didn't get a chance to say anything because she had left for Mexico with Chago. I tried to do the same over Christmas, but she'd left with her mother and Mr. Mulligan to reconnect with her mother's family.

I had given up on seeing her, but the day before I was due back, I met her outside of Starbucks. We shared banalities and talked about the weather. All I had meant to tell her stayed stuck in my throat. I saw she was already hurt and lost, that her guards were up. What good would it have done to tell her I ached for her every minute of every day? I would get on my flight anyway and she would stay here, her head full of doubts.

No matter how much I wanted the pain to ease, hers and mine, I couldn't help but keep up with her life through my old friends. Who would have thought Doug and the others would end up rooting for us? I knew Stanford had accepted both Chago and Charlie. I felt both proud and pained about that. I was proud because she'd gotten what she wanted and pained because it meant three more years away. I knew even if I ever got back home, it would be too late. Charlotte 'Charlie' Miller would not be mine anymore, but I knew Lottie, that small part of her, would always be mine as Briel would always be hers.

I looked at the clock in the kitchen, shaking my head. I still had one exam to take and I needed to concentrate on that, at least for a little while. A trip to the library would ease my mind. The only time I was not thinking of her was when I was studying, which was why I was spending most of my free time with my head buried in my books. On the bright side, it had helped me ace all of my classes and get that prestigious internship we had all fought for. I would have the whole summer to mope over having lost my Lottie. I put the pictures back on the fridge with the little guitar magnet I'd bought one day because it had made me think of her.

I was about to go to the bathroom when my phone started to ring. I looked at it idly despite knowing I would ignore it anyways. Except the name flashing on the screen made my heart jump in my chest. 'Lottie'. I reached for the phone with such a rush that it almost slipped out of my hands.

"Hello?" I answered breathlessly.

"Hey, Briel. Am I catching you at a bad time?"

"No, of course not." I closed my eyes as the pain in my chest eased immediately. It felt so good to hear her say my name, to hear her voice.

"I wanted to tell you I graduated."

"I know. I've heard." I smiled sadly. "I bet you were gorgeous in your graduation gown." I knew she had been gorgeous in her graduation gown. Doug had sent me photos. He had also sent me photos of them going to prom together. Part of me was quite pleased Doug had had to retake his senior year because even if he would never admit it, I knew he'd purposely cockblocked any potential boyfriend.

"Yeah…" She trailed off. I could almost picture her biting her bottom lip like she did when she was thinking. "I've been accepted to Stanford too," she added with a small voice.

I nodded stupidly as if she could see me. At the same moment someone knocked at my door, but I ignored it. Nothing could stop me from talking to her. I hadn't heard her voice for so long. My heart literally expanded in my chest.

"That's fantastic" I marveled, not able to stop my voice from breaking. "That's what you wanted."

"Do you miss me, Briel?" she asked me out of the blue. I hadn't expected her to touch this sensitive and hurtful subject.

"What do you want me to say?" I asked honestly, pacing the room.

"The truth, always," she replied as the person behind the door knocked even louder.

"I miss you every second of every minute of every day, Lottie." I let out in a sigh. "I want you so much, I am chasing our ghosts. Your face still haunts my dream. I just – "

The person knocked again impatiently. *There will be a major ass kicking!* I thought, getting red with anger.

"What is it?" she asked.

"Give me a second," I growled, opening the door before briskly freezing on the spot. Here she was, standing in front of my door, a duffle bag at her feet.

"Because you see, I was also accepted to Columbia." She continued to talk on the phone. "And I accepted that offer before even knowing if you still wanted me as much as I wanted you."

"Oh, Lottie." I cursed myself because she was blurry as my eyes filled up with tears.

"You told me that one day you wanted someone to love you as much as Juliet loved her Romeo, ready to make the sacrifices that needed to be made. I don't see my choices as sacrifices, you know, since they lead me to you." She took a tentative step toward me, hanging up the phone. "I don't want us to be a tragedy anymore, Briel. I want us to be an epic love story."

I hung up the phone, not even knowing what to do, what to say. I couldn't believe that she was standing before me.

"So since I'm moving to New York too, I was wondering if you wanted a roommate?" she asked, trying to sound teasing, but the tremor in her voice gave her emotions away.

I pulled her toward me and kissed her hard with all the love, pain, and despair I'd felt during the last year.

"Is that a yes?" she asked breathlessly when we finally broke our kiss.

I rested my forehead against hers. "It's more than a yes, Lottie. Now that I have you back, I will never let you go again."

"That's good since I don't intend to go anywhere," she replied, wrapping her arms around my waist.

"What about Chago?" I asked, somehow surprised that her overprotective best friend had let her move across the country without a fight.

She arched her eyebrows with a teasing smile. "You really want to talk about Chago right now?!"

I shrugged. "I just can't help but wonder how he'd taken the move."

Her smile widened. God, how I missed that smile. "He is fine with it."

I cocked an eyebrow. I didn't believe that.

She laughed. "Okay, okay. He said, and I quote, 'Tell the gringo there are a few planes a day and that I can get to New York in five hours. If he makes you cry once more, I will destroy his kneecaps.'"

"It's fine. I get that, but I fear nothing because you are my forever. I love you, Lottie Miller," I whispered before giving her a chaste kiss.

"As much as I love you, Briel Johnson," she replied, standing on her tiptoes to kiss me back.

THE END

ABOUT ME

I'm a trained lawyer, world traveller, coffee addict, cheese aficionado, avid book reviewer and blogger.

I consider myself as an 'Eclectic romantic' as I love to devour every type of romance and I want to write romance in every sub-genre I can think of.

When I'm not busy doing all my lawyerly mayhem, and because I'm living in rainy (yet beautiful) Britain, I mostly enjoy indoor activities such as reading, watching TV, playing with my crazy puppies and writing stories I hope will make you dream and will bring you as much joy as I had writing them.

If you want to know any of the latest news join my reader group R.G. Angels Group on Facebook or wvisit my website www.rgangel.com to join my newsletter

Keep calm and read on!

R.G. Angel

ALSO BY R.G. ANGEL

The Patricians series

1- Bittersweet Legacy
2- Bittersweet Revenge
3- Bittersweet Truth
4- Bittersweet Love (Coming in early 2021)

Standalones

1- Lovable
2- The Bargain (Coming in November 2020)

Printed in Great Britain
by Amazon

79246730R00140